Mikala raised her gaze to the heavens and raged. "Why? Why? Why?" With every word, she slammed her palms into the frozen earth. "Why did you have to steal my child? Why didn't you just take me? Why did you give her to me only to reclaim her a few short years later? She was a baby. She hadn't had a chance to live yet." Sobbing, Mikala doubled over, her body wracked with pain. "Please, just take me to be with her. I can't do this anymore on my own. I don't want to. Please have mercy."

Mikala could beg all she wanted, but no one was listening. Her little butterfly had flown to heaven six months ago. Never again would Mikala wake up to the melody of her sweet giggles or revel in the warmth of her tiny body as it settled against her own. Mikala couldn't caress Molly's pudgy cheeks, tickle behind her ears, or inhale her fresh little-girl scent after a bath. She couldn't tangle her fingers through her wild mane of curls or get lost in those bottomless blue eyes that stopped most people in their tracks with their unusual color and their ability to see right through them.

Worst of all, Mikala didn't know who she was. No longer was she a mother. She would never hear the word *Mama* coming from her daughter's bow-shaped lips, giving meaning and worth to her life. Without her child, and without that title, Mikala was no one—no one special.

Praise for Mona Sedrak

Themes woven throughout SIX MONTHS including hope, love, the meaning of family, and guilt, offer something for everyone who has dealt with life's tragedies. Relateable, emotional, and worth the read!

~Kimberly Ann Miller

I'd recommend this novel to people who love a second chance tale with real depth to the characters and a storyline that is heart-wrenching but in the end, uplifting like a butterfly's wings.

~Jules Dixon

From the first scene, Sedrak takes the reader on an emotional rollercoaster ride. The pain and gut-splitting agony protagonist Mikala feels at the loss of her only child is real, palpable, and pours from the pages in a writing style so intimate and descriptive, you can't help but viscerally feel every emotion Mikala goes through as she experiences it.

~ Peggy Jaeger

Sedrak delivers real characters with realistic feelings and a natural flowing dialogue. Using the theme of butterflies, the novel, *SIX MONTHS,* brings tears, laughter, and ultimately a sense of peacefulness for the soul.

~Colleen Driscoll

Six Months

by

Mona Sedrak

Six Months

Cover Art by *Diana Carlile*

The Wild Rose Press, Inc.
PO Box 708
Adams Basin, NY 14410-0708
Visit us at www.thewildrosepress.com

Publishing History
First Mainstream Fiction Rose Edition, 2018
Print ISBN 978-1-5092-2302-2
Digital ISBN 978-1-5092-2303-9

Published in the United States of America

Dedication

To my husband, Samy, who has always supported me
and believed in me, even when I lost faith in myself. I
treasure every second of the thirty-two years we've
spent together.

Chapter One
Daisies in February

"Catch me, Mama!" Molly called over her shoulder as she ran across the newly cut grass, filling the air with her sweet, little-girl giggles.

Her auburn curls bounced in a frenzy around her face, cascading down her elfin body in waves, catching the sun and the eye of every person enjoying the warm spring day at Lighthouse Point Park. Mikala followed her blue-eyed nymph, unable to stifle her own laughter and the tug to her heart strings.

The park was crowded, New Havenites and their animals coming out from their winter hibernation to enjoy the first warm day of spring. But Mikala wasn't concerned. Molly was impossible to miss—dressed in jeans, an oversized hot-pink and purple sweatshirt, and matching high-tops—as she raced across the lawn on her tiny but powerful legs chasing butterflies.

Molly skidded to a stop, spun her head in Mikala's direction, and flashed her crystal-blue eyes. A wide grin spread over her freckled face. "Too slow, Mama," she announced in a sing-song voice. "Here I come." She narrowed her eyes and launched herself at Mikala. "Catch me!"

Mikala had seconds to prepare. She'd played this game dozens of times before with Molly. She was familiar with the impact the ball of mischievous energy

1

hurtling toward her would make on her body and heart.

Molly didn't waver from her path. With complete abandonment, she threw herself into her mother's arms. Often, Molly jumped from her bed or from the side of a pool right into the deep end and into Mikala's arms. She would let herself go, trusting Mikala wouldn't let her down and would catch her and keep her safe.

Mikala had reassured Molly, time and time again, mamas had a special job. To catch and to hold, and to love and to protect—that's why God made mamas. She laughed and dropped to her knees. She opened her arms wide, preparing to be overcome, inside and out, by goodness and light. Instead of the soft spring grass she'd been dreaming of, Mikala's knees and ungloved palms crunched through the frozen landscape, sinking into the frigid ice-and-snow combination covering the cemetery and Molly's grave.

Molly's grave?

Tears filled Mikala's eyes and streamed down her face. Her palms and knees were lacerated, stung, and burned. Her arms, shoulders, legs, and back throbbed from the impact. The pain shooting through her limbs and torso was nothing compared to the agony ripping through Mikala as she once again faced the horror her baby girl no longer lived, no longer breathed, smiled, or laughed. Rather, she lay buried in this godforsaken place, beneath this frozen tundra, in the dark, and all alone...all alone.

She scanned her surroundings, shivering as she swiped at the locks of curls whipping across her face. The children's cemetery was deserted, as it usually was on her daily visits. The trees were barren, naked, and cold, and snow blanketed the ground, covering the souls tucked beneath. Rarely did she see another sobbing and broken figure hovering over a tiny headstone of a baby stolen too early from the earth. When she did, her heart ached, and her grief compounded.

Mikala raised her gaze to the heavens and raged. "Why? Why? Why?" With every word, she slammed her palms into the frozen earth. "Why did you have to steal my child? Why didn't you just take me? Why did you give her to me only to reclaim her a few short years later? She was only a baby. She hadn't lived a full life yet." Sobbing, Mikala doubled over, her body wracked with pain. "Please, just take me to be with her. I can't do this anymore on my own. I don't want to. Please have mercy."

She could beg all she wanted, but no one listened. Six months ago, her little butterfly flew to heaven. Never again would Mikala wake up to the melody of her sweet giggles or revel in the warmth of her tiny body as it settled against her own. Mikala couldn't caress Molly's pudgy cheeks, tickle behind her ears, or inhale her fresh little-girl scent after a bath. She couldn't tangle her fingers through her wild mane of curls or get lost in those bottomless blue eyes that stopped most people in their tracks with their unusual color and their ability to see right through them.

Worst of all, Mikala didn't know who she was. No longer was she a mother. She would never hear the word *Mama* coming from her daughter's bow-shaped lips, giving meaning and worth to her life. Without her child, and without that title, Mikala was no one—no one special.

Mikala had lied to Molly. She didn't catch her, hold her, or protect her like she'd promised on the day

3

she was born. She could have and should have. But Mikala hadn't listened to her internal alarm bell—the one that came as an added bonus the day she learned she was pregnant with Molly, and the one that warned when her precious girl was in trouble. Instead, she'd listened to all the people around her who loved her and Molly, but they had no clue what being a mother was.

"Wake up, wake up, wake up," Molly had chanted as she bounced up and down on Mikala's bed early one Saturday morning in mid-August. "It's here. It's today. Daddy says to get you up and get me dressed." She dropped to her knees and crawled over Mikala, positioning her small body on top of her mother. Molly placed her head on Mikala's breast as her itsy-bitsy fingers tiptoed their way to Mikala's armpits and dug in.

Mikala smiled and grabbed Molly's hands in one of hers as her other arm banded around the giggling girl and pulled her even closer. She breathed in Molly.

Molly wiggled. "Mama, please get up. It's Daddy-and-me day."

No sooner had the words left Molly's mouth when a weird knot lodged in the pit of Mikala's stomach, accompanied by a finger of apprehension that walked its way up her spine. She shivered and sat up.

As Mikala dressed Molly and made pancakes for breakfast while David got ready, the niggling sense of foreboding that made its debut in her bed returned for a repeat performance. This time the warning was loud and obnoxious. Her fears were unwarranted. Molly was spending the day with David, shopping for kindergarten school supplies. Afterward, they were having lunch with his parents and would be home by dinner. The plan was simple, safe, and worry-free. So, what was the problem?

By the time David came down for breakfast, Mikala paced.

As usual, David was engrossed in his email. His fingers flew across the screen of his smartphone as he sat at the breakfast bar next to Molly and began eating without glancing up.

Molly happily hummed a Disney tune, as she swung her legs and licked pancake syrup off her fingers.

Mikala studied her family and shook her head. At thirty-nine, she had everything she ever wanted—a husband who'd loved her since the day they met when they were just nineteen, and a sweet baby girl, their miracle, God had finally graced them with. Life was good. Everyone was safe, happy, and healthy. She had no reason for the anxiety that gained cyclone strength and speed in her belly and chest. Still, she knew better than to blow off her internal alarm. "You know what, guys. I've changed my mind. I don't want to miss out on all the fun. I think I'll go with you instead of to the spa with Rena."

Both Molly's and David's heads popped up.

"Mama, no," Molly whined. "Today is Molly-and-Daddy day. Only us." She turned her gaze to her father. "You promised, Daddy."

David quirked an eyebrow, his gaze searching Mikala's. "It's okay, Princess. Mama can come. We'll have fun together."

Molly's eyes welled with tears, and her bottom lip quivered. "Daddy, no. It's Daddy-and-me day. Only you and only me." She turned her face to Mikala and whispered, "I'll watch him so he doesn't get lost, and I'll stay close. Please, Mama, please."

Mikala got lost in her daughter's beseeching eyes, and her heart melted. Even at five and a half, Molly had her father mastered and her mother wrapped around her finger. She was an intelligent child who missed nothing. Mikala and David argued about his unhealthy cell-phone obsession, a direct result of an overly demanding job as a defense attorney. Lately when he went out with them, if they didn't watch him, he walked into objects and people. Once, they even lost him in the grocery store. But he was a great dad, and when he had Molly on his own, his gaze didn't stray.

"Easy there, Princess. No tears for Daddy-and-Molly day." David smiled, picked up Molly, and put her on his lap. "It'll be okay, sweetheart. Go to the spa. Have fun with Rena. Molly will keep a good eye on me, won't you, baby?"

"Yippy!" Molly threw her arms around her father's neck and gave him a syrupy kiss. "I'll watch you, Daddy. You won't get lost. I promise."

Outnumbered, and against her better judgment, Mikala gave in. She didn't want to be one of those overprotective mothers, and generally she wasn't. She wished she understood what she was feeling. Taking a deep breath, she let it out. She'd smiled and nodded. "Okay, Butterfly, but don't go flitting away anywhere, especially if he is looking at his phone."

Mikala recalled every detail of her daughter's face from that morning—from her dimpled chin to her toothy grin. The pain of losing her hadn't dulled in the slightest over the last six months. She shook her head and straightened from her crouched position over

Molly's grave. With the back of her hand, she wiped her face and nose as a cold wind blew.

Mikala searched in her coat pocket for a tissue, and then blew her nose. Her palms were a mess, and her fingers were stiff and painfully cold, but she didn't care. She cleared the snow from the butterfly sculpture balanced atop Molly's headstone, a magnificent piece of art Jake commissioned. Using her index finger, she traced Molly's name, date of birth, and date of death on the headstone. How fast the years had flown.

Closing her eyes, Mikala slowly replayed all the significant days with Molly. The day the doctor confirmed she was pregnant and she'd run home to tell David their little miracle was on the way. He crushed her against him and wept. The day Molly's heartbeat graced her ears for the first time and became her favorite symphony, followed by the first time Molly stretched deep inside her womb—a fluttering of a butterfly's wings. The day she pushed Molly into the world, heard her cry, and made her promises she hadn't kept. Then came the first time Mikala cradled Molly in her arms, and everything in her world clicked into place. Molly's first smile, giggle, word, step…her first everything.

Again, Mikala lost control as a fresh wave of anguish, followed by guilt and self-recrimination hit. She'd known without a shadow of a doubt, something terrible would happen that day, and she hadn't enjoyed the spa with Rena. Halfway through the day, she insisted on going home. When she couldn't reach David by three p.m., and his parents said he didn't arrive at their house, Mikala's heart skipped a beat. For just a few minutes, her brain stopped processing information, her vision blurred, and a roar filled her ears.

Wandering from room to room, she memorized every detail of the life she and David built—the family photos lining the mantel, the hand-carved jewelry box David bought her on their honeymoon in Salzburg, and Molly's tea set arranged on the coffee table for evening tea. A cold, hollow ache took residence in her belly where the knot of dread made its appearance that morning. The sensation expanded with alarming speed, dug in deep, and planted roots. Like an unwanted guest appearing without warning and bringing too many bags for just a brief visit, sorrow moved in, shifted, and stretched then got comfortable for the long haul.

When the house line rang, Mikala froze, and her gaze darted to the cordless on the couch. Her breath stuttered. Her heart seized. Clarity forced its way past the tentacles of sheer terror strangling, dominating, and paralyzing her. She shook her head and took a step forward, only to be hit by a wave of dizziness and nausea so tremendous, she doubled over wrapping her arms around her womb. Mikala's entire being, inside and out, shook as her heart tumbled about in her chest without a set time, tempo, or rhythm. Her breaths grew shallow and choppy, and her legs turned to rubber. The cord tethering Molly to her and this world had been severed.

The telephone rang four times before Mikala forced her body to cooperate. God, she hadn't wanted to answer. She hadn't wanted to know. She'd even considered not answering, protecting herself and her beautiful family from the annihilation of their world.

People said she was strong—the strongest woman they knew. They said in time she would heal. She would build another life. And God didn't give you more than you could handle. People were idiots. They had no idea how in her head she raged. She howled, and shrieked, and wailed…and begged, and pleaded for mercy. All day. All night. Every day. Every night.

Mikala wiped her eyes again and searched the heavens. Thick, gray clouds crowded the sky, heralding an impending storm. She took deep breaths, exhaling slowly as she prepared for the task that brought her here. It had to be done. Using her numb hands, Mikala brushed the rest of the snow off her daughter's headstone the best she could. She gathered the yellow daisies she'd dropped in the snow. They'd scattered over the grave and around a bouquet of white daisies she was certain Jake brought earlier.

Daisies had been Molly's favorite flower. Although finding daisies anywhere in Connecticut in February was impossible, Mikala was a good customer at Dixie's Flower Shop, and apparently, Jake was as well. Dixie made the impossible possible for this special day.

Molly had loved to color and paint, and every picture she created contained daisies and butterflies. "Daisies are happy all the time. That's why butterflies like them so much," Molly had explained, when Mikala questioned the smiley face Molly always drew in the center of each daisy.

Smiling, Mikala stopped gathering the flowers. They were beautiful, perfect as they were, blanketing her baby with bright, happy colors. She placed the few stems she'd collected at the base of the headstone. "Here you go, baby girl." Mikala traced the petals of one of the daisies with the tip of her finger. "Your favorite. So pretty and bright, my butterfly. Just for you on your special day, my sweet. Happy sixth birthday. Your mama loves you, remembers you, and can barely breathe without you."

Mikala closed her eyes and tilted up her head, digging deep for the strength she needed to utter the next words. For the briefest of moments, the sun peeked out from the clouds and kissed one of her cheeks as the wind whipped up and caressed the other. Her eyes flew open, and she gasped. Cupping her cheeks with her frozen hands, Mikala searched the heavens for the hole that was sure to be there—a conduit between the angels and those they left behind. Seeing only the clouds gather once more and the sun fade as quickly as it made its appearance, Mikala's tears started again. She brushed them away and cleared her throat. The time had come to sing Molly the song every child loves to hear on their birthday.

"Happy birthday, dear Molly. Happy birthday to you."

Chapter Two
All the King's Horses

Jake Santiago Cardona maneuvered Red through the narrow iron gates of the Gentle Winds Cemetery. He let the old truck find its way to the infant and children's section where he'd been countless times to visit his butterfly. His truck didn't need assistance. It knew its way by heart—every hill and turn and even the exact place he parked near the majestic oak tree.

Fuck, he hated this grim place—this section in particular. Jake slammed a hand against the steering wheel. So many tiny graves and so many little ones who never had a chance to make a difference in this world. He understood the circle of life and all that shit, but these babies were at the beginning of that circle. Some had lived a few years while others had only lived a few months. Still, some tiny souls had barely taken a breath. Mikala had insisted Molly be with other children, refusing to lay her to rest in the Jacobson family plot where all of David's departed family were buried. She'd been overcome and fragile. No one dared argue.

Molly had belonged to all of them. David and Mikala may have been her biological parents, but they'd shared her with Jake and Rena from the beginning, making them her godparents. The second Jake's gaze had connected with Molly, a few hours after she'd entered the world, and her tiny hand closed over his finger, he was a goner. She wasn't his, and yet she was, in every way that mattered. Molly claimed his heart that very second. She'd swallowed him whole. She'd shackled him to her for life, refused to let go, and made him happier than he ever thought he could be.

The weeks leading to Molly's birthday had been brutal. He'd cancelled his clients and flown in a couple of weeks in advance to be with his family. Although he did the best he could to console them, nothing would ever make up for losing their child. Last night, after Jake was certain David was calm, settled, and sober for a change, he'd spent an hour at the gravesite, talking to his butterfly. He described the places he'd been since she'd been gone and the things he wished they could've done together on her special day. He wished her a happy birthday, telling her how much he missed and loved her, and said his goodbyes in private. He didn't need an audience for his grief.

At this very minute, he was supposed to be on a flight to Los Angeles for a deposition he'd already rescheduled twice. He should have been buckled into his first-class seat, downing a Bloody Mary or three, reviewing the notes his paralegal sent him, and looking forward to an evening with a long-legged blonde named Elle. But somehow, Red drove him to the cemetery instead of the airport.

From the second he'd opened his eyes this morning, images of Molly flooded his head. A couple of times, he closed and opened his hand, certain Molly's tiny fingers were wrapped around his fingers, tugging, pulling, and begging for his attention. Although Jake anticipated the torture the day would bring, he nearly drove off the road when her pleading voice invaded his thoughts.

"Where's Mama? Uncle Jake, where's my mama?"

At first, Jake thought he dozed off while driving and dreamed of her. He hadn't slept much in days, and exhaustion took its toll. He pulled off the road and hopped out of his car, hoping the crisp February air would reboot his brain so he could get safely back on the road. He took deep breaths in and out as he circled the vehicle, climbed in, and turned on the radio as loud as it could go.

The second Jake pulled back into traffic and pointed Red toward the airport, Molly whispered her plea again. This time, he was certain he was awake. With shaking hands, he pulled Red off the road once more, closed his eyes, and rested his head against the steering wheel. He relented, telling himself he would give in to the fantasy of hearing her and talking to her just this once.

"Mama? Where's my mama?"

Jake swallowed past the lump in his throat and gripped the steering wheel with all his might. He anchored himself to this world as he entered the next. "Molly, baby. I miss you, sweetheart," he whispered into the silence of the truck cab. "We all miss you so damn much."

"Uncle Jake, where's my mama?"

"Butterfly, I don't know where your mama is. Wherever she is, she is missing you so damn much." Jake broke down. Gut-wrenching sobs ripped through him, and tears poured down his face. For months, he'd held his emotions in check. But now when he heard her angelic voice again as if she were standing right in front of him, he gave in. Sorrow, which had been escalating, intensifying, and consuming him, surged to the surface and spewed out.

"Find my mama. Please, Uncle Jake, find my mama."

Molly wouldn't give up, wouldn't let him sink into his grief, and wouldn't leave him until he did as she asked. Jake squeezed his eyes shut and shook his head. God, he heard her so damn *clearly*. Why was she here? Why was she doing this? Is this what Mikala experienced all these months? "Please, Butterfly, that's enough."

"Mama?"

Jake took a shuddering breath and succumbed to Molly's plea and impossible presence in his life once more. "Okay, Butterfly. Rest now, my angel. I'll find her. I promise. I'll take care of her, of all of them, as I always do. We'll be okay. Rest now, little one." He wiped his face with the back of his hand and steered Red into a U-turn. He'd lied to Molly. Jake knew where Mikala was, and Molly knew it, too. Maybe Mikala was right. Maybe some part of Molly was still with them, and she was telling them something. Molly was guiding them through this new life without her.

Shortly after Molly's funeral, Jake caught Mikala in Molly's room, talking and singing to a ghost only she saw and heard. Months passed, and she still did it—still locked herself in Molly's room and spent her entire day with Molly's ghost.

One day, Mikala's behavior became too much to hear and too much to see. Jake and Rena staged an intervention.

"I know you think I'm crazy, and maybe I am. But

she's here. I hear her, feel her, and smell her. Here in this room…she still is," Mikala insisted.

"Micky, sweetheart, she's gone. She's not here. She *is* gone." Jake's admission almost took him to his knees. The vise around his chest tightened, and his throat constricted. He wanted to give in to his grief, but he had to stay strong. Straining to fill his lungs, he willed his trembling legs to steady. He admonished his aching heart to ignore the torture it endured.

Jake squeezed Mikala's shoulders as he gazed into her tear-filled eyes. "You've got to stop this now." Mikala stiffened in his arms, and her gaze pierced him, straight to his soul.

"I know she's gone. You don't think I know she's gone? You don't think I know my baby is dead? You don't think I remember burying her broken body down the road in that cemetery with the other babies?" Mikala raged as tears ran down her face. "I remember. I remember every second of her life and every second of her death. *I* remember."

"Micky," Jake choked out. "Sweetheart, I…"

"No, Jake, no! Don't ask me to stop. Not yet. I can't. I need her. Let me have this time with her for a little while longer. Please, please…" She collapsed into his arms, broken and sobbing. She was undone.

What could he say? What could he do? In all his forty years, he'd never been so powerless. Helpless. Impotent to take away her pain.

Mikala and David, along with Molly and Rena, were Jake's only family. For the last twenty years, they'd been his everything. But despite all his power, influence, and wealth, when his family shattered, he was inept and incapable of sheltering them from the storm. Like all the king's horses and all the king's men, he could do nothing to put them back together again.

Sliding Red into Park, Jake scanned the cemetery, searching for Molly's grave. He scrubbed a hand over his face, blinked, and clenched his jaw. Mikala knelt in the snow beside Molly's daisy-covered grave—alone. Where the fuck was David? After spending the better part of a week talking, pleading, and listening to David as he cried and poured out his heart and soul, telling him things he didn't want to hear, and didn't want to know, Jake got it. The combination of the accident, Molly's death, and Mikala's grief was too much for one human to endure and overcome.

David's grief was compounded by an all-consuming guilt. He needed help—the kind Jake wasn't equipped to give him and the kind everyone in David's life had begged him to get for months. Jake could no longer wait for David to agree. Two weeks ago, he'd dragged him to the best shrink he could find.

Yesterday, after his third therapy appointment that week, David looked and sounded better. He seemed more settled, peaceful even. He was still devastated, but his sorrow was no longer a tsunami birthed by a deadly earthquake, leveling everything in its path. David seemed to be swimming stronger, smarter, and understanding how to manage the wicked riptides so they didn't pull him back into the depths of the dark sea where he'd been since August.

But Jake had sunk into the bowels of hell and was being shredded by wild dogs. After he left David last night, he'd visited Molly then drove to the nearest liquor store where he purchased the largest bottle of whisky they had and drove home. In the comfort and safety of his own home, with the help of Uncle Jack, he collapsed under the burden of all of David's sorrow, confessions, and guilt—not sure if he could ever rise on steady legs again. He now understood the biblical precept of helping to shoulder another's burdens when they stumble and stagger.

Once again, Jake closed his eyes and laid his head against the headrest. He understood Molly's plea for her mama. She didn't want Mikala to be by herself. "I've got her, Butterfly. I've got your mama, and I'll take care of her. I promise. Rest now." He sighed and swallowed past the lump in his throat. He would give Mikala a few more minutes before he went out, gathered what was left of her in his arms, and drove her home. Then he'd deal with David—again. Jake had no idea what to do. He was all out of tricks, and he was damn exhausted.

Jake ran a hand through his hair, to the base of his head and neck where an entire excavating team had settled in, their hammers and shovels doing a number on what was left of his sanity. Last night, he'd been certain David was ready to stand on his own feet and share his grief as well as his memories of Molly with Mikala, especially on a day like today. He was convinced David would find his way back to the woman who loved him and Molly with a depth of adoration and devotion Jake had never experienced. He couldn't have been more wrong or more disappointed in David. How could David leave her to deal with Molly's birthday on her own?

David had a right to mourn his child any way he wanted, but if he didn't take care, he would surface from his grief to find he no longer had a wife or a marriage. Six months ago, Mikala lost Molly and David on the same day—a double blow even for the strongest of people. David retreated into a world filled with deep sorrow, guilt, and self-recrimination. No one, not even Mikala, the love of his life, and the mother of his child, could crack the door open and find a way inside.

Jake straightened and rubbed his eyes. Time was up. He had to drag Mikala from Molly's grave. He'd done this dozens of times over the last six months and knew what it entailed—tears and heartbreak—for both of them. No one else had the ability to save Mikala from killing herself and joining Molly. David was lost, and Rena rarely came to the cemetery. Visiting the children's cemetery was too painful after her own loss. He couldn't ask her to come here, not even for Mikala.

Opening his eyes, he turned his head in time to see Mikala collapse on to Molly's grave and curl into a tight ball. That was it—he couldn't stay in the truck one second longer. "Sweet Jesus. She'll kill herself." The words left his lips in an agonized moan as he opened the truck door and hopped out onto the snow- and ice-covered gravel and into the freezing February air.

He'd given Mikala enough time with Molly—time to remember and be with her child the only way she could and time to say goodbye once more. But enough! The air was fucking cold. He couldn't lose her, too.

Without a word, Jake crouched next to Mikala's shivering form and scooped her up.

For the first time since Molly died, she didn't fight him as he carried her to the truck. Turning her face into his chest, she lay still with her eyes closed.

She weighed next to nothing, having lost much weight over the last six months. Her clothes hung on her as if she were nothing more than a wire hanger. Mikala was a solid slab of ice, and her breaths were shallow.

Jake panicked. Had he waited too long? Had she lost consciousness? He squeezed her and whispered in her hair, "Micky, sweetheart, open your eyes. Come on, open your eyes. Tell me you're okay, or I swear I'm driving you to the hospital."

Mikala's eyes fluttered open as he placed her in the warmth of the truck.

He breathed a sigh of relief, but the pain in her eyes almost did him in. When would it end? When would they all wake up from this fucking nightmare?

"Jake," she croaked. Her lips were dry and cracked, her nose ran, and her cheeks were streaked and wet.

"Yeah, sweetheart, it's me." But Jake wasn't who she wanted or who she needed to comfort and sustain her. He wasn't enough. How could he be? He wasn't David. "I'm sorry, Micky. I'm so fucking sorry." He took off his gloves and wiped the tears off her cheeks with his thumbs.

Mikala held his gaze for a few seconds, and then pulled away. She turned her face and body away, closed her eyes, and curled into Red's worn leather seat.

Jake sighed. The damage David had done by leaving Mikala on her own today couldn't be fixed. He reached over and secured the seatbelt around her shivering body, knowing she wouldn't bother. Then he rounded the truck, jumped in, and cranked up the heat as high as it would go. He drove Mikala the short distance home in silence.

When they'd reached Mikala's house, he parked in front of the two-story colonial and waited. He sensed she had something to say. No longer was she hunched over. Somewhere along the way, she'd straightened and squared her shoulders.

Mikala faced Jake. "I'm scared, terrified actually. I don't think I can do this much longer. He's gone, Jake. No matter how hard I search, I can't find him. When I call his name, and cry out, he doesn't answer. He won't come. He won't comfort or hold me."

Jake cleared his throat. "I'll talk to him. I'll make sure he goes back to Dr. Fieldhouse." He reached for her hand.

She jerked away.

"Micky, he'll get better. He's just—"

"Stop. Just stop. You've been great, really great. But this isn't your fault, and you can't fix this. You can't fix him. I understand he's wrecked, but he's not the only one. *I* need him. *I* need to be comforted. *I* need to be held. When I needed him the most, he abandoned me. He decided his feelings were the only ones that mattered. What about me?" She slapped a hand to her chest. "How do I go on? How do I do this without everyone I love?"

God, this whole fucked-up situation was slowly killing him. Jake had no idea what to do or say. He loved David like a brother, but if he could, he would punch him for being a selfish bastard and caring more about himself than his devastated wife.

Jake shook his head. He had to get his shit together. Mikala needed him. They both fucking needed him. "Micky, sweetheart. I'm here." He reached across the cab and caressed Mikala's cheek with the back of his hand. "You're not alone. I'd never leave you. I'll try to be around more often. Do your best to hold on.

David loves you. You know that. He'll find his way back. I know he will. He is so close."

Mikala brushed the tears from her face and glanced at the house. She took a deep breath and let it out as her shoulders sagged. "You know, for the first time I'm doubting the longevity of our marriage. We've been through a lot together. But this? This nightmare we can't wake up from has unraveled us. He can't get past his grief, even for a few minutes to help me cope with mine, and some days, I'm so angry. I'm angry he won't talk to me, mourn with me, and won't tell me what happened. And then I feel guilty because I shouldn't feel like this, and because I love him."

Mikala's voice broke as she turned toward Jake, and their gazes connected once more. "Go home, Jake. Go back to LA. Go back to Elle, Rachel, or whoever the flavor of the month is. Go back to your work. You can't fix us, Super-man. I love you for standing by us, loving us, and for trying to save us. But you can't."

Mikala kissed Jake on the cheek. She turned, opened the door, and stepped out onto the pavement. Before she shut the door, she hesitated and looked over her shoulder. "I know you're used to swooping in and saving us time and time again with your superpowers, but this time, we have to save ourselves. Problem is, I don't know if either of us has it within us to do so."

Chapter Three
Holes in Heaven

*"Why did he have to go, Mama? Was he bad?"
Molly wiped her eyes and nose with the back of her
hand and turned her sad eyes to her mother, searching
for the answer to a question most adults struggled with.*

*Mikala gathered her daughter's petite body in her
arms and carried her to the oversized wicker rocking
chair she'd rocked her in since before she was born.
She sat, placed Molly in her lap, and began rocking as
she searched for the words to soothe her daughter's
broken heart. "Butterfly, Stan was a good kitty. He was
just sick."*

*"But why did he have to die? Why couldn't you
make him better?"*

*With her fingers, Mikala wiped her daughter's
tears and cupped her cheek. "Sweetheart, mamas can't
always make things better, no matter how hard we try.
I'm sorry, Butterfly."*

*Molly's gaze met her mother's. "But where did he
go?"*

*Mikala kissed her daughter's head. "He went to
live in heaven. He'll be so happy there."*

*"Wasn't he happy here? I took good care of him. I
played with him, fed him, and gave him extra treats.
Didn't he love me anymore?"*

"Oh, baby, you took good care of Stan, and he

loved you so, so much. Sometimes, kitties die."

"Can I see him in heaven? Can we go visit?"
Molly's voice rose as she wiggled in her mother's lap
and turned her wide eyes on Mikala. "Can we go
tomorrow?"

Mikala sighed and wondered how on earth she
would settle Molly down for the night. "No, Molly. We
can't visit."

"But I want to see Stan. I miss my kitty," Molly
whined.

"I know, baby. But heaven is far, far away. You
want to know a secret about heaven though?"

Molly nodded, her eyes big and shining.

Like most children, she loved secrets, but she was
lousy at keeping them.

"Although you can't see Stan, he can see you."

A grin spread over Molly's face, and Mikala
breathed a sigh of relief. "He can? Really? How?"

Mikala smiled. When she was Molly's age, her
beloved grandmother died. Mikala's father had devised
an ingenious explanation that soothed Mikala's broken
heart. She never thought she would use this explanation
with her own child, but she was desperate. Molly had
been crying on and off all day, and they both needed
some rest. Maybe it would work on Molly.

"Stan can see you through the holes in heaven, of
course."

"There's holes?" Molly scrunched her forehead.

"Sure, that's how the sun shines through and how
the rain and snow make their way down. Stan will peek
through the holes and see you. He will purr and wag his
kitty tail. Although you can't see him, all you have to do
is close your eyes and raise your face toward heaven.

When you feel the wind on your cheeks and the sun warming your skin, you'll know he's sending you kitty kisses, like he used to when he woke you up in the morning."

Molly smiled, and she seemed to accept the explanation. She laid her head against her mother's chest as Mikala continued to rock her. After a few minutes, just when Mikala thought she'd succeeded in rocking Molly into a peaceful sleep, Molly's small voice broke the silence with the questions Mikala had anticipated but hoped she wouldn't have to think about.

"Am I going to die like Stan and go to heaven one day? Are you and Daddy? Will I see you there?"

Mikala gathered her daughter tight to her bosom and sighed. "No, Butterfly. You're not flying off to heaven, and neither are we. Not for a long, long time."

Mikala startled out of sleep to the insistent honking of a car horn. Molly wasn't in her arms. She was dreaming. Although the dream was sad, any opportunity to see Molly's sweet face once more was better than reality. Mikala rubbed her swollen eyes and groaned. God, she was exhausted. She turned her head and glared at the bedside clock. How could the time be nine twenty-two a.m. already?

Mikala closed her eyes once again. In twenty minutes, Rena would be at her door, forcing her to another god-awful session of hot yoga. She had to get out of bed and face the day, but she was too damn tired. All Mikala wanted was to swallow another magic pill her doctor prescribed and fall into oblivion. Every square inch of her body hurt. Even her eyelashes were too heavy for her swollen lids to carry each time she blinked.

Stretching, Mikala strained to hear any sounds coming from downstairs. The roar of the ancient furnace turning on and off as it forced warmed air throughout the house dominated the eerie silence. She needed to call a repairman before that monster exploded.

She took in a deep breath through her nose, praying for the blessed scent of java, her lifeblood. Coffee was the one thing David expended the effort to make. Each morning, he mixed, ground, and brewed her favorite blend. That ritual was the only sign he still cared and remembered she didn't follow Molly into the ground. This morning, though, she was denied that small gift.

Even though she was desperate for a hit of caffeine, Mikala showered and dressed first. She couldn't deal with David quite yet.

After Jake dropped her off the day before, she'd walked through the front door and found David sprawled on the family-room couch in another drunken stupor. He was surrounded by his usual friends, Jim, Jack, and Johnny. She'd held back the tears and called on the anger and hurt. Despite the time being only three p.m., Mikala had walked straight to their bedroom, changed, swallowed two pills, and crawled into bed.

Since Molly's death, Mikala often hid in her bedroom, huddled under the covers in the middle of the bed, and surrounded by a fortress of pillows instead of in the safety and comfort of her husband's embrace. In the first few weeks after Molly's death, she couldn't stand to be near or to be touched by David. But she had nothing to worry about. David spent his days and nights on the family room couch. He couldn't see beyond his own grief. Her suffering was of no consequence.

Most days she mustered all of her will not to scream, "You did this. You killed our baby. You were supposed to keep her safe and you failed." She wanted to strike him and rip him apart with her bare hands. She wanted to take her pain out on him and on anyone and everyone. But mostly, she wanted to know every detail of her daughter's last day, and David refused to give her even that small measure of comfort.

"Just tell me what happened. Please, David, please. Talk to me. I need to know what happened to our baby girl...our butterfly," she begged as he lay mute in the hospital bed after the accident, unable or unwilling to meet her gaze. She'd been consumed by grief. At one point, Jake had to drag her out of David's room and into the hall where she unraveled and had to be sedated.

David had sustained a concussion and a minor back injury. The doctors said his inability to recall the events of that day and refusal to discuss the accident came from the trauma, combined with the overwhelming grief of Molly's death.

While Mikala understood the explanation the doctors provided, she didn't care. She couldn't care. She simply lacked the capacity to be anything other than undone. David was alive. He would be okay, but her baby was dead. She'd entrusted Molly in his care, and he failed in the very worst of ways. He allowed their daughter to be mortally injured, and Mikala could not accept his silence.

The New Haven police were of little help. David was well respected in the community, and Jacobson Law was a big supporter of the New Haven Police Department. Lester Jacobson, David's father, was a very influential attorney. He pulled every string possible to move along the investigation. But at the end of the day, the police couldn't be certain of the cause of the accident.

"No drugs or alcohol were detected in Mr. Jacobson's system. Our conclusion is he simply lost control of the vehicle. Maybe he swerved to miss an animal. Possibly a deer. The road was wet, and the car hydroplaned, flipped several times, and ended up in a ditch in front of Nelson's Horse Farm. Unless Mr. Jacobson regains his memory, we'll never know conclusively what caused the accident," Sergeant Adams explained. He cleared his throat, and then met Mikala's gaze. "If it's any comfort to you, ma'am, she wouldn't have had time to even register what was happening or to be in pain."

Nothing was simple about losing their daughter, and imagining Molly's tiny body crushed on impact was far from comforting. All Mikala could think was Molly took her last breath without her there to hold and comfort her. Mikala needed to know beyond a shadow of a doubt what happened. She needed confirmation the accident was unavoidable, and her daughter's life could not have been spared. Without that knowledge, she didn't think she could ever find her way to acceptance and peace.

Like the steam that filled the bathroom, guilt surrounded and engulfed Mikala—guilt for not listening to her own intuition, not protecting her daughter, and not being more supportive of David. She had tried to help him, though. A few weeks after the funeral, Mikala had rallied. She threw herself into taking care of David. She took him to his doctor appointments, physical therapy sessions, and picked up his medications. Often, she asked him to accompany her to the cemetery, and each time he refused. When all her efforts to get David to share his feelings were unsuccessful, she gave up. David had alienated and shunned her, and her anger and resentment grew.

Now as Mikala went through her morning routine, she recalled Jake's plea from the day before. She should have more patience with David. Maybe Jake was right. She'd lost hope for her marriage and had to do better. She had to stop pushing David so hard.

The night before Molly's birthday, David had appeared better than he had in a long time. He was sober and even smiled a couple of times over dinner. After Jake left, she sat next to him on the couch and held his hand. "David, I know we've talked about the accident before, and you say you still can't remember, but could you try again? Please, David. I need you to walk me through your day with Molly."

David jerked away and walked across the room. He paced and wrung his hands. "I don't remember. I don't remember. How many times will you ask me the same fucking question? How and why the accident happened doesn't matter anyway. I know you blame me." He slapped his hand to his chest. "*I* blame me."

"David, I don't blame you." Mikala looked away. She didn't want him to see evidence of the lie she forced past her lips. "But every detail of that day and the accident does matter."

His gaze met hers, and he whispered, "I would do anything to trade places with Molly. I wish I'd been killed instead. I know you wish I was dead."

Mikala stood, and her eyes filled with tears. She took David in her arms and held him in a tight embrace.

"Oh God, David, sweetheart. No. I wish the accident never happened. I wish she were still with us. But I know the accident wasn't your fault. It wasn't anyone's fault." She cradled his cheek in her hand. "I'm sorry, sweetheart. I know you survived a terrible trauma, and you blame yourself. The details of that day are important, because I wasn't there with you and with Molly in her final moments. I think if I understood what happened I might find a sliver of peace. But I need you to know, I love you."

David's arms hung limply by his sides. He studied Mikala for a minute. He'd opened his mouth, and then closed it and looked away.

Mikala sighed, released a stuttering breath, and shook her head. A way to reach David had to exist. She closed her eyes and rested her forehead against the tiled shower wall, letting the last of the hot water beat down on her body. Once more, she chastised herself for being selfish and too caught up in her own grief to see David needed help. She should have been the one to drag him to therapy instead of Jake. If she wanted to save David and save their marriage, she had to wake up and stop feeling sorry for herself.

A minuscule smile played on Mikala's lips. David was the love of her life. They'd been married for thirteen years. Mikala still loved her husband, and he loved her, too. No more would she allow him to sleep on the couch. She needed his arms around her, and he needed her, as well.

Freshly showered and dressed in yoga attire, Mikala opened her bedroom door with a renewed sense of purpose. Today would be the day they turned a corner. Today, she and David would take one tiny step toward learning how to live in this new world without their daughter.

As Mikala stepped onto the second-floor landing, she noted the house was deathly quiet. No delicious coffee scented the air. David couldn't still be asleep, could he? She'd made enough noise showering and blow-drying her hair to wake him.

Just before her foot hit the first step, she paused once more and strained to hear any sounds coming from below. Something was off. The house was *too* quiet. A sense of dread washed over Mikala. She shivered, and goose bumps blossomed on her skin. She wrapped her arms around herself and let out a trembling breath.

A sense of déjà vu swamped her. The sensation of dread that built in her belly was all too familiar. She shook her head and whispered, "No. No!"

She was exhausted, emotionally spent, and was letting her imagination get the best of her. That had to be it. Hadn't she suffered enough? God couldn't be so cruel. Fear paralyzed Mikala. She willed her brain to settle and send the right signals to her body so she could move.

A minute passed before she stumbled sideways down the stairs, gripping the railing with both hands. When she reached the bottom, she halted.

The family room was semi-dark. One lamp was on, and the blinds were closed. From where she stood, Mikala couldn't see David's face. He lay on the worn leather couch in the same position he was in yesterday afternoon when she'd come home, but his head was turned away. He was dressed in gray sweatpants and a well-loved navy Yale T-shirt. Gone were the beautifully tailored suits he wore before their lives were obliterated. This attire was his new daily wardrobe.

She scanned the room. Bottles of liquor and dirty glasses littered the coffee table. The television remote control, along with David's reading glasses, were on the floor near the sofa where yet another pair of David's gym socks lay. The room was musty and reeked of alcohol.

Forcing her legs to move, she took three steps toward the couch and paused as her heart rate accelerated. David lay too still. From what she could see of his face, his eyes were closed. "David?" she whispered. "David, wake up." Her voice rose and trembled.

David didn't respond and didn't move.

A wave of nausea accompanied by vertigo washed over her. Her hands flew to her mouth.

No, no, no. Jesus. God. No.

Mikala rounded the couch and slid to her knees on the hardwood floor in front of David's supine form. Her gaze darted from his chest to his face. Her breaths became short and erratic.

He wasn't breathing. His chest wasn't moving.

She grabbed his T-shirt with both hands, shook him, and screamed, "David. David. Wake up." Over and over again, she slapped her palm against his cheek. "Breathe, damn it, breathe!"

Finally, Mikala froze. David's skin was cold. His lips were pale. "Oh God. No. Please, no," she wailed. She scanned the room. She had to get help. Where the hell was the phone? She had to get David to start breathing. How did CPR go again? What was she supposed to do first? Breathe in his mouth or chest compressions? She had to hurry.

Her mind raced, and her body shook. Did he have a heart attack? A stroke? Did he drink too much? She'd heard of alcohol poisoning. If she could just get him to breathe, he would be okay. But she had to get help first.

Mikala spotted David's cell on the side table. She righted herself and reached for the cell. David's prescription bottles clattered onto the hardwood floor—open and empty. Mikala focused on the bottles as they rolled in all directions. She gasped, and the cell slid from her trembling fingers. Eyes widening, she glanced from David's still cold body, to the liquor bottles on the table, and then to the four empty prescription bottles on the floor. "Noooo," she wailed. "Oh, God. Oh, David. Sweetheart, no. Not you, too. Don't leave me. Please don't leave me."

As tears streamed down her face, Mikala scrambled for the cell that had slid under the coffee table. With shaking fingers, she dialed 9-1-1 and ran to the front door, opening it as she waited for the call to connect. "1222 Hiawatha Lane. My…my husband has collapsed. Help me," she screamed into the phone as she raced back to David's side.

Dropping the cell, she positioned herself over her husband, crossed one hand over the other, and laced her fingers together as she'd been taught in the life-saving class she took at the Community Center before Molly was born. She began chest compressions. After thirty compressions, she tilted David's head and lifted his chin. Pinching his nose, she formed a seal around his cold lips and blew two breaths. She repeated this series, her arms and back aching, and her heart breaking.

The wailing of sirens came closer. Hands pulled her from David. Voices asked her question after question. What happened? When did she find him? How much did he drink? How much medicine did he take? Was he sick? Was he depressed? Had he tried to take his life before?

People flooded her house—police, paramedics, neighbors, Rena, Jake. When David was pronounced dead, she collapsed. Strong arms encircled her, picked her up, and cradled her.

David dead? How could that be? Molly was dead. David couldn't be dead. He was all she had left. David *couldn't* be dead! High-pitched screams followed by gut-wrenching sobs filled the room. She didn't know where the screaming was coming from, but someone was being mutilated as they lived and breathed. She fought the arms that held her. She wanted to go with David. She had to get to him. They'd made a terrible mistake. He wasn't dead. He wouldn't leave her. He loved her and she him.

People she didn't recognize, and didn't want to know, lifted David's lax form onto a stretcher and covered his beautiful face with a white sheet. Where were they taking him? She had to go with him. She couldn't stay in this house by herself. He needed her. She needed him.

Mikala fought like a wild cat. She screamed. She thrashed, clawed, and bit. But strong arms gathered her, held her, and begged her to calm down so she wouldn't hurt herself. Didn't they know it was too late? Didn't they know she'd already splintered, shattered, and exploded into millions of pieces?

A sharp prick penetrated Mikala's arm. Seconds later, her muscles and bones liquefied, and a thick fog oozed across the surface of her brain and was absorbed into every cell. Mikala closed her eyes and blessed darkness descended. She could no longer hear, see, smell, or feel. She welcomed the cessation of her senses and stopped fighting to stay in a world that pummeled her into a bloody pulp. Mikala drifted into a deep slumber, praying she would never, ever wake up.

Chapter Four
Watching a Corpse Rot

Jake parked Red in front of Mikala's house and sighed. The two-story, butter-yellow colonial with white shutters used to look as if it were smiling and happy with those it sheltered and protected. Since Molly and David's deaths, however, the house sagged under the weight of grief and sorrow. Today was no exception. The house stood dark, desolate, and depressed, covered in snow in the freezing February morning.

"I'm here, Molly. Rest now, Butterfly. I'm here," Jake whispered. Every day since he'd first heard Molly's voice on her birthday, she visited him and wreaked havoc with what was left of his sanity.

"Mama, Mama. Uncle Jake, where's my mama?"

For three weeks, Molly tortured him with her plaintive cries. Jake did everything he could to banish Molly's voice—tequila, music, and strenuous exercise. He even considered seeing a shrink, but he wasn't crazy. He knew why she was there.

Molly looked down through those holes in heaven on all the people she loved, and she didn't like what she saw. They were destroyed and distraught. They were lost. They were ruined beyond recognition with no hope of recovery. How did he get a ghost to understand that?

Jake rubbed his eyes, and for the hundredth time in

the last three weeks, he prayed for guidance and strength. People who thought they knew Jake would laugh at the preposterous idea he was a praying man, but those people—acquaintances, business associates, and even most he would categorize as friends—had no idea who Jake really was.

He was an intensely private man, and his trust and loyalty didn't extend beyond a select few individuals. Mikala, Rena, David, and his brother, Mateo, were the only people to earn his confidence and entry into his inner circle. With Mateo and David dead, his world shrank even more, leaving only Mikala and Rena. But Rena barely tolerated him.

Mikala. Gripping the steering wheel with both hands, Jake hung his head. What the hell would he do about Mikala? He couldn't lose her, too. If things didn't improve soon, he would. Jake was certain, losing her would lead to his demise. Why would he want to go on living in a world without any of the people he loved?

Until six months ago, Jake was convinced losing Mateo was the worst thing that could ever happen. He was wrong. Losing his brother had been a powerful blow, but losing Molly had brought him to his knees. David's death leveled him. The only reason he got out of bed was Mikala. He had to take care of her, and he had to do a hell of a better job than he'd done with David.

So heavy was the guilt he carried, Jake's shoulders slumped. He could barely breathe these days. Of all the people in David's life that could have predicted and prevented his spiral into the depths of agony, that person was Jake. But Jake had been deaf, dumb, and blind. He'd missed all the obvious warnings.

David, the man he'd thought of as his brother for twenty years, trusted him with everything in his shredded heart and tortured soul, and Jake did nothing to help him but take him to a fucking useless shrink who gave him the pills he used to kill himself. Some would say Jake did what he could, but Jake didn't agree. After all, David was dead.

Molly's and David's deaths were unfathomable, incomprehensible, and one hundred percent avoidable. No matter how many times he asked why, and how many times he beat himself up for not doing more to help David, the facts didn't change.

Molly was dead. David was dead. Mikala was in pieces.

Jake and Rena were left to pick up the remnants. Like fine crystal, Mikala had shattered into a million smithereens, some so miniscule, no matter how hard he searched, they would be impossible to locate. Even if he managed the gargantuan task of putting her together, parts of Mikala would always be missing.

He glanced at his watch—five minutes after seven. *Late*. His shift started five minutes ago. For the last three weeks, he and Rena took turns watching over Mikala. But Mikala no longer inhabited her body. Her heart beat, and once in a while, she responded to her environment. She rarely spoke, ate without nudging, or slept for more than a few hours at a time. Hell, Mikala barely willed her body to breathe. She was deteriorating at such a fast pace, he feared she would soon join David and Molly.

While Rena watched over Mikala at night, forcing her to shower daily and sitting next to her while she slept, Jake spent his days talking at her and begging her to eat. Taking care of Mikala was more than a full-time job. Although he was damned tired, and he was neglecting his clients and Elle, he didn't give a crap. For the most part, Jake's clients were filthy-rich assholes who didn't think the law pertained to them. He had the pleasure of cleaning up after them, and their spoiled children, and keeping their asses out of jail for a ridiculous amount of money. As far as Jake was concerned, those rich assholes could go fuck themselves.

And Elle? Mikala was right to refer to her as the flavor of the month. Elle, like all his flavors, knew the score—at least, he thought she did. He'd always been straight. He wasn't ready to commit to anyone and likely never would be. Jake didn't want any woman falling for him and giving up any part of themselves. Unfortunately, Elle decided he was worth reforming, and they had a difficult conversation the night before. In her wee mind, she had them riding off into the sunset. When he nixed that notion, she called him a few clever names and burst into tears.

Love was a dangerous thing when it was all-consuming. When people lost in the game of love, not only did they lose their hearts, they lost their minds. Case in point, Mikala and David. Jake had watched them find each other and tumble into the abyss of love. From the very beginning, he worried one of them would end up decimated. He was right.

David, Mikala, Rena, and Molly…his family. Jake's family was the most important thing in his life, and they'd always come first, before work and before women. He raked a hand through his hair, stepped out of Red, and trudged through the snow to the front door.

He opened the door and came face-to-face with Rena's flaming-red hair and scorching temper.

"It's about damn time you got here," she hissed. "I'm late again. Some of us aren't independently wealthy, for fuck's sake."

Jake met Rena's flashing green eyes and rubbed the back of his neck. "I'm sorry, Rena. I—"

"Look," she barked. "If you're too busy to do this, and I can't rely on you, just say so. I can handle Mikala on my own. Just get the hell out of my way so I know what I'm dealing with and can plan accordingly."

Jake's hackles rose. He had quite enough of Rena's holier-than-thou attitude. He didn't care if she was hurting. She wasn't the only one who loved Mikala, and this wasn't a fucking contest to see who could do more and sacrifice more. He didn't give two fucks if she liked him or not. The past was the past, and she had to get over herself. Mikala was his family, and he wouldn't allow Rena to shove him out of her life.

Jake grabbed Rena's elbow and pulled her through the front door and onto the porch. He closed the door behind them. "I said I was sorry, and I meant it. I'm doing the best I can. Enough is enough, Rena. Lose the attitude, and go to work. Take the evening off, as well. I've got her."

Rena put her hands on her hips and glared. "Well, your best isn't fucking good enough! You think saying sorry will fix her? No matter what you do or how much money you throw at the situation, you can't fix her. I can't fix her. Nothing will fix her." Rena's eyes welled with tears that spilled over and streamed down her face, replacing her freshly applied makeup with black streaks.

Fuck. Lately, Jake had a real knack for making women cry. He sighed and tried to pull her into a hug.

Rena stepped out of his reach as she swiped the tears off her face. She shook her head and looked to the sky. "Jake, we're over our heads here." She released a stuttering breath. "We need help. Mikala sat in Molly's room most of the night, just rocking in that damned rocker. I'm scared." She turned her gaze back to him. "Maybe we should call Dani or her mother and ask them to come back. Maybe we were wrong to send them all home."

After taking a deep breath, he let it out. He didn't know how to reach Mikala or how to guide her, or any of them, out the jungle of despair they were trapped in. But inviting all that pandemonium back into the house wasn't the answer. The week following David's funeral was a nightmare, and when her family and extended family converged, life in Mikala's house became a circus act. Everyone tried to help, but they made things much worse with their good intentions and their kind words. Each time Mikala emerged from her room, her family descended. They weighed her down and drowned her not only with sympathy, but also their confusion and grief.

Sandra and Joseph Cummings were compassionate and loving people who cared for their daughter. Although Mikala was close to her father, her relationship with her mother was strained. Mikala was also close to her older sister, but Dani had the burden of taking care of their aging parents and a house full of children. The only person Jake could call on now for help was Mikala's father. But he wasn't an option. Joe had dangerously high blood pressure and was recovering from a minor heart attack. The family insisted on keeping the reality of Joe's health from Mikala, and right now, Jake agreed.

To add to the tension, Mikala didn't want anyone to know the truth about David's death. Lester Jacobson used his formidable influence and wealth to have his son's death ruled an accidental overdose. Jake had no idea how the man did it, and he didn't want to know. For all intents and purposes, that story was the one they were all going with. No one, not even the witches of New Haven—David's older twin sisters and his mother—knew the truth. Jake, Rena, and Lester were left to keep the secret and carry the burden.

Jake shook his head. "I don't think bringing back Dani or her parents is a good idea. Joe's sick, and Dani has her hands full. They can't do anything." Jake looked to the front door, and then back at Rena. "Just go to work, take the night off, and get some sleep. Let me think through this mess a bit."

Rena sighed and glanced away.

The poor woman had dark circles under her eyes, and her once-fiery hair was dull and lifeless. She wasn't aware Jake knew she'd experienced her own devastating loss a few months before David died. One day, when they were all cramped into the house, watching Mikala unravel as they waited for the Coroner's Office to release the body so they could bury David, Jake walked in to the kitchen. He found Rena crying in Dani's arms and overheard their conversation.

"This situation is all too much, Dani. Micky lost her baby, and I've lost mine. Now David's gone. When will this senseless loss of life end? When will we wake up from the nightmare, and when we do, will there be anything left of us?"

Jake heard enough of the conversation to know Rena suffered in silence. Unable to share her pain with him or Mikala, Rena had turned to Dani for solace. He backed out of the room, feeling heartbroken and inadequate yet again. Someone had cursed their small family.

So far, he was the only one untouched by tragedy. Untouched? That was so far from the truth, it was laughable. On the outside, he was whole. But his insides should be declared a disaster zone. He couldn't eat, sleep, or think clearly enough to make decisions. He functioned on coffee and bourbon. But he would do what was necessary to keep going and stay upright. Jake straightened and lifted his chin. "Go, Rena. I've got this. You're already late. Drive safe." He gave her a half-hearted smile.

"Okay. Thanks." Rena's shoulders slumped. "Let me know if you need anything, or you change your mind. I'll see you after work tomorrow to take over as usual." Rena walked to her car, looked over her shoulder, and shook her head. Then she got in the car and drove off.

Jake took a fortifying breath, squared his shoulders, and walked in to the house. Something had to give. He and Rena had bubble-wrapped Mikala. They took care of her every need, mirrored her grief, and enabled her self-destructive behavior. If they continued this pattern, no hope existed for any of them to recover or survive.

Survival. Now that was a concept. Who wanted to survive the death of their only child or the love of their life? Who would want to put all that beauty, goodness, and perfection behind them and build a new life alone?

Not a single damn person he knew!

Yet, that's what he had to convince Mikala of...today. Today, he had to put aside his own grief and guilt and think of her. She was his responsibility. David wouldn't have died if Jake had done enough, and Mikala would still have her husband. Now, Mikala was Jake's to fix.

Resigned to his task, Jake opened the blinds and curtains in every room of the first floor and invited the sunshine back into the house. Not the joy, not yet, that was asking way too much. The sun was proof the world was reborn daily, even after the darkness of the night. They all needed proof of life.

Chapter Five
Barely Breathing

Jake made his way up the stairs in the silent house, past the collage of pictures of Molly since the day she was born, and then more pictures of David, Mikala, Rena, and him. His chest ached every time he saw their smiles. How naive they'd all been, thinking good and happy would always visit them—a gift they received without giving anything in return.

Stopping outside the master bedroom, he peeked in, knowing what he would find. The covers were pulled back, and the bed was empty. A multitude of pillows she normally hid behind and the body pillow that warmed David's side of the bed, were in their usual positions, undented. On the nights Mikala gave into her exhaustion, she closed her eyes, let go of this world, and fell into her dreams. Her breathing slowed and deepened, and she wrapped her body around the human-sized pillow, using it as an anchor. Even in a drug-induced sleep, she couldn't escape her grief. Tears tracked down her cheeks, shredding his already tattered heart.

Jake walked to Molly's room and stood outside the door watching Mikala. She sat in the old white wicker rocker she used to rock Molly in, clutching Molly's pink-and-gray stuffed kitty to her chest. The rocker faced the backyard where the snow-covered tire swing swayed in the breeze.

Closing his eyes, Jake rested his head on the side of the doorframe, remembering the first time he laid eyes on Mikala Cummings—Freshmen Orientation at Yale University. He'd been lost, out of his element, and he stuck out like an ostrich among lemmings. The second he saw her, even before their gazes met or he heard her voice for the first time, he was drawn to her. He had a gut feeling she would play a significant role in his life.

Mikala was different from the pampered, preppy crowd. Her curvaceous figure, long curly auburn hair, warm whisky eyes, along with her infectious laugh and welcoming smile, brought the boys to their knees. She may not have been the prettiest girl on campus or the most refined, but every person who saw Mikala Cummings knew something was special about her. The boys targeted her as their next lay, while the girls, well…they studied her every move.

Mikala stood a foot away from a tall redhead who also held court, but unlike Mikala, the redhead was at ease with her admirers. Jake's gaze connected with Mikala's across the green, and he recognized the panic and plea for help that beckoned him. He gave her a sympathetic smile, and he was powerless to stop his body from responding to her call. Ignoring every person around him, Jake pushed and shoved his way to her.

"Hi, baby." Jake looped an arm around Mikala's waist, interrupting the high-class hounds' attempt to charm her with their good looks and hefty bank accounts. "I see you've made some new *friends*." He emphasized the word "friends," delivering the message she was off limits.

Not missing a beat, Mikala grinned and turned her

full attention to him. "Hi, I thought I lost you. Want to grab lunch? I'm starved." She smiled into his eyes.

For a few seconds, Jake's brain short-circuited. Mikala ignored her new admirers and looked at him as if he was her whole world. He cleared his throat. "Sure." He smirked and lifted his chin. "Let's get out of here." Grabbing her hand, he led her away from the salivating pack.

Tugging on his arm, Mikala stopped and called over her shoulder. "Rena, you're wasting your time over there. Come on, girlfriend, Super-man finally showed."

"Do you know that girl?" Jake studied the red-haired siren who had half a dozen horny guys surrounding her.

"Just as well as I know you, Super-man." Mikala threw back her head and laughed. "We'll be the best of friends, you'll see."

From that second, Jake Cardona, Rena Henderson, and Mikala Cummings formed a friendship many envied. But Mikala and Jake's bond was unique and powerful. Although he'd grown up in a gang-ridden neighborhood of East LA and she in the farmlands of Ohio, they understood each other better than most people who lived a lifetime together. To Rena's disgust, Mikala and Jake shared many weird habits and obsessions—drinking ice-cold milk with pizza, eating cornflakes drenched in orange juice instead of milk, and watching reruns of 1970s sitcoms for hours at a time.

Then came David Jacobson, and Mikala was captivated.

Jake watched Mikala tumble, helpless to stop her fall, and he wasn't sure he wanted to stop her quickly forming infatuation with David. Jake's feelings for Mikala weren't romantic in nature. She was his best friend, and she understood him better than anyone ever had. David made her happy. Watching David and Mikala find each other and fall in love was almost too much to stomach.

He didn't believe in that all-consuming, forever-love shit. The only experience he had with true love was watching his mother love his father to a fault. Jake didn't want anything to do with love. He was certain David and Mikala wouldn't last. One or the other would falter, and he and Rena would be left to pick up the pieces. He was always concerned Mikala would leave him behind, and he would be on his own in the foreign land of Connecticut. But he was wrong.

David and Mikala's relationship thrived, and she didn't lose interest in her friendship with Jake or Rena. Instead, she wove all four of them together, forming what she called her Yale family. Mikala insisted Rena was the kind of girlfriend every girl needed—a little crazy and a lot loyal. And although Mikala had chosen David as her lover, Jake had been her confidant, best friend, and partner in crime.

Jake opened his eyes, straightened, and walked slowly to Mikala. He didn't want to startle her, although a little jarring might be beneficial. He walked into her line of vision and waited until she glanced at him. "Good morning, sweetheart. Have you had breakfast yet?"

Mikala shook her head and rocked.

Jake squatted in front of her and took her hands in his. "Micky, you're not eating or sleeping, and you've lost a shitload of weight. You're going to make yourself sick. You've got to try, sweetheart. Please let me help you. Let Rena help you. I know you're in agony. I understand, but three weeks have passed."

Mikala dropped her head to her chest and tried to pull her hands away.

Jake held on, refusing to let go. He wasn't giving in. "Micky." He used his most authoritative, no bullshit voice—the one he saved for the courtroom. "Look at me."

Raising her head, Mikala darted her gaze to him.

"No more, Mick. I'm not saying you can't grieve. I'm saying you need to take better care of yourself. I can't watch you waste away anymore. Trying to kill yourself won't change anything. Nothing will bring back David and Molly."

Mikala's eyes filled with tears that slid down her pale cheeks. "Get out," she whispered.

At first, Jake wasn't sure he heard her. But when she pulled her hands free, straightened her spine, and lifted her chin, he got the message.

"Get out." Although her voice was hoarse, it echoed loud and strong in the barren room. A furious storm built in her usually lifeless eyes.

Jake's pulse raced. In three weeks, this was the first time Mikala showed any emotion other than grief. Although she was pissed, fury was better than indifference. "Micky, let's go downstairs, have some breakfast, and talk. I know you're hurting, but you're not alone. We're all in pain. We're all devastated. We can heal with one another and survive this together."

Again, he reached for her hands, but when one of her hands connected with a slap across his face, his efforts were thwarted. His cheek heated and throbbed, and his eyes widened.

Mikala stood and flew out of the rocker.

Jake rocked back on his heels and almost fell backward.

She whirled to face him. Her long auburn curls whipped around her. Her hands fisted by her side. With her gaze, she tasered him to his spot. "Survive? Survive?" she snarled. "Did you just say that to me?"

Shit! Why did he use that word? Wasn't he just thinking that concept was unimaginable? What the hell was wrong with him? Why was everything he did and said so fucked-up? Jake rubbed his hands over his face. "Micky, please listen. That's not—"

"No, you listen. You stop, and you listen. *I* do not want to *survive* my daughter. *I* do not want to *survive* my husband. I do not want to *survive* at all. *I* want to be left the hell alone." Mikala's chest heaved. She pointed a shaking finger in his direction. "You have no idea what I'm feeling. None whatsoever."

Undaunted, Jake took a cautious step toward her. He lowered his voice, hoping to calm her. "I'm sorry, Micky. Of course, I don't know what you're feeling, but this behavior isn't what they would've wanted. David wouldn't want you to suffer, and Mol—"

"David?" She scoffed. "David doesn't have a say in what I feel or how much I'm suffering. When he was alive, he didn't give a shit. Why would he now? When I needed him the most, he abandoned me." She pounded her fist into her breastbone. "He left me to deal with Molly's death on my own. As if losing my baby, our baby, didn't shred me enough, he killed himself."

Standing straight and stiff, Mikala glared at Jake. "David took the coward's way out. He didn't care about my suffering, not for a second. He destroyed what was left of us—of me. Don't tell me you understand how I feel. You can't possibly understand my devastation or my loss. He took away everything."

"Mikala, David—"

"Don't!" She shrieked and launched herself at him. She pounded his chest with her fists. "Don't you ever mention his name to me again. Do you understand me? Never again."

"Micky, baby, stop now." Jake wrapped his arms around her, trying to hold her, absorb some of her pain, and harness the storm threatening to rip her apart piece by piece. His eyes filled with tears, and he struggled to contain his emotions. "David loved you so much. He was lost in his own grief and guilt. I'm sorry. I should've done more. I—"

Mikala slapped both palms on Jake's chest and shoved him backward. "You know what? You're right. You want me to say you did everything you could so you can feel better? Well, it's not happening." She jabbed a finger in his direction. "You should have done more." She stabbed a finger into her own chest. "I should have done more. I should have gotten him help earlier. I should have taken away his booze. I shouldn't have kept asking him about the accident, begging him to tell me what happened, and blaming him in my heart for her death."

Tears slid down Jake's face. "Oh God, Micky." His voice cracked. "David's death wasn't your fault. You didn't do anything wrong. You were as wrecked as he was. He chose to take his life. He was in such pain, and he carried so much guilt. He—"

"And he left me. He abandoned me not only to live

and breathe without my child, but now I'm supposed to live without him, too. I have to live with the fact I drove him to this."

Jake swiped at his face. He hung his head and swallowed hard. He wanted to ease her pain but was failing. All his efforts were useless, and he wished he had the skill to cut out the pain like the cancer it was. He would do anything and sacrifice anything for this woman. But nothing he said or did was enough—not for David, Rena, or her.

"Leave, Jake." She let out a long breath, and her shoulders sagged. "I don't need or want you here. The life we built—you, me, David, Molly, and Rena—is gone and buried. The sooner you accept that, and the sooner we all accept that, the better."

Jake raised his head and searched Mikala's vacant eyes. What was he supposed to do now? How could he reach her?

"You can't fix me, and neither can Rena. I want you both to stop trying. Everyone I've ever loved is gone. Get out, Jake. Just get out."

Shaken by her harsh words, Jake stepped back. He shook his head and did his best not to let the pain of her rejection show on his face. She was undone, and she had no idea what she was saying. Jake held up his hands in surrender. Nothing remained in his bag of tricks. Everything that came out of his mouth multiplied her pain.

Unable to bear the weight of her despair, he turned away. He walked to the door with his head hung low. At the door, Jake stopped and closed his eyes. Mikala's ragged breathing and weeping filled the room. His heart, a lacerated mess, bled for all of them. Jake considered his next words carefully. If he hadn't lost her already, he would once he opened his mouth. But she left him little choice. He had to save her, even if he sacrificed himself.

Mikala Jacobson would do anything for her child. *Anything.*

Exhausted and defeated, Jake steadied himself against the doorframe. "I'll go, Micky, but you should know one thing before I do." He turned and focused on Mikala. "You're not only hurting yourself here. You're hurting Molly. You're hurting your baby girl."

Mikala took a sharp breath, and with wide eyes, she glanced up. "What?" She searched his face. "What did you just say?"

"You heard me," he said in a ragged voice. "You think you're the only person she speaks to? I wish to hell that was true. Stop being so damn selfish." Jake straightened and clenched his hands. "Clean up your act, Mikala, so your daughter can rest in peace. Then maybe she'll stop begging me to help her mama, and I can get some fucking rest from this nightmare."

Six Months

August

Chapter Six
They're Still Here

"Mama, did you know butterflies have a thousand muscles? That's a whole lot. That's why they're so strong."

"Wow, I didn't know that." Mikala lay next to Molly, basking in the warm summer sun at Lighthouse Point Park. She turned her head toward her daughter and smiled at her beautiful girl.

"Mama, did you know butterflies eat with their feet?"

"Really? That sounds kind of gross, baby."

"Yup. Uncle Jake says the red ones are red 'cause they eat too much spaghetti like me." Molly giggled.

Mikala sighed. "What else did Uncle Jake teach you this time?"

"He said they can fly two thousand miles. That's why they need four wings in case the first two get tired. Caterpillars have six legs. Bet they never get tired. I wish I had six legs and four wings. No, maybe six legs and six wings. I'd never, ever, ever get tired. Mama, are you tired? 'Cause I'm not."

Mikala burst out laughing, rolled toward Molly, and wrapped the child in her arms. She buried her face in Molly's wild curls. "Whoa there, baby girl. If you had all those wings and feet, I'd never, ever, ever keep up with you, and I'd always, always be tired."

Molly rested her head on her mother's belly and searched the sky. "Mama?" she whispered as a light breeze rushed through the trees and ran its fingers through their hair.

"Yeah, Butterfly?"

"I see them now."

"You see what, sweetheart?"

"The holes. The ones you told me about. Stan is watching right now. Isn't he Mama? I feel the sun and the wind. My kitty is watching me and purring."

Mikala stretched, opened her eyes, and turned her face to the morning sun. She smiled. These days, dreaming of Molly brought a smile to her face. Molly didn't visit Mikala as often as she used to, but her daughter still had a way of sending her the right message at the right time. She asked questions Mikala had difficulty answering and begged Mikala to do things she found impossible.

One year.

Molly had been gone for one full year. Mikala sighed. How quickly and how agonizingly slow time elapsed. So much changed. Nothing in her life today resembled the beautiful life she took for granted one year ago. The very fabric of her world was torn to pieces and re-stitched—forever altered.

Few thought she'd survive, including herself. If not for Molly, she probably wouldn't have. In those early days, she had no will or desire to live. But even when others abandoned her, Molly persisted. Mikala closed her eyes and sucked in a breath, remembering Jake's parting words.

You're hurting Molly.

Jake's words had haunted her sleep and her every

waking moment until she thought she'd go mad. They tortured her and propelled her into the next phase of her life—existing without her husband and child, most of her friends, and without him—without Jake.

In the beginning, Mikala used all her strength to get out of bed and into the shower. Some days she was exhausted by the time she dressed and dried her hair, but she forced herself to go downstairs and swallow a piece of toast. Every time she wanted to give up and stay in bed, she remembered the three words Jake said. They were a catalyst to rebuilding her world. She fought her way back to the land of the living. Although she'd survived the war, she'd sustained deep wounds that left her scarred, inside and out.

"You're off the hook, Rena. Go back to your life. You don't have to babysit me any longer," Mikala told Rena the day after Jake left, with all the bravado she could muster.

Rena wasn't easily convinced.

Mikala had to just about throw her out.

Still, Rena didn't scare easily. She showed up daily before or after her shift, bringing food, flowers, books, and anything else she could think of to capture Mikala's interest. She used her key and, without a word, put her offering on the kitchen island. She left a note telling Mikala her work schedule and reassuring her she would return the next day.

A week after Jake left, Dani showed up on Mikala's doorstep. She begged Mikala to come home to Ohio for a few months.

Mikala loved her older sister, but she didn't appreciate the surprise visit or Dani's suggestion. Ohio was the last place on Earth Mikala wanted to be. While

Dani was happily married to a farmer and lived three miles from their parents' farm, Mikala escaped the farm the second she could and never wanted to return.

Her family's property was vast. One acre bled into another and finally merged with the neighbor's farm, which was also massive and eventually merged into yet another farm. While Dani found the routine of farm life rewarding and small-town living comforting, Mikala felt trapped and stifled. Often, she wanted to tear out her hair from sheer boredom. She hated the small-town gossip mill and found the people nosey and judgmental. Returning to Ohio was the last thing Mikala needed. Home was New Haven, not Ohio.

When Dani couldn't convince Mikala to go home, she put the one person on the phone Mikala would do anything for—her father. "Dad, I know you and Dani mean well, but coming home won't work. Mom and I will be at each other's throats in seconds. That's the last thing I need right now."

"Nonsense. She loves you, Micky. She has her own way of showing it, but she loves you and wants to help."

Mikala sighed. "She's called once since I saw you six weeks ago. You and Dani may want me home, but she doesn't." Mikala hated to admit she was hurt by her mother's actions. Although Sandra's behavior was nothing new, Mikala was more vulnerable than usual. Despite their differences, Mikala loved her mother. But she wasn't certain her feelings were reciprocated.

As a child, Mikala tried Sandra at every turn, and Sandra pushed back just as hard. Mikala was the definition of a strong-willed child. Even as a girl, Mikala understood she was different than Dani. Dani was the good child—the easy child. Mikala acted out, craving her mother's attention and understanding. Instead, she regularly received her disapproval and disappointment. Often, Mikala heard Sandra excuse and explain Mikala's existence and behavior to her friends.

"God has a sense of humor. Dani was such a good baby—angelic. I had no idea why people complained about having children. So, I lost my mind and had Micky. The good Lord wanted to teach me a lesson. Jesus in heaven, that child's a trial. If I survive her, it'll be due only to God's mercy."

Years of misunderstanding and resentment built until Mikala was certain her mother didn't know who she was at all. She craved her mother's attention, but she was resigned to the fact she would never receive it. While Mikala's father often defended her mother, this time fact was fact.

Joe cleared his throat and sniffed. "Come home for your old dad then. I'm worried about you, my girl. Having you in the house again will do me good. What do you say?"

Mikala's eyes filled with tears. She missed her father, and something in his voice told her he needed her as much as she needed him. She wished she could feel his arms around her, but she couldn't go to Ohio now, not even for a brief visit. "I can't leave them." Her voice broke. "They're here in this house with me. I can't leave them yet. It's too soon, Dad."

Joe stopped pushing and directed Dani to leave Mikala alone and return home. Instead, he called Mikala weekly and talked about life on the farm.

Mikala listened, finding comfort in her father's warm, comforting voice. Joe understood her grief better than she did. He didn't push for conversation or ask her to do more than she could. He was the best of men.

Unlike Joe, Rena, Dani, and her father, the majority of Mikala's well-meaning friends and family gave up on her. They were busy with their own lives. People had no idea what to say. She made them uncomfortable, and they avoided her like she had a communicable disease—as if they got too close, her devastation and ruin would spread to them.

Mikala didn't blame them. She appreciated their distance and the silence left in their wake. She craved silence. She found solace in the stillness of the day and night. Over the last year, her life had changed so fast. She survived a whirlwind and a maelstrom. Now, next to Rena, silence and stillness were her best friends.

The oddest things comforted Mikala. She reveled in early morning walks on a nearby abandoned beach when the air was crisp. The biting wind against her cheeks, the roar of waves crashing against the shore, and the fog of her warm breath hitting the icy atmosphere reminded her she was alive. Her soul was renewed as the sun rose over the ocean.

Mikala sat for hours curled on the family room couch where David took his life. She found comfort there, feeling closer to him somehow. She didn't turn on the television or play music. Instead, Mikala listened to the rhythmic tick-tick-tick of the grandfather clock her father gave them as a wedding present. At night, she fell asleep to the sound of her own inhalations and exhalations, reminding her she was still alive.

Shaking her head, Mikala forced herself to abandon the past and get out of bed. She had to move. Soon, Lester Jacobson would be at her doorstep. She refused to share this day with anyone, including Rena. But she couldn't deny Lester. Their growing relationship was the only good that rose from all the destruction and ruin of the last year.

After showering quickly, Mikala gathered her hair in a messy bun. Other than the diamond studs and wedding band she never removed, she didn't bother with makeup or jewelry. She scrutinized herself in the mirror. She didn't recognize the woman staring back. Her eyes were familiar and maybe her lips. That is where the resemblance ended. The woman's face was thinner and more angular, with prominent cheekbones. The rest of Mikala's body was even less familiar.

The day Molly died, Mikala stopped wearing her hair down.

Molly liked to *style* her mother's hair every morning to resemble her own wild mane. "See, Mama, we're twins." Molly would proclaim with a huge grin that lit up her face and Mikala's world.

Now, however, Mikala had no reason to endure the heavy weight of her hair on her shoulders. Most days, she either gathered and stuck her hair on the top of her head or pulled it into a ponytail so she wouldn't be reminded of what she'd lost. Mikala also lost at least twenty-five pounds, maybe more. She'd gained weight during her pregnancy and never made the effort to lose it. She was thinner than she'd ever been in her life. The weight had melted away.

"We're going shopping." Rena had declared one Saturday morning. "You're drowning in your clothes. I bet your underwear don't even fit. This is ridiculous. Enough!"

No matter how much Mikala protested, Rena didn't

let up until they were strapped in Rena's car, headed toward the local mall. Mikala was miserable, but Rena was right. Nothing fit Mikala. Not even her bras. Although Rena made the outing fun and light with lunch at Mikala's favorite restaurant, Mikala couldn't enjoy herself. She was overwhelmed by the crowd and the noise. She begged Rena to take her home, take her credit card, and buy whatever she deemed necessary.

The next day Rena went to town on Mikala's credit card. "*This* is what happens when you let others take charge of your life." Rena dragged one bag after another from her car and into Mikala's house.

Mikala stared in disbelief and horror.

Rena glared. "Girlfriend, I love you, but you're a pain in the ass. Don't even think of returning anything. I've got all the receipts, and you'll have to prove the clothes don't fit before I relinquish the receipts. You'll also have to return the items yourself." She turned and walked to her car. "Oh, by the way. A friend of mine from the thrift store is stopping by tomorrow at three. Have your circus-sized clothing, and anything else you're ready to part with, packed."

Mikala wanted to kill her best friend, but like a coward, Rena fled and didn't return calls or texts until seven p.m. the next day.

Then she appeared at Mikala's door with enough Chinese food to feed the neighborhood and a massive bottle of Chianti.

By that time, Mikala's anger cooled, but sorrow set in. She'd spent the day packing David's clothing, and she had been emotionally drained.

Mikala blinked at her reflection and shook her head. She entered her walk-in closet that was now too big for only her clothes and searched for something to wear. Daily, she discovered a new piece of clothing, makeup, or shoes she didn't remember owning and wouldn't have chosen to wear in her previous life as Molly's mother and David's wife.

She sifted through her clothes, hoping to find something light. The day would be hot and humid. Rena swore she purchased a few Mikala-style dresses, long, flowy, and comfortable—clothes she could hide in and under. Mikala had yet to find a single dress fitting that description.

Frustrated and running out of time, she turned to her right and continued searching. She spotted an ankle-length, cream-colored sundress with tiny pink and purple butterflies scattered throughout. The dress was on a hanger, but the hanger was angled so the dress hung in front of the other dresses.

Clipped to the dress was a note written in Rena's handwriting. "For you and for Molly. I'm with you, as she always will be."

Chapter Seven
A Good Man

Lester arrived promptly at ten a.m., holding a large bouquet of daisies.

Mikala opened the front door, and her heart did a little flutter. Lester looked like an older version of David. The resemblance was remarkable and never failed to remind her of the years she would never have with David.

Lester was a tall, broad-shouldered man with silver hair, a square jaw, and piercing blue eyes. He wasn't heavy, but he wasn't lean. He filled any room he entered with his imposing presence, self-assurance, and strength of will. Some called him arrogant, but not only was he brilliant, he was terrifying in the courtroom. David had worked hard to achieve and project the same aura of stability and self-possession as his father, but he could never quite pull it off.

Before Molly was born, Lester rarely said more than a few words to Mikala at a time. For years, he intimidated her. But Molly was Lester's first and only grandchild, and when she arrived on the scene, he became a reformed man. Molly captured Lester's heart and brought him to heel.

When Molly and David died, something inside Lester broke. While he was supportive and understanding after Molly's death, when David passed, he kept to himself and mourned on his own. Over the last six months, however, he eased himself into Mikala's world. While she had little tolerance for anyone else, Lester fit into her new life.

"Good morning, sweetheart." Lester kissed her cheek. "Ready to go?"

"Good morning, Les." Mikala smiled. She didn't think she'd ever seen Les wear anything but a suit. Even in ninety-degree weather, the man was decked out in a three-piece charcoal suit, crisp white shirt, and silk tie. He looked like a distinguished English gentleman, complete with a cane. "I'm ready. Thanks for picking up the flowers."

Together they strolled in silence, arm in arm, as they often did. Les was a man of few words and spoke only when he had something important to say. Unlike most people, he was comfortable with silence and didn't push to fill the void with mindless chatter.

A few weeks after David's death, Mikala ran into Lester at the children's cemetery. He was visiting David's grave and stopped to visit Molly as well. When he broke down and fell to his knees, Mikala followed and held him in her arms, sharing in his grief.

"Have lunch with an old man, please," he pleaded when he composed himself.

Lester never asked anything of her. Since David's death, he did everything in his power to ease her burden. He took care of the police, coroner's report, the funeral, the media, and the execution of David's will. A few months after David's death, he handed her the title to her house. Lester had paid off the mortgage in its entirety. Even the company that held David's life insurance policy stopped their inquiry and paid out his enormous one point five-million-dollar policy.

Mikala didn't have the heart to turn away Lester. He was different from her father in many ways, but he was a good man. Lester took Mikala to the Timeless Tea House where he introduced her to the pomp and pageantry of high tea. From then on, he stopped by her house once a week and walked with her to visit Molly. After, they went to the Tea House for high tea.

At first, Mikala and Lester talked little. But over the months that followed, she opened up to him and he to her. A strange and wonderful bond formed. The only thing that bothered Mikala was Lester's refusal to discuss the deadly accident that took Molly's life. "I know you spoke with the police at length when I was distraught. Did they shed any light on the accident?" Mikala asked him one day over tea.

Lester stopped stirring his tea and dropped the spoon with a clatter. He raised his head and scrutinized her. His lips pressed together as his hands closed into fists. "There's nothing to discuss. Nothing you need to know. Nothing that will bring back Molly." He studied her with his ice-blue eyes. "Mikala, we will never talk about this again. Am I clear?"

Mikala straightened her spine and squared her shoulders. She opened her mouth to argue, but as Lester picked up the spoon once more, she noted his hand shake. She barely heard his next words.

Lester's face paled. "I can't. It's done." Agony suffused his features and ran through him like a live current. He trembled.

Mikala understood the pain that came with revisiting the accident and Molly's death, but Lester's reaction made her wonder if he knew more than he was telling her. Despite all the questions Lester's reaction raised, Mikala dropped the subject and never brought it up again. She loved Lester, and she couldn't bear to witness his pain.

Allowing Lester to spend the one-year anniversary of Molly's death with her was an easy decision. Rena offered to come, but Mikala refused. Rena admitted she found the cemetery overwhelmingly sad. Although visiting Molly wasn't exactly joyous, Mikala felt Molly's presence and found peace in the stillness of the cemetery.

Mikala wanted to show Molly she was better. She'd relearned the basics—breathing, talking, and walking. She even learned to eat a meal and sleep on her own. Like a survivor of a devastating illness or injury, Mikala rehabbed enough to master the basics— the activities of daily living. Now came the bigger challenge. She had to move on to higher levels of functioning—finding purpose in her life. Maybe one day she'd even find happiness. She wanted Molly to find eternal rest and peace, knowing her mama would be okay.

Mikala stumbled and would have fallen if Lester didn't support her with a fortifying grip at her elbow. She glanced up, surprised to find they'd neared Molly's grave.

Lester studied her. "Are you okay, Mikala?"

She nodded, but her attention was on her daughter's butterfly-topped headstone and the man kneeling by the graveside. Mikala's entire body and all its functions came to a grinding halt. For a few seconds her mind blanked, her lungs seized, and her heart paused.

Jake. Oh God, he was back.

After the initial shock eased, the elephant that rested against Mikala's chest since the day Jake walked out of her life shifted and tumbled away. Mikala inhaled, filling her lungs to capacity for the first time in six months.

Mikala studied and cataloged every inch of Jake—muscular thighs, narrow-waist, flat abdomen, broad-shoulders, square jaw, flint-colored eyes, and jet-black hair. Some described his eyes as cold as steel and calculating as a predator, but he'd always regarded her with affection and understanding. She closed her eyes and savored his presence back in her world. Then reality hit.

Six months. Six months of silence. Six months of pain and loneliness and a growing anger that turned to downright rage at his abandonment. Tears traveled down Mikala's cheeks. She took another luxurious deep breath and, with a trembling hand, swiped away the tears.

Mikala shook her head. She couldn't deal with Jake. Not today. She scanned the cemetery and noticed the old battered truck parked under the oak tree. Why hadn't she noticed Red before? Jake had no right to be here. And Jake had every right to be here.

Mikala gritted her teeth and again shook her head. She should behave like an adult, shove aside her feelings, and be more understanding. After all, he too must be hurting. But...*screw it!* She didn't have to pretend. She didn't have to make nice, and she didn't have to justify her actions. What for? Who for? She made excuses for David's behavior after Molly's death, and where had that gotten her? Abandoned and alone.

Like David, Jake had abandoned her when she needed him the most. Whatever she'd said or done shouldn't have mattered. She'd been crazed with grief. If he loved her the way he said he did, and if he were truly her family, how could he leave when she was broken and needed him the most? Mikala shook with rage. This day was hard enough without him.

"Mikala?"

Turning her head, Mikala met Lester's gaze. "I need him gone. I can't do this. I…" Her voice broke. "Please, do this for me. Tell him to go. Please, Lester." Mikala dropped her chin to her chest, and her shoulders slumped as more tears spilled down her cheeks.

Lester pulled a handkerchief out of his pocket and dried her cheeks. "Are you sure this is what you want? Maybe the time has come for you two to talk and clear the air."

Mikala raised her head. She focused on Molly's grave, and then on the man she'd called her best friend and super-man.

Jake stared back.

Mikala's breath hitched. Nothing had changed. Jake still resembled the sexiest Latino version of a superhero on the face of the planet. But even from a distance she saw the guilt and utter anguish written all over his features. The man was the picture of misery with his head hung low and his shoulders slumped.

God, she couldn't deal with him right now. The confusing and opposing emotions—the push and pull—she experienced each time she looked at him were dizzying. She wanted to run to him, hold him and comfort him, and allow him to comfort her. But she also wanted to slap him and shake him until he promised to never again walk away, no matter how hard things got.

Mikala glanced to the side. "No, Les," she whispered. "Tell him to go. This isn't the place or the time for the conversation he and I must have. I'm not ready. I won't do this here." She swallowed past the lump in her throat. "Today is not about me and Jake. Today is about honoring my daughter's memory, and although I get why he came, I can't have him here right now."

Lester touched Mikala's chin. "Just like you, that boy's hurting. I don't know why he left, but I'm certain he had his reasons. Why don't you hear him out?"

Mikala squared her shoulders, and her hands closed into fists at her sides. Why was Lester pushing? Why didn't he understand the war raging inside her? She wanted to let in Jake. She longed for Jake. But he destroyed her trust, and she couldn't open herself again to more pain. She had nothing left to give anyone, including Jake. "Tell him to go. For me, Les, tell him to go."

Lester stared for a minute, and then he nodded.

As she watched Lester pick his way across the gravel road toward Jake, Mikala doubted her actions. Was Lester right? Should she hear out Jake? Maybe she should be stronger, more reasonable, more forgiving and understanding. Mikala shook her head. What the hell was she doing? Why was she putting herself through this agony? She lived with enough guilt and self-doubt to last her a lifetime. Her life was one big carnival ride, and she didn't need Jake's emotional tilt-a-whirl, or Lester's roller coaster of guilt. They could both go to hell and leave her to deal with the avalanche of emotions she was holding at bay.

The conversation that ensued between Lester and Jake was long and seemed heated at times, but Mikala wasn't worried. Lester was a powerful man and a gifted litigator. He wasn't one to be argued with. Jake respected him and would listen. Jake was also a good man. He wouldn't like what she asked of him, but he would respect her wishes. He would go...eventually.

Seeing Jake suddenly swing his head toward her, she gasped. Unable to witness his anger and pain, she dropped her head and didn't raise it again until a car door slammed. Mikala shivered in the stifling midday heat and sighed.

Jake was gone. Again.

Mikala stumbled to her daughter's grave and forced all thoughts of Jake out of her mind. With the bouquet of yellow daisies clutched in her hand, she sank to her knees. She smiled and glanced to the heavens, blinking against the glare of the sun. A warm summer breeze caressed her cheeks. Dropping her head, Mikala focused on the words engraved on the headstone, *Molly Ann Jacobson—Our Butterfly*. "Hi there, Butterfly. It's your mama. I feel you, baby. I know you're here." Mikala laid the yellow daisies next to Jake's white ones.

For the last six months, every week a fresh bouquet of white daisies lay at Molly's grave. Although some days Mikala was tempted to throw them away, she never did. Jake forgot her, not Molly. Molly was his butterfly, too, and Mikala wouldn't deny her daughter the beauty of those flowers or the love that came from a man who had considered her his daughter.

"I miss you, baby girl. God knows how much I

miss you. I'd be lying if I said I was all healed. Baby, don't ask that of me. That would be impossible. But, Molly, I'm better, and I promise I'll work on getting my act together even more. Daddy's with you now. Give him a hug and a kiss for me. Tell him..." Mikala's voice broke, and she cleared her throat. "Tell him I love him." She closed her eyes, waiting for the inevitable question. For the last six months, Molly asked the same question.

"Mama, where's Jake?"

Mikala could finally provide an answer.

Chapter Eight
His Daily Friends

One look from Mikala incinerated Jake where he stood in front of Molly's grave. Did he expect Mikala to forgive him? Did he think she would open her arms wide and welcome him back after he walked out? He was a clueless idiot.

All Jake knew was he needed his family. He needed Mikala. He couldn't have his family as it had been—safe, sound, intact, and untouched by tragedy. The time for miracles had passed. But he'd be damned if he lost Mikala, too. He had to find a way to heal the hurt he'd inflicted.

Jake and Mikala had never been this angry, hurt, or distant from one another. The path to forgiveness and recovery was uncharted and filled with potholes and fallen debris. Had they gone too far in their pain and said too much to forgive and forget? He hoped not, because without her, his life would never be complete. But that fact was nothing new.

Since the first time Mikala smiled at Jake across the crowded lawn at Yale, whenever she was anywhere in his vicinity, he never failed to sense her. No matter how far they drifted from one another, some things would never change. She would always be a part of him, and he would always know where she was. He only wished he knew what she needed to ease her pain and bring back even a hint of her alluring smile.

Jake would give anything to see any semblance of the happy, carefree woman Mikala used to be. The woman who stood shooting daggers at the gravesite bore no resemblance to the confident, sassy girl he first met at the age of nineteen. She also wasn't anything like the talented woman who earned a law degree, scored a position in one of New Haven's coveted law firms, and then gave it up for an even more prestigious position—Molly's mother. Jake ran a hand through his hair and watched as Lester walked slowly toward him.

Lester leaned on his cane. "I'm sorry, son, but she wants you to leave."

Six months. Jake was gone six months, and in that time, everything and everyone he knew in New Haven changed. The Lester Jacobson standing before him was nothing like the man Jake knew for the last twenty years. Lester had aged and now used a new accessory he never needed in the past. The deep grooves of sorrow transecting his face, gravelly voice, slumped shoulders, and the shadows of grief lurking in his now-dull blue eyes, told the story of loss and devastation. He was a broken man.

"I won't presume to understand why you took off the way you did. I'm certain you had your reasons, but today..." Lester's voice broke, and he exhaled raggedly. "Today, son, isn't the day for explanations and absolution. She's barely holding on."

Swallowing hard, Jake shook his head. He should have stayed away, but he couldn't. He had to come. He had to pay his respects to his little butterfly. Surely, Mikala knew he would come? He didn't think she would begrudge him this time with Molly. He hoped she was ready to forgive him. After all, she'd asked him to leave, and against his better judgment, he'd done as she asked.

At the end of the day, Jake fucked up everything. Like an idiot, he returned without a plan. He couldn't take away the pain and anger that still festered in her. He couldn't give back her child or her husband, and he couldn't explain why he left. Why the fuck did he return?

Mikala blamed him for David's death. She'd said he didn't do enough, and she was right. Maybe she spoke in the heat of the moment and in grief, but no words were truer. Jake spent the last six months coming to grips with the fact had he paid more attention, and had he listened closer, he could have saved his best friend and brother.

Jake turned toward Mikala. She dropped her head and even from a distance, he saw her painfully small frame shake. He hurt her. He added to her sorrow. He was a selfish bastard. Guilt, remorse, and self-condemnation were his daily friends. Since the day David died, they took each breath and each step with him. Now they reappeared.

He hung his head, and his shoulders slumped. He shouldn't have come. He wasn't ready to face Mikala, and she didn't want anything to do with him. They were still lost and shattered. Maybe this is how they will always be, but he hoped that wasn't the case.

The last six months had been hell. At times, the weight of David's confessions was too much to bear, and no end was in sight. He alone would carry them for a lifetime. Sparing Mikala and Lester was the least he could do. Six months wasn't enough to grow a set or to find a way to stand tall under the weight of his burdens without his shoulders sagging, and his back aching. Jake shuffled toward Red.

"Jake."

He stopped, turned, and met Lester's gaze.

"She needs you, boy. She's better, but she needs you. The time has come for you to return home and for both of you to heal together. David would want you to take care of her and she of you. She doesn't comprehend you two were meant to be together, but you do. Don't you, boy?" Lester scrutinized Jake. "Neither of you will be whole ever again without each other."

Jake ground his teeth and shook his head. He had a great deal of respect for Lester, but the man didn't know what he asked. Over the years, Jake and Lester had their differences, especially where David was concerned. But they also forged a relationship and a bond few knew about or understood. Underneath his gruff exterior lay a kind, loyal, and compassionate man who loved deeply and would do anything for his family.

Lester was caught in the trappings of his own upbringing and tradition. He loved the only way he knew and raised his children in the manner he was raised—with a firm hand and an unforgiving voice that set unbearably high expectations. He was a well-respected, highly sought-after litigator. Jake didn't believe a smarter, savvier, and more insightful attorney existed. To this day, Lester was an icon at Yale Law. He continued to train the best and the brightest interns in his renowned law practice and was one of Yale's biggest benefactors. Molly inherited his penetrating blue eyes and shrewd, discerning mind.

Staring into Lester's eyes, Jake couldn't deny the truth. Lester was right. For twenty years, he, Mikala, David, and Rena functioned as a unit. At nineteen, Mikala was transplanted to New Haven, escaping the farmlands of the Midwest, while Rena stalked across the border from Manhattan, taking Yale by storm. Almost from the beginning, Mikala and Rena loved Connecticut and Yale. They adapted easily to their new environment.

David grew up in New Haven and was right at home at Yale. His family had deep roots in the community and the University. David had no choice but to follow his grandfather and father to Yale Law School.

Unable to hold Lester's gaze, Jake studied the cloudless sky. Jake's story was altogether different. New Haven was nothing like East LA. Jake didn't fit in, and he didn't give a flying fuck. He went to Yale to make something of himself and make Mateo proud. He didn't come to form new friendships, and he certainly didn't expect to find a family. But Mikala, Rena, and David entered his life, and within a few short months, the kid who never had a real family or friends he could count on, suddenly had both—so much perfection and so much beauty. He had a hard time trusting all the good filling his world was real.

Mikala fell in love with David. Rena, with her brazen beauty and her trash-talking, sassy mouth, set her sights on Jake, despite his insistence he wasn't interested. Over the months that followed, Mikala and Jake's friendship grew, and they became inseparable. David was wise enough to understand, if he wanted Mikala, Jake was part of the package. He and Jake formed a strong friendship and a brotherhood based on respect and loyalty.

Jake was grateful to David for sharing Mikala, and neither he nor Mikala crossed the line that bordered between friendship and passion. Jake was certain if he'd made an effort, however, he could have won Mikala's heart and claimed her. But stealing her from David would have exploded the precious friendship they forged.

Early in their relationship, Jake determined Mikala deserved better than what a poor kid on scholarship with a fucked-up childhood could offer. Before their deaths, his father and brother had been members of one of the most violent gangs in LA. And Jake's mother worked herself into an early grave, caring for two children on her own and paying off her husband's endless debt.

Clearing his throat, Jake focused on Lester. Jake may have escaped the life he was born into, but he was still not good enough for Mikala Jacobson. "She doesn't want me here, Lester, and I can't blame her. They were my family. The only family I had, and she's everything to me." Jake swallowed hard. "But I...I can't fix our shattered lives. I should've done..." Jake's voice broke, and he looked away. How would he find the words to explain to Lester David's tragic death could have been prevented if he'd acted faster and did more?

"Jake, son, look at me."

Jake couldn't meet his gaze.

He let out an exasperated huff. "Come on. Look at me, boy."

Jaw tight, Jake glanced at Lester.

"David's death wasn't your fault."

Jake shook his head. "You don't know—"

"Don't interrupt me." Lester stood to his full height and straightened his shoulders. "I know what I'm talking about. You think you're the only one my boy confided in? Do you?"

Jake's mouth opened and closed, and his eyes widened.

Lester's hands fisted. "Well, you're wrong. I knew well before you did."

Stiffening, Jake stopped listening and stopped breathing. Lester knew? God! Lester looked like he had one foot in the grave for a reason. What a fucking nightmare.

"Are you listening to me, boy?"

The older man's voice thundered in Jake's ears. He scrubbed a hand over his face. "I'm sorry, Lester. I had no idea he called you. I assumed I was the…"

Eyes narrowing, Lester's face turned to stone. "You listen to me and listen good. David was my boy. I'll carry his sins to my grave. You don't have to. I wish to God I wasn't on this earth to see the mess he made of not only his life, but of all our lives. But the good Lord refused to spare me or you. I made my son who he was. I will take responsibility for that, but I won't add his death to my burden, and neither should you."

Jake closed his eyes, and for just a few seconds, the knot in his gut loosened. Perhaps he wasn't to blame for David's death. He opened his eyes and shook his head. He may not be entirely responsible, but he hadn't done enough. "I wish I could absolve myself of his death that easily. David was your son, but he was my brother. I loved him and accepted him for what he was. He was deeply troubled. I let him down."

"Son, you're a good man, and I know David loved you and leaned on you—too much. But that's a conversation for a different day." Lester swallowed hard, and then cleared his throat. "The fact is, David did what he wanted to do, as he always did, without considering the consequences of his actions. He didn't think about you, Mikala, Rena, or the rest of us. He decided to end his life. Nothing you or I said or did would have stopped him. He was lost. Death was his choice, and the sooner we all wrap our heads around that, the better off we'll be." His eyes filled with tears, and he hung his head as he leaned onto his cane once again.

Jake wanted to reach out to steady the man who aged and shrunk in front of his eyes. But he knew better. Lester would not appreciate the gesture. Instead, Jake stayed silent, giving the old man time to lasso his emotions. Although nothing was left to say, and he'd heard enough, Jake waited out Lester. He'd been around the man enough to know, Lester had yet to complete his closing argument.

"My boy did a terrible thing. He made a terrible decision, and in a split second, he lost everything. He couldn't own up to it. He wasn't a man. My boy was weak. He was a coward. I expect better of you."

Chapter Nine
Men Don't Run, Men Don't Hide

Jake stood speechless. His heart raced, and blood roared in his ears. He needed time to think and to digest Lester's words. He didn't condone David's actions, and he had difficulty understanding David's decision to take his life, but he didn't think of him as a coward.

Running a hand through his hair, Jake looked toward the heavens, praying for understanding and wisdom. He searched for the right words to say to the man who'd opened doors, supported him, and fathered him more than his own father ever had. But the heavens were silent.

Once more, Lester cleared his throat. "You were the strong one, Jake. You held them together. You spent almost twenty years fighting David's battles, cleaning up after him, and saving his ass."

"Lester, you don't know what you're—"

"Stop!" Lester commanded, stamping his cane into the earth. "I may be old, but I'm hardly senile. I know everything. You could have left at any time, chosen a different path, and a woman of your own. But you chose this life. You chose to stay guarding over a woman who loved another. Now is the time for you to step up. Be a man." Lester pinned Jake with his gaze and pointed a finger. "Be a better man than my boy was."

Be a man.

Jake closed his eyes and absorbed the familiar words. He'd heard them before coming from another's mouth. His heart pounded against his ribcage with strength he didn't think the little organ possessed. Lester never minced words, and he didn't take up the habit now. But Lester said too much. He wasn't wrong, but he said more than Jake was capable of handling at the moment.

Without a word, Jake turned. He walked to Red, jumped inside, and slammed the door. He drove out of the cemetery gates and onto Grove Street, gripping the steering wheel hard enough for a sharp pain to radiate from his clenched fists through his wrists and forearms. He controlled the impulse to push Red as fast as she could go until he hit I-95. Then, he gave in to his need for speed. He had no idea where he was headed. He had to put as much distance as possible between him, Lester, and Mikala.

Halfway to Jersey, Jake eased his foot off the gas pedal and slowed Red. He steered the truck off the highway and pulled into the parking lot of a dilapidated diner. Jake released a ragged breath and raked a hand through his hair. He was tired of hurting, grieving, thinking, and running. Running and working long-assed days that never ended was all he was good at lately. Neither filled the hole in his heart or soul, and neither brought him any closer to a solution. He should talk to someone. But most of the people Jake normally called when he needed someone to lean on were either dead or didn't want to hear from him—Mikala, David, and Mateo. The only one left was Rena.

Jake rested his head against the headrest and closed

his eyes. He wondered what Mateo would have thought about the wreck he'd made of this life. He was certain his brother would have reduced this sordid mess to the basics—family, friendship, loyalty, brotherhood, taking responsibility, and being a man. In the world Jake and Mateo grew up in, those bonds and virtues were the essentials of life.

Be a man.

"You want to be a man? A good man? Work hard and stand on your own legs. Take responsibility...for your life, family, woman, decisions, and actions. No excuses. Men don't fucking run, and men don't hide like pussies." This mantra had been Mateo's, and he ingrained it in Jake from a young age. With a father in prison, and a mother working three jobs to support her boys, Mateo had reared Jake.

Jake idolized his big brother, the man of the house. He wanted to make Mateo proud, and those words seemed easy enough to live up to. As Jake grew, he learned better. He opened his eyes and shook his head.

Men don't run. Men don't hide.

Running and hiding. That's what he'd been doing––from himself and from Mikala. Six months ago, after his encounter with Mikala, he'd driven to Rena's house and sat in his truck. She found him at the end of her shift, hiding from the world and having his own pity-party.

Rena banged on the driver's window, startling him. She gestured for him to follow her inside. As Jake explained what happened, her face turned crimson, and her anger knew no limits. She raged and called him every name in the book. Like Lester, that little redhead never minced words. "I get it. You don't give a shit about me. You never have, but what about her? How the fuck could you walk out on her?"

"Rena, you know that isn't true. I love you both. You're my family. You're the only people I have left that give a fuck about me, but I'm doing more harm than good. She blames me for his death. Hell, she can't stand to look at me. For God's sake, just listen." Jake broke down as he'd never done before.

Rena stopped ranting and listened. They sat for hours, pouring out their hearts to one another and confronting old and new hurts. "We can't protect her from the world. We must push her to live in her new reality. Right now, you're no good to each other. You feed off each other's pain and grief. I can see that now. You can't save her, Super-man. She must do that on her own and in her own way. Go home, Jake. She'll be ready to hear from you again one day. That day, however, is not today and won't be tomorrow."

For the first time in two decades, under the very worst of circumstances, Jake and Rena forged a friendship. A friendship built on years of love and hate and hurt and happiness. That night, Rena turned from enemy to ally.

When they were in college, she gave him her heart. But when Jake didn't return her feelings, Rena's resentment grew. To make things worse, Jake committed the ultimate asshole move. After Mikala and David's wedding, Jake and Rena ended up in bed. Fulfilling all clichés, they celebrated their friends' nuptials in their own drunken way. Later, when Jake apologized and showed no interest in furthering their relationship beyond one night, Rena declared war.

Over the years, Rena's anger dulled, but she

disliked and distrusted him. With her sharp tongue, she took every opportunity to launch arrows his way, stopping only when Molly was nearby. But they'd finally put the past to rest and now often talked deep into the night once she finished her nursing shift. Rena gave him the Mikala updates he required to stay sane, and he gave her the friendship and support she longed for.

Jake turned on the interior truck light and checked his watch. Five-fifteen p.m. Rena's shift started at seven p.m. He dialed.

"I've been waiting for your call."

Rena's somber voice rang in his ears. "Guess you know me pretty well by now."

"I don't know about that. But I do know you need to stop running and talk to her."

Jake ran a hand over his face. "I went to the cemetery. I tried to, but she—"

"Yeah, I know. What did you expect? The cemetery isn't a great place for explanations. Not today."

"Okay." Jake sighed. "I get it. My timing was lousy, but that fact doesn't matter anyway. She's not ready. She still doesn't want me near her."

"For God's sake, buck up, man. You want me to tell you what to do? Fine. She misses you. She's hurting. Go. Explain your ass. Apologize. Tell her you've been a dick, and you love and miss her. Kiss and make up. She needs you, and you need her. Hell, I miss you and need you, and that's saying a hell of a lot." Rena huffed. "Are you listening, Jake?"

Jake smiled and sat up straighter, experiencing a burst of energy accompanied by a zing of hopefulness rushing through his veins. "Yes, General, I hear you. I understand my orders and will do my best to execute them."

"Very funny. Go to the house. She's there by herself. Call me when you're done."

"I'll do that. Bye, Rena."

Jake bounded out of the truck and went into the diner. He ordered a large black coffee, hopped back into Red, and headed for Mikala. All the way there, he prayed he'd find the right words to say what needed to be said. Two hours later, he parked in front of the dark house. He stepped into the warm August night and leaned against Red.

For a few minutes, he closed his eyes and listened to the conversations of the creatures of the night. He was a night owl. When he was in Connecticut, he enjoyed sitting on the porch deep into the night when most humans were at rest, and the other creatures that inhabited the earth came out to play.

Moving to Connecticut all those years ago had been like immigrating to a foreign country. Although he understood the language, people spoke with an uppity lilt he couldn't imitate. He couldn't even find a decent Mexican restaurant in New Haven. He was miserable and wondered how he would survive four years. But then he discovered the peaceful, stillness, and beauty of the night.

Jake grew up with horns blaring, people shouting and arguing, and even gunshots filling the nighttime hours. But in New Haven, he was introduced to a new orchestra that gathered and composed when the sun went down and the moon lit the stage—the rustling of leaves as squirrels and chipmunks gathered and hid their bounty, the swaying of branches and tall grass as the wind swept through the city, and the nightly melodies of crickets and cicadas. For once, when the sun set, his heart rate slowed to a healthy pace, and he breathed easy. He was safe. Each and every time he experienced the wonders of Mother Nature his soul was renewed.

Sighing, he opened his eyes and straightened. He walked to Mikala's front door. He still had no idea what to say. The drive hadn't been as helpful or as enlightening as he hoped. He had no idea if Mikala was awake, but the time was only eight-thirty. The door opened before he knocked.

Jake dropped his arm to his side as he took in Mikala from head to toe. She was at least thirty pounds lighter than the last time he saw her. Her auburn curls were piled on her head with loose tendrils falling around her face. Her whisky eyes, framed by thick lashes, blazed in her pale face. Her chest rose and fell with ragged breaths, and her pulse galloped at the column of her long graceful neck. She was barefoot and dressed in jean cut-offs and a black tank.

Eyes wide, Mikala inspected Jake as he scrutinized her. She blinked and refocused on his face. Her lips set in a tight, thin line as she worked to control her breathing.

Jake was taken aback. She'd changed, and that change went deeper than her physical appearance. Gone was the girl who taught him how to laugh, love, and forgive. Gone was the vibrant woman who lived large, always wore a smile, and radiated joy. The angry, bitter woman standing before him was not his Micky. Jake cleared his throat and took a small step forward. "Hello,

Mikala."

Mikala stepped back and used the door as a shield between her and Jake. "What are you doing here?"

He rubbed the back of his neck and breathed out. "I'd like to talk to you. Can I come inside?"

Licking her lips, she shook her head. "No. I have nothing to say. Please leave."

As she shut the door, Jake shot out his hand, and his palm connected with the door.

She darted her gaze to his and gasped.

"Micky, please. Wait. A lot needs to be said, a fuck of a lot. You don't have to speak. Just let me talk. Just listen."

Mikala's grip tightened on the doorframe, and her knuckles turned white. She looked at her feet. For a few seconds, they stood in silence.

He waited, praying she would give him a chance. When Mikala raised her head and glanced at Jake, the pain and distrust evident in her beautiful eyes made his gut twist with bitter self-loathing. He'd put that look there. He'd hurt her. "I'm so damn sorry. I shouldn't have pushed you. I shouldn't have said the things I did, and I sure as hell shouldn't have left. I've regretted that conversation and those few minutes every day for the last six months. Please forgive me. I miss you so damn much." Jake raised his head and met her gaze again. He shoveled a hand through his hair and took a steadying breath. She didn't let him inside, but at least she didn't slam the door in his face.

Tears ran down Mikala's face.

Jake ached to put his arms around her and draw her into the comfort of his embrace, but he didn't think she was ready to accept his touch.

"Why?" she whispered. "Why did you go?"

Jake's stomach clenched. Jesus, she wanted to know why? What could he say? I killed David. Your husband drowned in guilt and shame. I knew, and I did nothing. I couldn't deal with any of it—Molly's death, your sorrow, and the crushing weight of David's secret. I was a weak son of a bitch. Was that what he was supposed to say? Would those confessions comfort her? Fuck no. Telling her would unburden him but hurt her. Hadn't she been through enough?

"I don't have a good excuse for my behavior. But I wasn't good for you, Micky. I wasn't good for anyone. I was a wreck." Jake dropped his gaze and rested his forehead against the door for a few seconds before swallowing hard and straightening. His gaze slid up to meet hers. "I'm sorry. I should have stood by you. Please forgive me."

Mikala studied him.

She gazed deep into his eyes and right through to his soul, disappointment evident in her gaze. His answer was lame. In fact, it wasn't much of an explanation at all. But he didn't know any other combination of words that would soothe her.

"I'm sorry, Jake." Mikala shook her head. "That's not good enough. You left me just like he did. I trusted you, and you took off when I needed you the most. I can't do this, and obviously, you can't either. Picking up where we left off as if nothing happened is too hard. Too many memories and too many disappointments lie between us. I'm sorry." Her shoulders slumped, and she stepped back, retreating to the safety of her home.

Jake's heart squeezed in his chest until breathing was almost impossible. He raised his arm and brushed the tears off her cheek with the back of his fingers. He wouldn't, couldn't, cause her any more pain. Rena and Lester were wrong. She didn't need him, and she didn't want him back in her life. Jake swallowed past the lump in his throat and choked out. "I'm sorry, sweetheart. I'm so damn sorry." He let his hand fall, willed his body to turn, and his legs to move toward Red and away from the only family he had left on this earth.

Six Months

February

Chapter Ten
Surviving the Un-survivable

"Goodbye, Jen. Have a good day, and thanks for coming in so early again," Mikala called over her shoulder as she walked out of the New Haven Community Center and into the frigid February day. She glanced at the heavens and smiled. The snow had stopped falling, and although the air was frigid, the wind didn't blow half as bad as it had earlier. Jennifer and the rest of her grief support group met at the community center for breakfast. They were a tight-knit group who stood by each other through thick and thin, and Mikala was grateful to have found them.

Getting through the day without breaking down would be challenging, and the group wanted her to be in the right frame of mind to survive it. Several volunteered to spend the entire day with her, but Mikala wanted to walk this road alone. She needed to prove to herself and everyone in her world, she was better and stronger. Mikala even sent Rena to the Bahamas with her new boyfriend, and she insisted Lester, who had developed a nasty cough last week, stay home.

Today was Molly's birthday and the one-year anniversary of David's death—the good and the bad rolled together into a pill most found impossible to swallow. After studying several headstones in the children's cemetery and seeing how short of a time some parents had with their babies, she no longer dreaded the anniversary of Molly's birthday. Instead, she celebrated every second she'd been gifted with her precious girl.

The anniversary of David's death was a different thing altogether. Mikala valued her grief support group's wise counsel. Often, she replayed her group leader's words, hoping one day soon she would believe them.

"David chose to take his life. That is the way he chose to deal with his pain. His death was not your fault," Liana counseled.

"You can be sad and angry, but you can't let those emotions consume your life forever," another group mate reminded her. "You're still alive. If you try, you can find joy again. You did nothing wrong, and you deserve to be happy."

A year had passed since the last time Mikala melted into the circle of David's arms at the end of a long day, leaned into his frame when the weight of the world overwhelmed her, enjoyed the scent of his musky cologne, or reveled in the caress of his lips against hers. In actuality, she lost David a year and half ago. Months before his death, he denied her the gift of his touch as well as his tenderness, understanding, and compassion. The very second Molly's heart stopped, Mikala lost everything she desired and required to connect with him, and to feel safe, secure, and loved.

Mikala still struggled with the concept of surviving her daughter and husband and building a life without them, but her new friends shared her experience and never judged. Each had their own heartbreak to overcome. Their stories differed, but the book was about loss and surviving the un-survivable. Each member contributed their own unique chapter.

As she gingerly made her way across the icy parking lot to her car, Mikala sighed. Silently, she thanked Rena and Lester for dragging her to the grief support group seven months ago. She stopped with her hand on the driver's door. A shiver of awareness ran through her, and she turned.

Jake.

All week Mikala felt the weight of someone's gaze tracking her every movement. She wasn't the least bit concerned. In fact, when goosebumps blossomed on her skin or the hair on her forearms stood, Mikala paused, surveyed her surroundings, and smiled. Jake was her little stalker. He watched over her, deciding when and if to approach.

Time and time again, she'd proven to Jake he couldn't sneak up on her. They shared a unique connection. Mikala never experienced this bond with another person on earth—not her mother, father, sister, Rena, or even David. She and Jake sensed when the other was around or in trouble. On many occasions, one or the other called or showed up on the other's doorstep.

In the beginning, David had been troubled by their weird relationship. But once he understood Jake wasn't a threat, he found humor in their odd ability. "You two are like twins separated at birth. You're creepy. I swear you guys were born with internal sonar systems. You know…like dolphins or whales that use high-frequency sounds to find each other?"

"Ooh, I bet we could make some money if we lent them to the bio or psych department for experiments,"

Rena had joined in.

Mikala scanned the vicinity. Although she couldn't see Jake, her sonar pinged, alerting her he was near. The only time her sonar failed her was the last time he surprised her at Molly's grave. She'd been too self-absorbed and drowning in her grief to hear the messages her heart sent. No matter how far or hard she pushed Jake, he wouldn't stay away for long. Thank God. A part of Mikala knew Super-man would make his way back into her life. Their story was unfinished. She wondered when he would show himself.

Six months passed and much changed. That old saying about time healing all wounds may have a hint of truth. Six months ago, Mikala thought that saying was total bullshit. She couldn't see past her pain to entertain the concept of healing. She doubted *all* wounds could mend, but hers were scarring over. The scars covered her from head to toe and went too deep for a plastic surgeon to be of any use. No amount of intervention would restore the Mikala who was David's wife and Molly's mother. While she would never again be intact and unblemished, she was functional.

Opening the driver's door, Mikala hopped inside before she froze. She turned the ignition and pushed the seat-heater button. Two weeks ago, she traded her luxury sedan for a spacious SUV, and she loved it. The car had plenty of room to lug stuff back and forth to the community center and the food bank where she volunteered. The sedan had been a gift from David on her thirty-fifth birthday, and although she told him she loved it, the car wasn't her style. The SUV was more her—the new Mikala.

Inside and out, Mikala was transformed. She was

in the process of rebuilding and redefining her life one step at a time and finding her way in a world missing so many of the people she loved. She was a different woman from the one who rejected Jake's apology and asked him to leave, unable to witness the guilt and pain washing over his features each time he looked at her. Understandably, she was also different from the woman she was when they were whole, before their lives were obliterated. But she tortured them both.

Living without Jake was her decision. She forced this choice upon them both, and to this day, she stood by her decision to deal with her grief in her own way. Now, she understood people dealt with loss in different ways. In one year, she experienced a double blow, and she no longer felt guilty for the methods she used to survive and thrive.

Driving out of the icy parking lot, Mikala scanned the area searching for Red. The truck was nowhere in the vicinity. Was she disappointed or relieved? Probably a little of both. She feared Jake would repeat his disappearing act if she allowed him back into her life.

Mikala didn't understand why Jake left in the first place. When she asked him, he lied. But whatever he held back made no difference now. Time diluted the sting of his abandonment. Jake dealt with his grief in his own way, just as she had.

Mikala shook her head. She had to get her act together. Next to David, Jake was the person she trusted most in the world and the person who knew her best. She needed him back in her life so she could breathe. Yes, Rena was a close and treasured friend. But Jake fulfilled every role, every need, but one—lover. That role had only ever been David's.

Jake was Mikala's best friend and confidant. He was her big brother, partner in crime, and her superhero—all rolled up in one. She shared her dreams and her darkest fears, and he never let her down—not until a year ago.

Mikala parked in front of Dixie's Flower Shop. She stepped out of her car and scanned the street. Anticipation accelerated her heartbeat. But Super-man was nowhere in sight. Sighing, Mikala squared her shoulders and rounded the car. She climbed over the pile of snow between the street and the sidewalk and made her way into the flower shop.

"Here you go, hon. Daisies for Molly." Dixie laid the flowers in Mikala's arms as her mouth turned up in a smile.

"Thanks, Dixie." Mikala smiled at the plumb, petite woman with a cherubic face. "Did you have any trouble getting them?"

"Nope, and this time I doubled the order. Strange, I had another person order daisies as well—the white kind. The place that usually supplies them couldn't find any."

Mikala froze. "Did he pick them up already?"

Dixie scrunched her forehead and studied Mikala. "How did you know the customer was a he?"

Mikala shrugged.

"He picked them up early this morning. Good-looking fella—tall, dark, and delicious." Dixie leaned forward and raised her eyebrows. "Do you know him?"

Mikala nodded. Dixie described Jake perfectly. "Actually, I do know him. He was Molly's godfather." Before Dixie could ask any more questions, Mikala thanked her and left the shop on wobbly knees. Her imagination hadn't been working overtime. Jake *was* in town.

As she drove to the cemetery, Mikala wondered if Jake would be there. She missed him almost as much as she missed Molly and David. Now was the time to fix things between them—forgive and move on. Now was also the time to admit she lashed out and hurt him. He wasn't any more responsible for David's death than she was. Plus, she had to ask for his forgiveness.

What would Jake think of her now? Would he approve of the new life she forged? Her life was simple, quiet, and predictable. Most days she worked from home in the morning, doing legal research for several firms in the area—a cushy job Lester helped her carve out. She didn't need the money, but the work gave purpose to her day. She was her own boss, and she accepted as many or as few jobs as she wanted. In the afternoons, she attended support groups or did volunteer work.

On occasion, Mikala had lunch or dinner with Rena, but those times were becoming fewer now that Rena had a steady boyfriend. Mikala was happy for Rena. For so long, Rena had been her rock, and she'd made too many sacrifices. Mikala could never repay her.

Recently, Rena had admitted she'd been pregnant, but she lost the baby a few months after Molly died. "I couldn't tell you. I wanted to, but you were devastated by Molly's death, and then David died, and I…I lost the baby at seven weeks. I barely had time to come to grips with the fact I was going to be a mother."

Mikala's eyes filled with tears. She reached for her

friend's hands and held them. "I'm so sorry, Rena. I'm sorry I wasn't there for you. I wish I hadn't been so self-absorbed. My world collapsed, and I couldn't see past my own pain."

Rena shook her head and looked away. "Don't beat up yourself. No one could have done anything. I guess, the precious life I carried wasn't meant to come into the world. Anyway, I would have had to raise the baby on my own. Ben took off the second I told him he was going to be a daddy." Rena glanced at Mikala. Tears trickled down her face. "You know, Micky, I wasn't even sure I wanted to be a mother. Then I lost the baby, and the pain of losing my child cut deep. Although I didn't know her or him, I still grieved, and I understood your pain better than you knew."

During that traumatic period in Rena's life, she didn't have anyone to lean on. Mikala realized she'd been a heavy burden on the people she loved. Rena, Jake, and Lester paused their lives to keep her whole and sane. Mikala did her best to show Rena she could stand on her own, and Rena was slowly letting go and building a life of her own.

Lester, however, was another story. No matter what Mikala did or said, he hovered. He called her daily and often invited Mikala to high tea or family dinners. Tea was a treat, while dinner with the family was torture. David's mother, Sylvia, drank her way, martini after martini, through most dinners, while David's older sisters, Leslie and Priscilla, did their best to make Mikala feel small.

The Jacobson twins were aggressive, man-eating attorneys who never married. Neither sister had believed Mikala was good for David, and their respect for Mikala hit an all-time low when she chose to give up a prestigious law career to care for Molly.

"God, Mikala, we don't live in the 1950s. Why on earth would you sacrifice your career to play pat-a-cake full time?" Leslie's mouth twisted in a sneer. "Honestly, that's what nannies are for."

Priscilla rolled her eyes. "If you want to do the mommy thing, stay home for a few months. Don't make changing diapers a fulltime job. Your career will never recover. God, you're wasting your education."

"I don't want a stranger taking care of my child," Mikala argued. "I don't see my choice to stay home with our daughter as a sacrifice. Raising her fulltime, without being pulled in a thousand directions, is a privilege and a choice many don't have."

When David was alive, Mikala tolerated the witches and their opinions because they rarely saw his sisters, and she didn't want to make trouble for David. Now, she found family dinners absolute hell. Mikala attended Jacobson family dinners because she loved Lester, and the poor man didn't find any comfort in his family's arms. But keeping her mouth shut was a formidable task.

Like her, Lester struggled with Molly and David's deaths. While he and Molly had shared a close, almost magical bond, Lester's relationship with David had been rocky at best. Often, Lester had been critical and cutting with David.

"Why can't you be more like your sisters? They get it. They know what must be done to win a case. Where's your spine, boy? Use your backbone. Apply some pressure to your opponent, and maybe you'll actually win some of these cases."

Over the years, Lester launched those hurtful words and many others at his son. Although Mikala and Lester never discussed Lester's relationship with David, she was certain he now regretted every one of those damaging words. How could he not? David died without having his father's approval or feeling his father's love. That must be a heavy burden for any person to carry.

David never stood up to his father. He'd wanted to make Lester proud. To gain his father's approval, David tolerated his family's harsh treatment and worked hard at a job he hated. David insisted Mikala not interfere between him and Lester, but she struggled to understand their relationship which was so unlike the one she shared with her father. The few times she'd spoken up, Lester turned around her words and used them against David.

"Now you can't even defend yourself. You need your wife to do it. No wonder you can't win a case. I should've hired her. Too bad she won't have me."

In the past, when Jake was in town and agreed to join the family for dinner, he became embroiled in these arguments. He, however, succeeded at tempering Lester's comments. Lester respected Jake much more than he respected his own son. When Jake spoke, Lester listened. In Jake's presence, Lester occasionally praised David for a small accomplishment. But those times were rare and treasured occurrences.

Mikala may not have liked the manner in which Lester treated David, but when she witnessed the love suffusing the man's features the first time he laid eyes on Molly, her heart softened. When Molly entered the world, and when he was in her presence, Lester became a different person altogether. He transformed into a soft-spoken, doting grandfather who was fiercely protective of Molly and Mikala. Lester was two different people—tough and unrelenting with David and gentle, loving, and supportive with Mikala and Molly.

While Sylvia and the witches barely acknowledged Molly, Lester more than made up for their neglect. He not only showered Molly with presents, he gifted Mikala and Molly with his time and devotion. Lester was one of the few people who calmed Molly when she cried as an infant. Each time Mikala called, he dropped what he was doing and came over at all hours of the day and night.

When Molly was a few months old, Mikala had been desperate. Molly wailed for almost three hours straight, and Mikala joined her for the last hour. Exhausted, she called Lester sobbing. He canceled a full day of clients and rushed to the house. Within twenty minutes, he stood in front of her door ready to take over.

"Now, now, Molly-mine," he crooned as he paced through the house in a three-piece Armani suit and a burping towel on his shoulder. "Tell your old grandpa who pissed you off, and I'll take care of them. You tell me what you want, my angel, and Grandpa will do whatever it takes to get your heart's desire. Nothing is too big or too small. Would you like a car? Would you like a pony? Would you like a castle? Would you like a sailboat? How about a small pink airplane?"

Lester comforted Molly for hours by murmuring these and other ridiculous questions. His tender words and touch worked that day and every day Molly was in a temper. The second she heard his voice, Molly calmed and stared into his eyes as if she understood every word. When Molly learned to talk, she and Grandpa Lester would spend hours walking hand-in-hand and talking about everything under the sun, including the art of fly fishing and world politics.

At the sweet memory, Mikala sighed. For the few years she was on this earth, Molly brought joy to many people's lives.

Mikala parked her car as close as possible to Molly's grave, grabbed the daisies from the passenger seat, and stepped out of the car. She followed the fresh footprints to the butterfly headstone that was cleared of snow. Daisies lay as bright as the sun against the fluffy white snow blanketing Molly's grave. Once more, Mikala was too late. Jake had come, and he had gone.

Chapter Eleven
Christopher Columbus and the New World

Mikala laid her daisies beside Jake's. "Hi, baby girl," she whispered. "It's your mama, sweetness. Happy birthday. I can't believe you're seven. Where has the time flown?" With the back of her hand, Mikala wiped the few tears that trailed down her cheeks. At times like these, David was the lucky one. "I know you're with Daddy, Molly. Tell him I love him and miss him."

Closing her eyes, Mikala tilted her head to the heavens. She waited, breathing in and out. Molly always came. She always blessed and soothed Mikala with her touch. Sure enough, the clouds parted, and the sun warmed Mikala's face as the wind kicked up and ran its fingers through her hair.

Holes in heaven.

Mikala smiled and opened her eyes. "I know you're here, Butterfly. You'd be so proud of your mama. I miss you, and I don't think that feeling will ever change. But I'm doing better."

"Mama?"

Mikala's heartrate sky-rocketed, and her hand flew to her chest. She hadn't heard Molly's voice in some time. The sound of her baby's voice never scared her, but she was troubled by the plaintive tone in Molly's voice.

Hadn't she done all the right things? She rebuilt her life, and each day she improved. She was learning to live again. Why wasn't her baby-girl at rest? What was Mikala missing? "Butterfly," Mikala whispered as she traced the butterfly wings of the headstone with the tips of her fingers. "Every day, I feel stronger and more hopeful. Rest, my darling. Your mama will be just fine. Rest, my sweet."

"Mama, where's Uncle Jake?"

Mikala gasped. *Where's Uncle Jake?* She closed her eyes and hung her head. Molly was much wiser than her mama. She knew who was missing in Mikala's life—Jake. Mikala wasn't lying. She was better. But Molly had been a perceptive child and held her mother's feet to the fire. She wouldn't accept Mikala's half-hearted declaration of, "I'm fine. I'm better."

Was Molly only worried about Mikala, or was something wrong with Jake? Mikala's eyes flew open, and she sank to her knees in the snow. Rena spoke with Jake on a regular basis, and he and Lester kept in touch. Neither Rena nor Lester mentioned anything being wrong. But they wouldn't. Mikala banned conversation about Jake.

Until today, Mikala hadn't paid close attention to her own internal sonar. She closed her eyes once more and searched for Super-man. After a few minutes, she gave up. The only emotions she tapped into were sadness and loneliness. Nothing new there. Every time Jake crossed her mind in the last year, she felt the same thing—sad and lonely. How *was* Jake doing now?

Jake didn't allow many people in his life. His group of friends was limited, and his love life was non-existent. He had a series of brief affairs all ending when the poor girl wanted more than he could give. The man refused to commit to anyone and was hopeless with relationships.

Over the years, plenty of women fell for Jake. He was irresistibly delicious eye candy. When he stopped brooding, he was charming. But as far as Mikala could remember, other than the disastrous relationship he had with Alison Pennington in law school, he never again allowed anyone to get close.

Alison Pennington had been a sophomore at Yale when she set her sights on Jake. She was the only daughter of a well-known business magnate, rivaling Bill Gates. Eight months after they met, young Alison, having kept their relationship a secret from her parents, introduced Jake over July Fourth weekend.

Mr. Pennington wasn't a fool. He knew about Jake and had him investigated. When Jake declared his love, and his intention to marry Alison after graduation, Mr. Pennington made his opinion on the matter clear. Jake Cardona wasn't good enough for the Pennington Princess. In a move everyone but Jake saw coming, Mr. Pennington threatened to disinherit Alison if she continued her relationship. With hardly a tear, she immediately cut off Jake.

Mikala shook her head. Jake's experience with Alison fed into his insecurities. When the subject of relationships came up, he would turn to Molly and say, "My heart belongs to Molly. Isn't that right, Butterfly? I'm yours and…?"

"You're mine, all mine, Uncle Jake," Molly would say, giggling.

Sighing, Mikala stood and brushed the snow off her coat and pants. Without Mateo, David, or her,

Jake's world would have narrowed to Lester and Rena. His variety of women and long list of business acquaintances didn't count. He wouldn't depend on them or take them into his confidence.

Mikala had her support group as well as Lester and Rena, but she was certain, just like Lester, Jake wouldn't seek help to deal with his grief. Sharing with strangers wasn't his style. Was Jake feeling as lost and as lonely as she? Did he need her as much as she needed him? "Molly, is Uncle Jake okay?" she asked the butterfly headstone.

Molly stayed silent.

A knot formed in Mikala's stomach. Molly was gone. She'd delivered her message and retreated into Mikala's heart for safekeeping. Mikala didn't care what anyone thought or said about her conversations with Molly. Until she'd lost Molly, she wasn't a believer. Now Mikala didn't doubt Molly was with her in spirit. She guided her and gave her what she needed to move on with her life.

Mikala spent a few more minutes talking to Molly and enjoying the peacefulness of the cemetery. After saying her goodbyes, she drove to the other section of the cemetery where David was buried. She grabbed the roses from the passenger seat and made her way to the gravesite. There, too, Jake had been already.

Laying her flowers next to his, Mikala said a small prayer. Initially, she'd waited two months before she visited him. But now she stopped by every few weeks. She'd loved David with all her heart, but he left her. When Molly died and he retreated, Mikala lost David for good. She mourned Molly along with the loss of her marriage.

David hadn't been perfect, but he was hers. They built a life together spanning two decades. He was her friend and lover, and the man who fulfilled her little girl dreams. He was her Prince Charming. She loved the life they built, the child they created, and she trusted him with her heart.

Mikala closed her eyes and recalled David's engaging smile, the angle of his jaw, and the way his hair was always in disarray. From the second Mikala had met David at the age of nineteen, he fascinated her. He wasn't like any boy she dated in her hometown of Easterville, Ohio. Like her, he was spirited and driven. He was easily bored and had an endless desire to live life to its fullest. Lester allowed David four years to live as he desired, before he had to toe the line and attend law school. David took advantage of every second and ran wild and free.

In everyone's eyes, David was a young, out-of-control rich kid, but Mikala understood him. Like her, he'd broken free from the confines and pressures of being someone everyone wanted him to be and not who he truly was.

Rena was concerned Mikala made a mistake and she expressed her concerns freely. "Why do you put up with his array of shit? You're gorgeous and smart. You could have anyone. If Jake didn't continually save his ass, David would have been expelled, or worse, a long time ago. Are you sure you know what you're doing?"

Mikala sighed and nodded. "Of course, I know what I'm doing. He makes me feel alive. I know he's a bit on the wild side, but he's good to me. He's like a horse that's been confined in his stall too long. Now that he's been freed, he's stretching his legs, throwing up his head, breathing in fresh air, and galloping free." She smiled. "You wait and see. In time, he'll slow down and come to pasture."

Opening her eyes, Mikala stared at David's headstone and shivered. Like all relationships, their marriage had its ups and downs, but he loved her and Molly and the beautiful life they built together. Didn't he?

When David took his own life, Mikala was ripped apart by every emotion possible—shock, sorrow, anger, guilt, pain, and despair. Often, she replayed their last days, weeks, and months together, and she found another reason to blame herself for his death.

"Even before Molly died, I could tell the pressure impacted him," she'd said to Rena in one of their many Rena-led therapy sessions. "He often worked late, and sometimes, he never made it home 'til morning. He drank more, and he was even short with me a few times. I should have done something or mentioned his behavior to Lester. Molly's death compounded the strain."

Rena squeezed Mikala's hand. "Stop it, Micky. Stop finding reasons to blame yourself. Blaming yourself for David's death or Molly's death is utter nonsense. You couldn't have done anything."

Mikala suffocated under the weight of grief and guilt until Rena and Lester dragged her to the community center. Then her world changed. She still didn't understand how David could love her but take his life. Suicide was a selfish act. Still, David's choices had been his own.

She couldn't hold back her tears from sliding down her face. Once upon a time, she had perfection.

Sometimes, her imagination got the best of her, and she questioned the life they built. But in her heart, she believed they'd been happy. Now, she made an effort to remember something good she and David had shared, and she had many beautiful memories to choose from.

Smiling, Mikala wiped away her tears and remembered the day after Molly was born. The nurses and doctors pressured Mikala and David to name her. At first, they'd thought Anne was the perfect name, but somehow the name didn't fit.

"How about Molly?" David suggested as he admired his daughter suckling at her mother's breast.

Mikala tried the name on her lips. Molly. Molly Anne Jacobson. The name was perfect, and the baby agreed as she opened her eyes and stared at her parents.

"Micky and Molly—the sweetest gifts a man could be given." A huge smile stretched across David's face.

David ordered dozens of personalized candy boxes with Micky and Molly's names and gave them to everyone they knew. He was the proudest father she'd ever seen, and he had been a damn good father.

As she absently rubbed her chest, Mikala studied the dates carved into David's headstone. God, he'd been so young. They had their whole life before them and years and years to live and dream. Now those years and dreams were all gone. All wasted. "Hi, David. I hope you've found peace. I wish I understood. I really do." She shook her head, and her voice broke. "I'm working on understanding, and I'm working on forgiving. I'm working on putting my life back together without you and Molly and finding meaning and purpose once again. You can rest easy. I'm healing. Every day is better than the last."

Mikala swallowed past the boulder in her throat. The wind had picked up, and she no longer felt her toes. Time to go. She shoved her hair out of her eyes and turned to walk back to her car. But after reaching the paved path, she paused. She had more she *needed* to say. No matter what anyone said, a part of her believed she hadn't done enough. One of these days, she would let herself off the hook but not today. She turned and walked back to the gravesite.

"I'm sorry, David. I'm sorry I didn't pay more attention. I'm sorry I didn't do more to ease your suffering, and I kept pressuring you to remember the accident." Mikala shook her head, and a strangled sob escaped. "I was in such pain, but that's no excuse. I hope you forgive me. I'll try to forgive myself for being less than what you needed and you for leaving me."

Mikala kissed the tips of her fingers and touched David's headstone. "I love you, David. I always will, my darling. You were my first real love, and I'll carry you in my heart, along with our child, always and forever." Wiping her eyes once more, she walked to her car and slid in. She turned the ignition and rested her head against the steering wheel. She'd survived the day.

Mikala took a deep breath and let it out. Is this what the rest of her life would be—a series of firsts accomplished on her own? God, she hoped not. More had to exist in life. How did people find meaning in their lives when everything they planned for and everything they dreamed of was no longer possible? Her life used to be busy and loud, but now the exact opposite was true. Silence no longer comforted her because lately, it was accompanied by loneliness and a tinge of fear.

Mikala reached into her bag that lay on the passenger seat. She searched for her phone and scrolled through her contacts. When she found Jake's name and selected it, his picture displayed. No matter how sad she was, She couldn't suppress the smile that stretched across her face. The picture showed Jake rubbing noses with Molly—one of Mikala's favorite pictures. Mikala had asked Jake to leave, and he did. Now, she had to beckon him home. Perhaps, together they could begin the process of rebuilding their lives in a meaningful way.

Over the last six months, she had been tempted to call Jake on a number of occasions. Somehow, the timing was always wrong, and she justified her inaction with a series of lies. She told herself if he wanted to see her, he would have stayed and fought harder when she asked him to leave after David's death and again six months ago. But he'd left, and now he didn't deserve her. She could live without him. He no longer meant anything. He was part of the past and not the future.

Every word was ridiculous and utter nonsense. Mikala invented some remarkable lies to keep herself going, but now was the time for a reality check. Jake was, and would always be, an important member of her family. She'd loved him for as long as she could remember, and she couldn't heal or go forth into this new world without him.

Rena and Lester started the journey of healing with her, and now, Jake had to join the expedition. Jake was strong, and he was a good man. He'd survived hell before. He lost everyone he loved, and he rebuilt his life. Like Christopher Columbus—well, maybe better than Columbus—Jake knew how to navigate all the twists and turns to the New World.

Mikala took a deep breath and let it out slowly. Her hands trembled, but she gripped the cell tighter and typed the three words she was certain he would understand.

Fly home, Super-man.

Chapter Twelve
Super-man's Kryptonite

Jake settled against the leather sofa in his living room. He let the warmth of the crackling fire in the hearth sink into his bones. Staring at his cell, he reread the words Mikala sent.

Fly home, Super-man.

Home. Jake swallowed past the knot in his throat. Home was always where Mikala was. Since the summer of their freshman year at Yale when Mateo had been killed in a drive-by shooting, and Rena, David, and Mikala rushed across the country to be by his side, the group became his family and his home. They stood by him day after day, refusing to leave his side.

Mateo was fifteen years older than Jake and the only family Jake had left in the world. Jake's father was killed in prison when Jake was eight, and his mother died when he was ten. When Mateo died, Jake's navigation system short-circuited. He didn't know where he fit in the world or what direction to travel. Jake lost his motivation to return to school.

As he remembered the younger, angrier version of himself, he ran a hand through his hair. Fueled by rage and grief, he'd decided to stay in LA and seek vengeance for his brother's murder. But, thank God, his Yale family had stepped in.

"I know you're hurting, but leave this to the

authorities. There's nothing you can do. You don't belong here." David grasped Jake by the shoulders and squeezed. "You never did. You know it, and so did Mateo. He wouldn't want you to seek revenge and throw away your life."

"You don't get it. You don't know what the fuck you're talking about. His life was a constant struggle for survival. My life was supposed to be the same." Jake pounded his chest with a fist. "I walked away unscathed. He never will. He sacrificed everything. I can't leave—not again. I know who did this. Everyone knows. His death can't go unanswered and ignored." Jake clenched his teeth and spat out, "He was worth more than to be shot like a dog in the street."

Mikala pulled Jake to the sofa, forcing him to sit next to her. She held his hands. "You're right, Jake. His memory should be honored. Do you think the best way to honor his memory is with more violence and, in all likelihood, with you being killed? Is that what his sacrifices were worth? From what I can see"—Mikala scanned the apartment Jake shared with Mateo before going to Yale—"his life was worth more than that."

Located east of the LA River in Boyle Heights, the two-bedroom apartment was a rundown hovel situated in the heart of gang territory that even the local law enforcement found difficult to police. Pictures of Jake, and the awards he received over the years covered every surface of the cramped space. The apartment, and everything in it, was evidence Mateo adored his brother and was proud of his accomplishments.

"You were his greatest gift and a source of joy and pride." Mikala cupped Jake's cheek. "Don't you think the best way to honor him is to fulfill his dream? For you to rise above? To succeed?"

Jake stared into Mikala's eyes, and then broke down in her arms and cried. "I don't know how to do this on my own. This place is the only one I've known as home. He was my only family."

Mikala wrapped her arms around him. "You're not alone. Look around you, Jake. I'm here. David and Rena are here. We'll be a family and make a home together. I swear to you. You'll always have a home with me."

Before Jake could change his mind, his newly formed family had packed him up and loaded his ass on a plane back to New Haven and back *home*.

Jake smiled, turned, and picked up the picture of David, Mikala, Rena, and himself sitting on the side table. They huddled around a bonfire drinking beers, teasing each other, and laughing. The photo was old and taken during one of the many parties David threw in the backyard of the rundown house they rented during law school. They were so innocent and carefree––their lives untouched by turmoil and tragedy. Jake loved that picture of his family in their first home.

Tracing their smiling faces with a finger, Jake recalled how each of his friends played a unique role in their makeshift family. Mikala was the matriarch, and the glue that kept them together, guiding them back to the fold when they strayed. Jake was the protector, keeping them safe and out of trouble, caveman-style. Rena nurtured, fed, and watered. Despite their many protests she would kill them, Rena also practiced her newly acquired nursing skills.

David was their child. Unfocused, privileged, and a bit impulsive, he was constantly in trouble—alcohol, marijuana, partying. David used and abused anything and everything to cope with the constant family pressure. Despite all the trouble he landed in, David had a huge heart. He was loving, generous, and kind. His sense of humor was wicked. Keeping David focused and out of his father's reach, however, was a fulltime job Rena, Mikala, and Jake shared. After all, someone had to give a damn about David, and someone had to love and accept him as he was, because his family certainly hadn't.

Jake shook his head, clearing the memories of the past and allowing in the troubling present and tenuous future. He placed the picture back on the table, stood, and paced his small living room. With every step, he surveyed the minimally decorated room. Jake's main residence was in LA. Although he rarely used it, he bought this small condo after he won his first big case and earned a tremendous bonus. The condo was a waste of money because most of his free time had been spent at David and Mikala's. The problem was, neither his house in LA nor the condo felt like home.

As he stared at Mikala's message, Jake's heart pounded. His fingers hovered over the telephone screen, waiting for his brain to engage and fashion the appropriate response. He needed the right words to express how sorry he was for his past fuck-ups and how thrilled he was to hear from her. He was dying to see her. He longed to jump in his car this very second and drive to her house.

Jake tamped down his excitement. He didn't want to fuck up the chance to redeem himself. He couldn't. He had to do and say the right things. After taking a deep breath, he let it out slowly. He stopped pacing long enough to look at the picture again. He ached to see Mikala's smile once more. He couldn't lose her again. But although he had a lot to say, some truths would never leave his lips.

Mikala was his most precious relationship. She'd cut him off and shunned him from her presence for a year. The few words they'd exchanged in front of her house six months ago shredded him. Jake felt cornered, and he chose to hurt her with lies than destroy her with painful truths. He longed for her and the days when they shared every aspect of their world.

Worst of all, his fucking sonar thing was malfunctioning. Jake couldn't tell if Mikala was still in survival mode or if she'd found her way out of the dark and discovered life was worth living. He prayed his sonar was repairable with no permanent damage.

Rena had kept him apprised of Mikala's progress. "Time to come back and try again, Jake. She's ready. She's calmer, healthier, even happier. But she misses you."

Jake was grateful for her updates, and perhaps she was right this time.

Lester, in his own way, was just as insistent Jake return to Connecticut. For the last six months, he'd called Jake every week with trivial law-related questions. Jake saw right through Lester's ploy, because the man was widely published on most of the topics. Every once in a while, Lester threw him a bone and shared details about Mikala's life.

"She's rejoined the land of the living once more and so should you. I've even spied her smiling a time or two. She's healing. What about you?" Lester asked Jake a few weeks ago.

Jake sighed. "I'm okay, Lester. I'm okay."

Lester huffed. "You're full of shit, boy. I know it, and you know it. You'll never be okay without your family."

Jake scrubbed a hand over his face and walked to the bar. He poured himself a generous portion of whisky and took a healthy gulp. He'd put up with Lester's weekly lectures, because he owed the man a debt he couldn't repay. If talking helped Lester, Jake was glad to do it. Lester had few people he could confide in and even fewer he could trust.

"I need you to come home, Jake. I need you, boy," he'd insisted a month ago during one of his calls.

Jake frowned. "What's the urgency, Lester? Is something wrong?"

"I'm not discussing the issue on the damn phone. I've never asked you for anything. Now, I'm calling in my chips. I need you. Will you let me down?"

Jake sighed. "Give me some time to finish things here, and I'll come." He let too many people down already. He couldn't have added Lester to the mix.

He stared into the amber liquid that resembled Mikala's eyes. He pictured her heart-shaped face, creamy skin that got burned at the hint of the sun, and her long auburn curls that ran as wild as Molly's had. He never thought of Mikala as petite, but the last time he saw her, she appeared fragile—smaller than her five-foot-five frame.

Downing half the glass with one swallow, Jake walked to the bay window. He studied the darkening sky. After setting his glass on the sill, Jake let his fingers fly across the cellphone screen. He composed the message he'd typed over and over again the last six months but never sent.

—Forgive me. I'm sorry.—

This time, Jake sent the message and closed his eyes. He rested his head against the cool window and waited. Within seconds, his phone pinged with an incoming message.

Only if you forgive me. I'm sorry, Super-man.

Jake blinked and read the text again. Forgive her? For what? She'd done nothing wrong and even if she had, he would always forgive her. He might have once been her super-man, but she was his kryptonite, and she'd never understood that. He would do anything for her—anything. Even though leaving her just about killed him, he walked away, and he gave her space—a year's worth.

Twenty years ago, Mikala saved him. She loved him unconditionally. When he would have thrown away his life—and most likely gotten himself killed—she gave him a family and a future. Her support never wavered.

Jake took a deep breath and let it out slowly. His heart hammered as he typed his message.

—You shouldn't be asking for my forgiveness. I'm the one who fucked up. I walked away. I hurt you, but I never meant to. I swear. I broke us. Please let me fix us.—

He wanted to apologize for much more. He longed to confess his sins just to unburden his soul. But he couldn't travel down this road of redemption. Mikala wasn't his priest, and no amount of apology or explanation would bring back David.

Jake didn't want to reopen old wounds. He spent the last year dealing with David's death in his own way and reached some conclusions. Jake did the best he could. Every chance he could, he stood by David's side and found him the best of care. But his best wasn't enough. No matter what Mikala believed, Jake wasn't Super-man.

Forgiving David for taking his own life and putting this unrelenting guilt to the side would take time. One day, Jake hoped he would achieve forgiveness. He understood David's motivations, but he didn't understand his actions.

Mateo's words rang in Jake's mind. "Men don't run, and men don't hide." What the hell did David think would happen to them after he died? Did he think they would carry on as if their lives weren't destroyed? And why the fuck did David confess to him *and* to Lester of all people? If he planned to kill himself, why didn't he take his secrets to his grave?

Jake couldn't absolve David, and neither could Lester. David needlessly burdened them both with his sins, and then left this world. He left them shattered even more than they already were. Jake had loved David like a brother, but his love was not blind. Like all humans, David was imperfect. Despite his shortcomings, Jake had loved him. But his confession nearly destroyed Jake.

Raking a hand through his hair, Jake resolved never to share David's ugly secrets with Mikala. Telling her had been David's responsibility, but he'd been weak. He covered up for David one too many times. He did so to protect Mikala and Molly. His continued concealment of the facts surrounding Molly's death was his final act of deception for his friend and brother. Some secrets you took to your grave, because exposing them to the light gave them power to mutilate and destroy the innocent.

Jake picked up his glass and downed the rest of the whisky. He made his way back to the sofa and waited for Mikala's text. When he read her message, he was glad he sat.

The past is over with now, Jake. He's gone, and she's gone. There's only you, Rena, and me. We're still here—left behind. We were a family. I don't know what we are now. So much has changed. Have we?

Have we? A few seconds passed before Jake understood what Mikala asked. Her question—two little words—confirmed Jake had fucked up in the worst of ways. He inhaled sharply. Mikala said the past was the past, and she forgave him for leaving. But her question revealed how badly he'd injured and scarred her. Distrust and apprehension laced Mikala's words.

Message received—loud and clear. Mikala and Jake's relationship was built on love and trust. He let out the breath he'd been holding in a long-ragged sigh. In the twenty years they'd known each other, as far as he knew, Mikala never doubted their friendship. But even a diamond wasn't immune to a stress fracture.

Jake dropped his head in his hands. His gut burned. He doubted the sensation was due to indulging in too much whisky on an empty stomach. His mouth filled with the sour taste of self-loathing and disappointment. He hadn't been much of a man. Mateo would be disappointed in him. Jake had run and hid like a fucking pussy. Before David's death, Mikala would never have questioned his sticking power or commitment. Now, he had to gain her trust once more.

They weren't whole, and their lives would never be

the same. But he, Mikala, and Rena survived the super-storm that imploded their world. They were still a family, and they had a solid foundation to rebuild on. Jake remembered who they were enough to begin the renovation.

After several minutes of contemplation where the only sounds that accompanied his racing thoughts were the occasional hissing of the fire and his steady breathing, he raised his head and stared into the dying embers. At least, Mikala opened the lines of communication once more, even if he didn't like what she said. He squeezed the cell and thought for a minute before he typed. Mikala didn't need flowery words or promises. What she needed was the truth—straight from his heart.

—You're right, Micky. You, David, Molly, Rena, and me—we were a beautiful family. We can't go back, but we can go forward. *I* know who we are. *I* remember who we are. So much has changed, but *we* have not. Let me prove it to you.—

Jake was ready to prove to Mikala *they*—he and she—were still whole. They'd been through hell, but he was still her super-man. He was ready to help her build a new future, keeping David's secrets to himself. He prayed for strength. He prayed he made the right decision, and he prayed for mercy if she ever found out the truth. Standing, he stared at his phone, and then typed.

—Be brave, sweet girl. I won't hurt you again. I won't let you down. I swear to God, I won't. Let me come home.—

After a few minutes, he received the words that had him looking up toward heaven and mouthing the words,

"Thank you!"

Okay, Super-man. Fly on over.

A huge smile stretched across his face, and he pumped his fists in the air, feeling as if he just won the Super Bowl, the World Series, and a gold medal in the Olympics for the Decathlon.

—When can I see you? I am in town.—

I know you're here, you idiot.

Jake sensed the smile in Mikala's tone, and his smile grew even bigger. Of course, she knew he was in town. She always knew when he was around.

By the way, stop stalking me. It's creepy.

He hadn't kept his presence a secret. He had been losing his mind and was pulled to her. For the last few days, he stalked her, tracking her movements from a distance.

—Okay, no more stalking, but when can I see you?—

Holding his breath, he waited. He was anxious to have this first meeting over so they could get past the awkwardness and move on to more common ground. He was convinced he could get them back to being Jake and Micky. They wouldn't be exactly who they were before losing Molly and David. How could they be with the trauma they experienced? But Jake would do his damnedest to get them as close as possible to whole once more.

Dinner tomorrow?

He exhaled, relieved she wasn't making him wait too long.

—Where would you like to go?—

Come to the house at seven. Let's eat in. But you should know, Rena's not here.

Jake laughed, and for a second, the sound of his own laughter shocked him. He hadn't laughed or felt true joy for what seemed like years. He reminded himself he hadn't done anything wrong or illegal. He was allowed to be happy, and it was about damn time Mikala did too. They had to learn to live again.

Rena's not home was code for *bring food*. Mikala didn't have to say anything else. She was testing his memory—the silly woman. He knew everything about Mikala Jacobson.

She was a crappy cook. The woman couldn't even brew a cup of coffee, and that was a tragedy considering she was an addict. Rena, on the other hand, was a fucking genius in the kitchen. She could've opened her own restaurant. Who fed Mikala when Rena was gone?

—Vinnie's okay?—

Vinnie's always okay. Don't forget…

—The cheesecake. Got it.—

Jake hesitated, and then typed,

—I haven't forgotten a thing, Micky. Not a damn thing.—

Chapter Thirteen
A Good Woman

Jake woke up the next morning, feeling better than he had in a long time. The temperature outside was still cold, and the snow wouldn't let up, but everything in his world was warmer and brighter. The second he finished making dinner plans with Mikala the night before, like an excited teenaged boy who'd gotten a pretty girl to agree to a date, he'd texted Rena. He figured the poor woman had gone through enough with them. She deserved to hear they were on a better path.

—I'm home.—

Yeah, so?

—No, I mean, I'm going home. I'm having dinner with Micky tomorrow. I think we'll be okay.—

Fucking damn time. You people are tiresome and not very bright. A Yale education was wasted on both of you.

Jake laughed.

—You need me to say it, don't you?—

Yup…I'm waiting…and hurry because you're interrupting a potentially spectacular orgasm.

Jake shook his head.

—Fuck, Rena. I didn't need to know that. You were right. Go back to Tyler or Tom or whomever you're screwing these days.—

*You're an ass. His name is Ted, and for the

record, I'm always right. Good work, Super-man.*

Jake grinned. He'd pleased Queen Rena. His smile didn't dissipate as he showered and dressed. Twenty minutes later, as he maneuvered Red through the falling snow, a ridiculous grin stretched across his face. Slowly, his world righted itself. The women in his life welcomed him back into the fold. Now, all he needed to figure out was what the hell Lester was up to.

Jake was meeting Lester at Grinds, a popular coffee shop on Chapel Street. Located near the University, the coffee shop would be filled with students. Lester insisted they meet at Grinds and not his office or one of the many restaurants in town, and Jake gave in to the old man's request. He'd have a hell of a time parking, but at least he'd get a decent cup of coffee.

Arriving at the coffee shop, Jake frowned. A long line of partially awake humans waited for their morning fix. He scanned the busy establishment, looking for a distinguished-looking man dressed like he walked off the set of a British drama series.

Dressed in his usual three-piece suit, this time navy pinstripes, Lester sat in an overstuffed leather chair near the window with a to-go cup. Jake didn't appear as imposing as Lester. He was outfitted in slate gray wool slacks, a black fitted cashmere sweater, and a black leather coat. Although Jake understood the message a well-crafted suit sent—and he had a closet of Armani suits to prove it—when he wasn't working, he opted to dress less formally.

Jake picked his way through the noisy crowd. "Morning, Lester. Interesting place you chose." He took off his coat and leather gloves and nodded at the coffee cup in Lester's hand. "I need one of those magical drinks before we start talking." Glancing over his shoulder at the long line forming in front of the barista, Jake sighed. "I'll be a while, but I'll be back."

"Morning, Jake. Have a seat, boy." Lester picked up his cell. "You'll get your drink. What do you want?"

Jake raised an eyebrow. "You've got connections here, too?"

Lester shrugged.

Jake sighed. He didn't care how the caffeine arrived, as long as it came quickly and in copious amounts. "Black, monster size."

Lester finished texting and glanced at Jake. "Your drink will be here in a minute. Think you can make any sense before the Java hits your bloodstream?"

"Well, if you talk real slow, I think I can keep up." Jake made himself comfortable in the chair across from Lester. "I'd rather solve this mystery sooner rather than later. You summoned. I came. What's going on?"

Lester slowly raised his cup and took a slurp. He swallowed then took another.

Jake crossed his legs and waited out Lester. The man moved like molasses on a cold winter day. Finally, his piercing blue eyes, so like Molly's, focused on Jake.

After setting down his cup, Lester cleared his throat. "The time has come for you to return home, boy. For good."

Jake nodded. "I get it. I'm here. I'm meeting Mikala for dinner. I'm certain we'll work things out. I won't disappear again."

"I know you're meeting her, and you damn well better not disappear again." Lester lifted his chin and scowled. "Your disappearing act is not what I'm talking about."

Jake's gut clenched. He deserved Lester's reproach. Mikala wasn't the only one Jake had let down. But something else was troubling Lester. Before Jake could ask him what was on his mind, a young man wearing an apron and holding two to go cups approached their table.

"Here you go, sir." The server handed Jake one of the cups then turned toward Lester. "I brought you a fresh one as well, Professor Jacobson." He handed the other cup to Lester. "Anything else I can get you, sir?"

"No thanks, Peter. This cup is perfect." Lester smiled and nodded. "Before you run off, though, I want you to meet Jake Santiago Cardona. He is one of the finest litigators you'll ever meet. Who knows, if you play your cards right, you might have the opportunity to work with him."

Jake's mouth fell open, but he didn't have time to respond.

"Good to meet you, sir." The kid licked his lips and stuck out a trembling hand. "I'm familiar with some of the cases you've tried over the last few years. Didn't you defend Alexander Evenson? I followed the case in the media. Meeting you is an honor."

What the fuck was the old man up to now? "Ah...yeah. That was my case." Jake shook the kid's clammy hand and stared at Lester. Why the hell would Jake ever work with this kid? Jake didn't take on interns. "Thanks for the coffee." He pulled his hand out of the kid's grip.

"Peter here is one of my best interns. I think he's got quite a future ahead. He reminds me of you."

Like a proud papa, Lester smiled at the kid. Jake

didn't take the bait. No way would he encourage whatever delusions Lester enjoyed. Jake smiled and nodded, hoping the kid would hurry back to his current career choice.

A couple of minutes passed before Lester gave up his attempts to engage Jake in further conversation with Peter.

Peter hung his head and retreated.

Coffee in hand, Jake settled into his chair and glared at Lester. "What the fuck was that about? You know I don't take interns."

Lester frowned. "Watch your mouth, boy. This isn't LA, and you're not in the hood."

Sighing, Jake rubbed the back of his neck. He took several gulps of coffee before he again focused on Lester. "All right, Lester. Let's start again. Why am I here?"

"I'm not beating around the bush." Lester narrowed his eyes. "The time has come for you to take your rightful place in the practice. I need you right by my side. Tell me what you want, and I'll see what I can do."

Jake exhaled. *Shit, this again.* He shouldn't be surprised, and yet, he was. Lester had been hounding him to join Jacobson Law since the day he passed the Bar. Although he had no intention of ever practicing in the Northeast, he'd sat for the Bar in Connecticut, in addition to sitting for the California Bar.

The topic of joining Jacobson Law hadn't come up in a while. He and Lester covered this terrain too many times to count. To Lester's frustration and disappointment, Jake wouldn't entertain his offer, no matter how good. Ten associates made up the practice and, currently, two partners existed, Leslie and Priscilla. David had been the third partner. Lester ran the show as managing partner.

Jacobson Law wasn't Jake's cup of tea. The practice was a high-stress, cut-throat operation, and he wasn't interested in being under the witches' thumbs. Although those reasons were valid, the main reason he wouldn't consider joining the practice was much more delicate. Although the words were never spoken, he and Lester both knew why.

Jake had graduated at the top of his class and had his pick of offers at graduation. To Lester's great consternation, practicing in Connecticut wasn't an option Jake would entertain. He insisted on returning to LA.

Once he started making money, he bought a condo in Bel Air—one of the many ritzy neighborhoods Mateo used to drive them on the weekends. Anytime they could escape, or when Jake complained about the hours of homework and the social life Mateo prohibited him from having, Mateo loaded a cooler and a sullen Jake in his rusted truck. They visited Bel Air, Santa Monica, the Hill Section and Sand Section of Manhattan Beach, Malibu, and Pacific Palisades.

"This life is what you get, when you have an education." Mateo lifted his chin toward the street. "These homes and these sweet rides don't come for free, bro. No, this sweet life comes with blood, sweat, and tears." He pointed at the beautiful homes that lined the street and the expensive cars gracing the driveways. "You can have a life filled with beauty, but you got to *earn* it, by using this." Using his fist, he double knocked Jake on his temple. "Nothin' is for free in this world. Not even the shit apartment we live in."

Jake scowled and waved his hand toward the street. "What if I don't want this—a fancy car and an expensive house that looks more like a museum than a home real people like you and me live in? This world is what *you* want. Not what I want." He clenched his fists and raised his chin. "What's wrong with what we have and where we live? The apartment and our life were good enough for Ma and you. Why aren't they good enough for me?"

Mateo's eyes narrowed, and his face flushed. "You don't know what the fuck you're talking about," he snarled. "You want to live in that shit-hole your entire life—running drugs and guns, fighting to stay alive every day, every fucking day? Ma didn't have a choice. I don't have a fucking choice. You—you have a fucking choice. You hear me, bro? You feel me?"

Mateo grabbed Jake by the shoulders, pulling him until their noses were inches apart. "You got a brain, bro. You just too damn lazy to use it. We don't live. We fucking survive. They—" Mateo pointed to the houses lining the street— "they fucking live."

Resting his forehead against Jake's, Mateo shifted his hold and grabbed Jake by the back of his neck. "You'll work your ass off. I'm counting on you, Jake. You'll live for both of us. You get me?"

Jake never again fought his brother and never forgot his words. On the day he moved into his Bel Air condo, Jake bought a six-pack of Tecate, Mateo's favorite beer. At sunset, he'd sat on the deck, toasted his brother, and drank the entire six-pack, letting the memories flow.

Everything in Jake's life had dramatically changed

since Lester first asked him to join the firm. Still, committing to the practice didn't feel right. Maybe with David gone, managing a large law firm had become too much for Lester? Perhaps the old man was ready to slow down or retire.

Jake would do anything for Lester, but he couldn't grant him this request. He hated disappointing the man who'd always treated him like a son. Jake cleared his throat and scrutinized Lester. "We've been here before, Lester. My answer hasn't changed. I have a good practice in LA, and you have Leslie and Priscilla. Surely, one of them could step in? Have you discussed this with them? Maybe you should take on another partner or two? I'm certain one or more of your associates would jump at the chance."

A pulse ticked in Lester's jaw, and he sat forward, spine stiff. "Don't speak like I'm senile and presume to tell me what I need, boy. I know what I need, and before you spout any more bullshit, we both know we haven't been here before. Things are different. Do I have to say the words out loud? Do I, boy?"

Jake kept his mouth shut and ground his teeth, his gaze never leaving Lester's. This conversation wasn't one he wanted to have.

"He's not here anymore. There, I've said it. Feel better? You're finally free. You've been laid off as David's protector—his super-man. He's no longer your responsibility." Lester collapsed in his chair.

Jake hung his head. No, he didn't fucking feel better. Although David was gone, he couldn't swoop in and take what was his. Jake had stayed away from New Haven and refused to join any law practice in the area, because New Haven was Jacobson territory—David's territory. He refused to be in competition with his best friend. He and David competed enough in school, and he wouldn't continue that nonsense after they graduated.

Where Lester was concerned, David needed a fighting chance to succeed. David had no business being a litigator. Hell, he shouldn't have attended law school. He didn't have the drive or the stamina. He lacked the animal instinct to go after an opponent and take them down. Even though the law was literally in his blood, David didn't *love* the law.

What had been difficult for David was second nature to Jake. Maybe Jake's courtroom battle skills came from his childhood where every day was a game of survival of the fittest. Finding an enemy's weakness, plotting their takedown, strategizing their demise, and finalizing the win were in Jake's blood.

Jake applied to Yale Law School on a whim. He was one of Yale's token minority students and received a full scholarship for his undergraduate studies. Paying for a Yale graduate degree, however, was out of the question.

Then, Lester entered the picture and changed Jake's life. After a painful Jacobson Thanksgiving family dinner Jake, Rena, and Mikala had been summoned to, Lester called Jake into his office. He sat behind his massive mahogany desk, nursing a snifter of brandy. Before Jake sat, Lester came to the point. "I hear you've been accepted to law school. You'll attend. Your tuition and fees will be paid and will continue to be paid as long as your grades are to my standards."

Jake stared open-mouthed at the intimidating man.

"You'll tell no one of this matter—not David,

Mikala, or Rena. This arrangement is between you and me. You will tell them you've been awarded a scholarship, and you'll maintain your pizza job. Every semester I want to see your grades, and when the time comes, you'll intern at the firm. Do you understand me, boy?" Lester barked, jarring a shocked Jake out of his stupor.

Jake licked his lips and cleared his throat. Lester offered him a future and opened the door to higher education so Jake could fulfill every one of Mateo's dreams. But Jake wasn't stupid. In the world he grew up in, everything came with a price. "What do you want in return?"

Lester smiled and steepled his fingers. "Nothing."

Jake shook his head. "Nothing? I don't understand."

"Nothing, boy. You think I haven't been watching you over the last few years? Your relationship with David? I doubt very much he would have made anything of himself without you, and that girl he's in love with, keeping him focused and his ass out of serious trouble. So, no strings."

Jake dropped his head and ground his teeth. He stayed silent for a minute as he reined in his galloping heart and the anger charging through him. With his hands fisted at his sides, he raised his head and met Lester's gaze. "My friendship with David isn't for sale. You don't have to pay me off. David's the closest thing I have to a brother. I'll always have his back. If you bothered to look, you would see he's a good man. All he wants is your love and approval."

Eyes narrowed, Lester's smile faded. "Do not speak as if you know my boy better than I do. Don't insult me by insinuating I'm buying your friendship. I'm offering you a future. This proposition is a one-time offer. Do you understand? We'll never discuss this topic again."

For a long moment, Jake studied Lester, and then he swallowed hard. He let out a deep breath and raked a hand through his hair feeling both deflated and hopeful. Lester *was* offering him a chance of a lifetime. He'd be a fool to pass it up, but nothing came without a price. With a trembling voice Jake said, "I'll pay you back every dime the first chance I get. I swear."

Lester's smile returned, and he sat back in his chair. "I believe you would, but recompense isn't necessary."

Jake shook his head. "But…"

Lester held up a hand. "If you *insist*, however, I can respect that."

Jake squared his shoulders and lifted his chin, waiting for the blow.

"I'm not interested in money. I've got more of that than I need." Lester took a drink of his brandy and focused on Jake. "You'll owe me a favor, and one day I'll collect."

Was Lester now calling in his favor by insisting Jake join the practice? Jake took another swallow of his coffee, and then raised his head and met Lester's gaze. He cleared his throat. "I can't be him. I can't fill his shoes. Walking into his office and claiming it as mine isn't right. I won't claim his birthright."

Lester dropped his cup on a nearby table and leaned forward. "Now, you listen to me, Jake. *You* cannot be David. *You* will never be David. No one can take his place. No one. You think I didn't know my boy and didn't love him just because I was tough on him?" Lester's face turned crimson, and his breathing was labored. "You have no idea what you're talking about. No idea at all." He shook his head and looked away. "I wasn't the best father, the most patient, or the most understanding, but I loved him. I made some serious mistakes. Those mistakes cost him his life. I will never forgive myself—never."

Jake stayed quiet, waiting for Lester to gather his thoughts. All the Jacobson men used him as their dumpster. They unloaded their guilt and pain without regard for his feelings. They were his family, and God knows they'd been there when he needed them, but at times, his shoulders drooped under the weight of their troubles.

Sighing, Lester turned to Jake. "David wasn't cut out for the law like the two witches I sired."

Jake inhaled sharply, and he darted his gaze to Lester.

"Didn't think I knew about that sweet nickname?" Lester smirked. "Well, my girls earned it. They're like me—too much. They live for the chase and the kill." Lester's smile faded. "David wasn't like them, and he wasn't like you or me. He tried. He worked and worked. He wouldn't give up. I should have stopped him." Lester's shoulders sagged. "Long hours, drinking, gambling, and that woman…" He shook his head. "He had such a beautiful family—Mikala and Molly. But he couldn't keep his eyes on what was important."

Lester *did* know his children. Jake was surprised at Lester's admission and yet, he wasn't. The man was an expert at reading people. He had to be in his line of work. Jake wrongly assumed Lester had been too blind to see his children for who they really were.

Lester cleared his throat. "You protected David and cleaned up after him. I pushed him and pushed him. I wanted him to wake up and wise up before Mikala did, and he lost her and Molly. I went about it the wrong way." He stared right into Jake's eyes. "But so did you."

Jake shook his head. Was Lester blaming him for David's mistakes? If given the chance, Jake wasn't sure what else he could have done to protect the innocent— Mikala and Molly. "What do you want me to say, Lester? What would you have had me do? They were my family. Just like you, I did what I thought was best to keep them intact and happy."

Lester sighed and rubbed his face. "I'm tired, and I'm old. I can't lose any more children. I can't destroy any more lives. If I leave the practice to the girls, they'll kill each other competing for managing partner. They're sharks in and out of the courtroom. They have no leadership ability, and they'll destroy the practice. I can't have any more carnage on my hands. I need you by my side."

Would he forever be saving Jacobson men? Jake's gut clenched, and he hung his head. Was that his lot in life? His superhero's cape was tarnished, and its weight caused his shoulders and back to ache. Yet, Lester had never asked anything of him. "I would do anything for you. I owe you my career, but you're asking a lot. I don't know if joining the practice is the right thing to do."

"I know this transition won't be easy. My girls will fight you. No doubt about that. Jake, you may have everything you could ever want in LA, but you don't have her. She's here."

Jake couldn't help but be impressed. Lester was not only a master litigator; he was a master manipulator. The man pulled out all the stops and took no prisoners. Hell-bent on getting his way, Lester unloaded his entire arsenal on Jake. Damn if his aim wasn't precise.

"I've watched you over the years—all of you. This so-called family you four made revolved around my boy. Mikala loved David and would do anything to make him happy. You loved Mikala and bent over backwards to keep *her* happy." Lester shook his head, and his lips curved up in a small smile. "The three of you were so intricately tied to one another, none of you knew how to exist without the other. I was never certain what role Rena played, but she is forging a new life of her own. Now, only you and Mikala are left, and you must rebuild and redefine your relationship."

Jake let Lester's words sink in syllable by syllable. Lester spoke the truth. Of course, Jake loved Mikala. She was…is…his best friend. Wasn't she? No words in the English language existed that described their relationship. In his gut, Jake knew they were more than friends, but they weren't lovers. She was David's. She had always been David's.

Without David, who were they to one another? Wasn't that the question Mikala asked him? He doubted she fully understood the scope of her question. Could they become more than friends? The thought hadn't crossed Jake's mind. He rubbed his forehead. "What are you saying, Lester?"

Raising an eyebrow, Lester pinned Jake with his gaze. "You know exactly what I'm saying. That woman thinks the world of you. She can't function without you.

I'm an old man, but even I know what you two share isn't just friendship."

Jake cleared his throat. "To be honest, I have no idea who Mikala and I are to one another now that David and Molly are gone. So much has changed." He swallowed hard. "All I know is I need her in my life."

Lester nodded. "David needed her, and she was a wonderful wife. Molly needed her, and a better mother didn't exist. Rena needed her, and for years, she stood by her side. You needed her, and she told you to come home. Did any of you ever stop to wonder what she needed? What she wanted? Don't you think you should do that? Get your head out of your ass, boy. Pay attention to what matters and to what's in front of you."

Chapter Fourteen
Endings and Beginnings

Mikala walked from room to room, straightening pictures that didn't need to be straightened and fluffing pillows that were already full. Jake would knock on her door at any moment, and she was jittery. She woke up early, drank three cups of coffee, ran five miles on the treadmill, showered, dressed, and vacuumed the entire house—all before ten a.m. Then she spent the rest of the day pacing and obsessing over things she couldn't change.

In the past, Jake's visits weren't anxiety producing. Today was different. Although she missed Jake—the long talks they used to have, and the laughter they'd shared—they weren't lighthearted and carefree anymore. They were scarred, and Mikala was traumatized, not only from losing Molly and David, but also from Jake's abandonment. Mikala was transformed. She barely resembled the woman Jake once knew, and she worried their relationship was damaged beyond repair.

"I not only blamed him for David's death, I raged. I sent him away, not once but twice. I know I was needy and difficult. Maybe he had enough. Maybe I was too needy, too angry, and too much of a handful," Mikala had admitted to Rena a week before Rena left with Ted to the Bahamas.

Rena reached for her hand and squeezed. "You've been through hell and back. No one can blame you for what you said or did during that horrific time. I am certain Jake didn't leave because of anything you said or did. He thought he was doing what was best for you. He, too, was pretty messed up."

Mikala hadn't been sure she believed Rena. She wasn't certain of anything. She'd believed Jake was indestructible, and the kind of man who would never walk out, no matter how hard the going got. But her anger and grief had been too heavy a burden to lay on anyone. Jake was human, and humans had their limits.

She didn't want to drive him away again. She was still bruised, but she wasn't broken. Shaking her head, she sighed and surveyed the family room. She studied the pictures of friends and family decorating her mantle. Some were gone, but many still graced her world. She wished she'd been stronger, but she, too, was human.

Today, however, was a beginning. When Jake arrived, Mikala would do her best to tuck away the past, deep into the recesses of her heart for safe keeping and focus on the future. She walked up the stairs and opened the door to Molly's room. Months ago, she'd packed and given away David's clothes, but Molly's room was intact. The time had come to pack her baby's belongings and share them with children in need. She was almost ready to do so…almost.

Smiling, Mikala scanned the room. Powder-pink paint covered the walls, and a variety of butterflies in flight decorated the room. A canopied daybed with pink netting and metal-scrolled lines in a silver finish took up the corner of the room. The bed resembled an elegant carriage fit for a princess. A whitewashed dresser littered with Molly's beaded jewelry and plastic bracelets stood in the corner, and the massive rocker Mikala used when she was still in her belly, under her heart, faced the sheer lace curtains and the backyard.

Over the last year, Mikala spent many days rocking one of Molly's many stuffed animals. Molly loved this room. She adored all the butterfly books, posters, and stuffed animals her uncle Jake spoiled her with.

Once Jake discovered Molly's interest in butterflies, he read up on the delicate creatures and spent hours showing her pictures of butterflies from all around the world. He took her to her first Migration Festival at Lighthouse Point Park. For days after, all Molly talked about were the amazing birds, butterflies, and dragonflies passing through the park.

"When you're older, we'll leave your mama and daddy and go to Mexico for the Annual Monarch Butterfly Migration. Millions and millions of beautiful butterflies will fill the air, and if you stand still, they'll kiss your nose." Jake had touched the tip of Molly's nose with his finger. "Then they'll kiss your cheeks and even your lips." He touched her cheeks and lips.

Molly's big blue eyes were wide, and a smile stretched across her face. "Daddy will be busy, but we have to take my mama."

"Oh, why is that? Aren't I enough for you, Butterfly? Aren't I your super-man?" Jake's lips puckered in a pout.

"Yup, but you're Mama's, too, and she'll be all alone here while Daddy's at work. She'll be sad without you." Molly had wrapped her tiny arms around Jake's neck and tugged him toward her, kissing his chin.

Mikala smiled.

Molly had been wise—too wise somedays. A memory of Molly sitting on David's lap giving him a lecture came rushing back out of nowhere. Mikala sat on Molly's bed and held her daughter's beloved stuffed rabbit, allowing the memories to engulf her.

A few weeks before the accident, David had joined her and Molly for dinner—a rare treat. While Mikala cleaned the kitchen, David took Molly into the family room to set up a movie. Finished with the kitchen, Mikala entered the family room and found David sprawled on an easy chair with Molly straddling him. She cradled his face in her hands, and her expression was serious. As she listened to their exchange, Mikala grabbed her cell from her back pocket and snapped a picture.

"Daddy, Mama says you work too hard. You have to stop 'cause we miss you, and Mama's sad."

David took Molly's hands and kissed them. "I'm sorry, my Butterfly. Daddies have to work hard sometimes."

"But you work hard *all* times, and Mama's all alone. You have to stop."

"Mama's not alone, sweetness. She has you." David poked Molly's belly with his index finger.

Molly squirmed and giggled. "Uh-uh, I'm going to Mexico with Uncle Jake. He says you have to stay here and take care of Mama 'cause you're hers, and Uncle Jake is mine." Molly turned her head, and her gaze met Mikala's. The little minx had actually winked at Mikala.

Standing, Mikala pulled her cell out of her pocket. She found the picture she took of David and Molly. She scrolled through pictures of her family enjoying holidays, barbeques, birthdays, and carefree beach days. She hadn't taken a single picture since the day Molly died. God, how she missed her family and the carefree, happy days they'd spent together. Those days were over. She couldn't have her Molly-David-Rena-and-Mikala family, but she had Jake.

Rena, with Mikala's prompting and blessing, had moved on. She freed herself from her troublesome past, as well as the anger and resentment she held for Jake. Few knew about Rena's troubled childhood. When Rena was three, her mother dropped her off at daycare and didn't return. Since her father was never in the picture, she was raised by her grandmother. Her tumultuous childhood negatively impacted Rena's self-confidence and self-worth. She looked for love and acceptance in all the wrong places.

Although Rena's Yale family gave her a home, acceptance, love, and a feeling of belonging, over the years her heart took a beating. Rena's early attraction to Jake and his rejection didn't help her misguided notion she was unworthy and unlovable. Just when Rena came to grips with the fact she couldn't have Jake, they let their guard down, got drunk, and got stupid. One senseless moment was all Jake and Rena needed to make a terrible mistake. They had been reckless with each other's feelings.

When Mikala had returned from her honeymoon, Rena and Jake both confessed. Mikala was furious and was tempted to slap them. They were adults, behaving like reckless teenagers.

"He sleeps with me, and then he throws me away like I'm trash. He treats me like I'm nothing more than a one-night stand." Rena cried in Mikala's arms. "He says he's sorry. He made a mistake. What the fuck does that mean? He's a man-whore and a dick. I can't believe you can stand to be in his presence."

"We were drunk. Drunk!" Jake raged as he paced Mikala's kitchen. "She didn't say no. If she had, I would have stopped. You know I would. She knew I didn't have feelings for her. For years, I've made that abundantly clear. We made a mistake. I apologized. I explained things as best I could. But fuck, what does she want me to say? We had one fucking drunken night of sex, nothing more, and she damn well knows it."

They were both right, and they were both wrong. Months passed before Jake and Rena had admitted they'd both screwed up, and they could be in the same room without ripping out each other's throat.

Mikala scrolled to one of the last pictures she'd taken of Molly. Jake and Rena stood on either side of her, holding her hands, swinging her high into the air, and her baby girl was laughing hysterically. Rena and Jake smiled at Molly, tolerating each other's presence on her behalf. Many days had been spent like this. They weren't outwardly antagonistic, but they didn't enjoy a friendship similar to what Jake and Mikala had.

But since David's death, something changed. Rena *talked* to Jake. She didn't lash out or throw barbs. Over the last few months, Mikala overheard Rena laughing and joking with him on the telephone. She even defended Jake and begged Mikala to call him. Once again, Mikala's world flipped upside down. This time for the good—enemies were now allies.

Ted entered their world, and Rena blossomed. Ted Reeves worked as an investment banker from New

York. Rena met him seven months ago after he sprained his ankle skiing and ended up in the emergency room where she worked. He adored Rena and spoiled her shamelessly. Rena glowed each time he was in the room, on the phone, or on her mind. She was a woman in love for the very first time. All she needed was a push from Mikala. The time had come for Rena to build a life of her own.

A few weeks ago, Rena admitted Ted wanted to take her away for a romantic week in paradise, but she refused his offer.

Mikala kicked Rena out of the nest. "He's good to you. He makes you smile, and he brings you Junior's Cheesecake every time he visits. What else could a girl ask for?" Mikala nudged. "He loves you, Rena. Has he said the words? Have you told him you love him?"

Rena looked away and turned as red as her fiery hair.

Mikala had her answer. "Stop resisting and start believing." She squeezed Rena's hands. "You're special, and you're worthy. He's a good man. Let him love you. Let yourself love him. Go to the Bahamas with Ted."

Rena swallowed hard. "The timing is bad. You come first. I want to be here for you. Molly's birthday is…"

Guilt overwhelmed Mikala. Not only did Rena have her own challenging past to overcome, but she also shouldered Mikala's problems and postponed her chance at happiness. "Stop it, Rena. Stop using me as an excuse to deny yourself any further. I love you for always being here, but I'll be fine. I promise. I need to find my own way, and you need to find yours as well."

After a few more days of nagging and cajoling, Rena gave in. Over the last few days, Mikala received a variety of texts and pictures from Rena depicting a deliriously happy and in love woman. Mikala hardly recognized her friend without her worry lines and the shadow of loneliness lingering in her eyes.

Not much good came out of the senseless tragedies Mikala, Rena, and Jake experienced, but Mikala swore from now on they would be grateful and celebrate every morsel of good and happy that came their way. Although tucking away the past and stepping toward the future was easier said than done, she vowed to lead by example.

Mikala scanned Molly's room one last time, gave Molly's rabbit a final squeeze, and stood. She left the door to the room open and walked down the stairs. She would no longer keep the room as a sanctuary to the past. She would force herself to look at Molly's room daily, and then to pack Molly's things. Her baby wasn't here any longer. Molly had immigrated, taking permanent residence in heaven and in Mikala's heart.

Endings and beginnings.

"Life is a series of chapters and a series of endings and beginnings, Mikala," her father had said the last time they talked on the phone. "Endings are often sad, and beginnings are what you make of them. You have to be brave, or you'll spend your entire life caught in the worst place of all."

Mikala huffed. "Where's that, Dad? What's worse than losing my child and husband?"

"Getting stuck in between forever."

"I don't get it." Mikala shook her head. "I'm moving on. I have no choice. I'm not stuck anymore."

Joe sighed. "Well, my girl, I think we both know better. Staying stuck in the middle where only blank space is visible after the last word of a chapter was written would be a damn shame. Don't be scared to flip the page and see what comes next."

Mikala hung her head and swallowed hard. "I'll try, Dad. I promise, I'll try."

Halfway down the steps, Mikala paused and listened to the chiming of the doorbell.

Beginnings.

Her heart fluttered in her throat, and all thoughts of the past were pushed aside. Now was the time for new beginnings. Jake had arrived.

Mikala took a deep breath and willed her body to move to the front door. She gripped the doorknob and rested her head against the front door. She sensed her super-man on the other side of the door. Her heart sped up in anticipation. She breathed in and out, raised her head, and opened the door.

Chapter Fifteen
Super-man's Flying Home

Jake stood outside Mikala's door with a small smile, a five o'clock shadow, and snow on his too long, unruly dark hair. The man was beautiful, and Mikala drank each inch of him in. He was a cross between William Levy and Eduardo Verástegui.

Jake's gaze travelled down Mikala's body.

She wished she'd taken more time with her appearance. She didn't have on any makeup, her hair was piled on her head in a messy bun, and her feet were bare. Like her, he was dressed casually in dark jeans and navy crewneck sweater, but he was delicious eye-candy…drool-worthy. Although she knew she looked better than she had in months, the fitted maroon cashmere sweater and skinny jeans she wore revealed her too thin, tragedy-ravished body.

God, she'd missed Jake! She wanted to launch herself into his arms, hold tight, make him swear he'd never leave, and let the dam of tears she'd been holding back all day break free. Instead, Mikala gave herself a mental slap-down and smiled tentatively. She had to get a grip.

Letting out a stuttering breath, Mikala dragged away her gaze from his beautiful face and to the bags he held. She inhaled the mouth-watering aroma wafting from the bags. "Hi, Super-man. Is that my dinner I smell?"

Jake nodded. "Lasagna, garlic bread, salad, and Chianti as ordered." He extended two large bags in front of him. "Am I allowed to enter?"

Mikala tilted her head and studied Jake. She couldn't remember him asking if he could come inside or even ringing the doorbell before. Now, he stood on her doorstep, shifting from foot to foot, cautious and uncertain. She was responsible for his hesitancy. The last time he stood at her front door, she'd refused to let him in. She'd hurt him. Smiling, Mikala nodded at the bags in his hand. "Well, that depends. Did you forget?"

A wide grin spread across Jake's features.

Jake's glorious smile eased her anxiety, and the ache in her chest subsided as some of the strain so evident in the furrow between his brows and the tightness in his jaw diminished.

"Micky, you know better than to even ask. You'll get your cheesecake as soon as you finish your dinner. Now move your ass, woman. It's fucking cold out here."

Laughing, Mikala shook her head. She turned and led him down the hall, past the family room, and toward the kitchen. "Some things never change. Watch your language, mister. Children are in the…" She stopped mid-sentence and mid-stride then dropped her head, and her eyes flooded with tears. Her shoulders slumped, and her hands fisted. Children no longer existed in the house. Jake could curse all he wanted.

When Jake's hands landed on her shoulders, Mikala jumped. Her spine straightened, and she squared her shoulders. Silently, she berated herself. She wouldn't fall apart again. She simply couldn't. Today was about beginnings and not about revisiting the past.

Jake turned her. With two fingers under her chin, he forced her to meet his gaze. "It's okay, go ahead," he whispered. "Let it out. I'm here now."

Jake's words were Mikala's undoing. She crumbled. Damn him. She'd been strong all day yesterday and today. She shed a few tears, but she kept moving forward. Now though, Jake was here. Despite her earlier resolve, she no longer wanted to follow the rules she'd carved out. Those rules were supposed to keep her from falling apart and build an illusion she'd healed and wasn't stuck between chapters. But screw the rules. Jake *was* here.

He drew her into his warm embrace, and her tears flowed. He held her and didn't say a word as her cries turned into sobs. When he picked her up, carried her to the couch in the family room, and sat, placing her in his lap, she cried even harder.

Mikala wept for everything and everyone she'd lost over the last year and a half—her baby, her husband, the man who had been hers before Molly died, and the broken one who suffered and took his own life. She cried for the devastation that tore apart her precious family and the life she'd planned on enjoying but never would. Finally, she sobbed because although he was back, she'd lost Jake for a full year.

When her tears stopped and all that remained were hiccups, she pulled away. She'd drenched Jake's shirt.

He handed her tissues from a nearby box.

She glanced up to find him studying her. Mikala shifted off his lap and sat next to him. Unable to witness the pain in his eyes, she focused on her lap.

"I'm so damn sorry for leaving you to deal with

Molly's and David's losses on your own. I behaved…"

Jake's voice was laced with sorrow and self-recrimination. Mikala wiped her eyes. She shook her head and sniffed. "It's okay. I understand. I don't know why I broke down. I'm much better now." She shredded the tissues in her hand. "I'm sorry for getting your shirt wet. Please just forget about this meltdown." Mikala pushed off the couch and stood. "Let's eat."

He grabbed her hand and pulled her back down. "Micky, look at me."

Mikala straightened her shoulders and raised her head.

"First, don't hide from me and don't ever deny your feelings. We've always shared our feelings with one another. Cry, scream, and throw things if you want. Whatever. I don't give a shit. I can take it."

Despite his earnest expression and the sincerity she heard in Jake's voice, Mikala shook her head. He could take it? Uh-uh, no way. She'd done as he said. She cried, screamed, and even threw a thing or two. How had he reacted? Jake just walked back into her life a few minutes ago. She couldn't lose him again. Taking a deep breath, she steadied her voice. "Jake, really, I'm good. I don't break down on a regular basis anymore. I won't fall apart again. I'm good. I'm better and stronger. I—"

Jake's eyes widened. "Oh, Jesus. Oh, God." He stood and ran a hand through his hair. "For fuck's sake, Micky. Do you think I'll leave again if you cry—if you fall apart?"

Mikala shifted and shrugged. She studied the tissues in her hand.

Jake exhaled and scrubbed a hand down his face.

"After all the years of friendship and all the challenges we've shared over the years, do you honestly believe I left because I couldn't deal with your grief?"

Mikala wrapped her arms around herself. She wasn't sure what she believed anymore, but she was certain Jake was vital to her existence. She used all her self-control not to throw herself in his arms and beg him to promise never to leave her again. The problem was, she had no idea why he left in the first place, and never is a long time. His behavior had been completely out of character. He'd abandoned her once, and he could do it again. Mikala shivered and tightened her arms.

"Micky, your devastation had nothing to do with why I left—not in the way you think. I was wrong to leave, but I left because I was guilt-ridden. I was a coward. I blamed myself for David's death and your pain." Jake's shoulders slumped, and he dropped his gaze. "To this day, I wonder if I could have done more to help him. I wish to God I had. I'm sorry. I let you down, and I let him down in so many ways."

God, they were making the same mistakes again. Mikala's stomach churned. If they traveled down the road of assigning blame, she would lose Jake. Mikala couldn't survive losing him again. Poor Jake. Because she'd blamed him for David's death, he blamed himself. She needed to set the record straight.

Mikala stood and faced Jake. "David made a choice to end his life. I don't understand why, and I'm not sure I forgive him. I'm learning to accept no one was to blame, and his death couldn't have been prevented. You must do the same." Mikala took Jake's hand and pulled him back to the sofa. "I owe you an apology. I—"

Jake shook his head. "No, you don't—"

She held up her hand. "No, let me get out these words." Mikala cleared her throat. "That day in Molly's room…when I completely unraveled, I was awful to you." Her voice trembled, and she bit her lower lip as she fought to keep her tears at bay. "I blamed you for David's death. I lashed out. You didn't deserve my anger. Hurt and angry at the world, I took out my grief on you. *I* made you go, and *I* left you no choice." Mikala swallowed hard. "Six months ago, I still wasn't ready to deal with the reality of my life and again sent you away. But those decisions were mine, not yours."

Jake reached for her hand and squeezed. "I should have stayed. You didn't make me do anything. You were hurting, and so was I. Your tears didn't drive me away. You did nothing wrong. I was fucked up. You guys were my family. I was supposed to protect all of you, and I couldn't."

Tears trickled down Mikala's face. "Oh, my superman—my sweet protector. Even you have limitations." She wiped her face and smiled into his eyes. "You couldn't have done anything. I know that, and I also recognize you're human. We need to convince you of that fact and do our best to put past hurts behind us. Okay?"

Jake dropped his head and studied their joined hands. He squeezed her hands, and then glanced up.

For a few minutes, they gazed into each other's eyes, saying nothing…yet, saying everything.

"Okay, Micky," he whispered.

Mikala nodded. "Good." She pulled her hands out of his. "Can we eat now? I'm starved."

Jake retrieved the bags of forgotten food from the front foyer, while she went to the kitchen and gathered the dishes and utensils they needed. As she reheated the food and brought everything to the small kitchen table where she, David, and Molly used to eat when they didn't have guests, she caught up Jake on her job.

"Do you like the work? Aren't you bored?"

"Actually, the work is interesting, and I enjoy setting my own schedule. When I'm not on the computer, I volunteer at the community center or food bank. My life isn't exciting, but it's fulfilling enough for now." Mikala tore a piece of garlic bread, dipped it into the lasagna sauce, and stuck it in her mouth. She closed her eyes and relished its spicy flavor. Since Molly's death, food had lost its appeal, but the lasagna was fantastic. She swallowed and licked the butter and sauce off her lips and fingers. "I have a routine, and I find comfort in knowing what I'll be doing from hour to hour. Keeping busy is a blessing." She peered up to find Jake studying her. He'd hardly touched his meal. "What?" She frowned.

"Nothing. I'm glad to see you eating, that's all." He picked up his fork and dug into his lasagna. "You look great, but you've lost a shit-ton of weight. What's going on?"

Mikala's cheeks heated, and she was certain her face was as red as the pasta sauce. She shrugged and glanced back to her plate. She was sensitive about her weight. Funny how she hadn't cared what she weighed or what she looked like before her world flipped. Now, though, everyone focused on her weight and what she ate. She was always under a microscope with everyone watching to make sure she didn't fall apart or disappear.

She was tired of being the center of attention and drama.

Rena and Lester often commented Mikala was too thin and encouraged her to eat more. Where once Mikala loved food and lived to eat, now she ate to live. She looked gaunt and haggard and wasn't the least bit attractive. Even the clothes Rena bought her six months ago were loose. Mikala made an effort to eat, but most of the time, she didn't have an appetite.

Jake stopped eating and set down his fork. "I'm sorry. I didn't mean to embarrass you, sweetheart. Like I said, you look great. I'm an idiot. Forget it."

Jake was kind. She resembled a walking skeleton. Mikala shook her head and exhaled. She had nothing to be embarrassed about. Jake didn't mean to hurt her feelings. He was gone for a while, and he'd missed a lot. Of course, he would ask questions as they became reacquainted. Making a big deal out of one caring comment was stupid. After all, he was her friend, not a lover studying her body.

Mikala shrugged. "Don't worry about it." But she'd lost her appetite and moved food around her plate. After a few awkward moments of silence, she sighed. *Enough of this weirdness.* She didn't want Jake treating her like fine china. She needed to get over herself and move on to a new subject. After taking a sip of her wine, she cleared her throat. "How long are you in town for?"

Jake glanced up and smirked. "Well, now that's an intriguing question, and I have an interesting story to entertain you with."

They finished eating and carried their wine into the family room where he built a fire. For the next hour,

Jake replayed his conversation with Lester.

Mikala couldn't remember the last time she was this content and at peace. She melted into the couch and took occasional sips of her wine. A smile played on her lips as she tracked Jake's long, lean, muscular body stalking around the room—building a case as if he were in the courtroom.

She wasn't the least bit surprised Lester offered Jake a position in the firm. She was shocked, however, he wanted Jake to come in as a partner and eventually buy him out. Once they got wind of their daddy's grand plan to take away their flying brooms and ground their asses, Leslie and Priscilla's heads would explode. Mikala grinned.

"What in the world are you grinning about?"

"Sorry, I was thinking about the witches." Mikala chuckled. "You should accept Lester's offer so I can see their faces when he tells them."

Jake returned her grin, but he quickly sobered. "Seriously, you think I should accept Lester's offer? Is that the right move?"

Mikala's smile dimmed, and she shook her head. "Uh-uh. No way, mister. This decision is too big. Huge. I can't tell you what to do." She tilted her head to the side. "What do *you* want to do? What would make *you* happy?"

He looked away. "Jacobson Law was never supposed to be mine. New Haven and Jacobson Law are David's turf."

"A lot of things weren't supposed to happen, but they did." Mikala shrugged. "We have to go on. We must build a new life without them. We can love them forever, but we can't mourn them forever. At least, that's what the members of my grief support group keep telling me."

"Your group is right." Jake sighed and nodded. "I've spent the entire day thinking about Lester's proposal and little else. There's a lot to consider. To be honest, I'm tired of LA and my too-rich-for-their-own-good clients who think money can buy them out of any shit they get into. I've enjoyed taking their money, don't get me wrong." Jake shrugged. "But I'm over that scene and lifestyle. While I haven't worked out the logistics, and I haven't decided the role I want to play at Jacobson Law, I do know one thing." He set his wine glass on the coffee table and sat next to Mikala. He took her hands in his and squeezed gently. "I–I want to come home, Micky." He glanced up and met her gaze. "I want to come home for good."

Had she heard him right? Mikala's breath stuttered, and she clutched his hands. "For good? You want to move back to New Haven? Permanently? Are you sure?"

Jake studied her and nodded.

Mikala glanced at their clasped hands and swallowed hard. Super-man was flying home...to stay. Her heart galloped and almost tripped over itself with excitement, while her brain generated question after question, warning her to slow down and proceed with caution.

Jake asked her if he *could* come home. What exactly did he want to know? He didn't need her permission. Why was he seeking her approval? Mikala raised her head. "So much has changed, Jake. Our family no longer exists. It imploded. Molly and David are together in heaven. Rena, I'm certain even if she's not, will start her own family with Ted, in New York. You and I are the only ones left."

Mikala remembered what she'd promised Jake years ago when he'd lost Mateo. As she spoke, she found clarity as well as confusion in her own words. "Jake, despite the distance that developed between us and the pain we needlessly showered on each other, you will always have a home with me. Where ever I am, you too will always be welcome. I just don't know who I am any more, and I have no idea how we go forth in this new life without the people we loved. How do we rebuild? Who are we to each other?"

Jake kept his gaze focused on Mikala. He brought her hands to his lips in the most tender and most gentle of kisses filled with promise. "We are what we've always been. We are Micky and Jake—two people who survived the deadliest of superstorms. We have loved each other and cared deeply for one another for...well...forever. That fact is the only one that's important. Don't you think? The rest, we'll figure out together."

Together—what a lovely word. Mikala swallowed past the lump in her throat. Jake was right about one thing. She'd loved him for what seemed like a lifetime. Perhaps with him by her side, she would find the strength to turn the page so she wouldn't get stuck in the middle. The time had arrived to let Super-man fly home!

Six Months

August

Chapter Sixteen
Sexy Latino Lovers

Mikala and Jake sat at The Purple Armadillo with all of Molly's favorite food laid out before them— melted *queso*, guacamole, salsa, nachos, beef and chicken tacos, tostadas, and taquitos. Today marked the second anniversary of Molly's death. Jake and Mikala decided to remember her by doing something she would have enjoyed.

Jake hated The Purple Armadillo. He swore nothing on the menu remotely resembled true Mexican cuisine, and the food was an insult to authentic Mexican chefs. But where Molly and food had been concerned, the crunch and mess factor were all that mattered. No matter how hard he'd tried to talk Molly out of coming to the restaurant, he always lost. She had been convinced this eatery was the best place on earth to eat.

Molly was enamored with the restaurant's flamboyant decor which matched her own sense of style—bold, flashy, and fearless. Bright red paint decorated the walls. Green, red, orange, and blue chairs circled neon-green-legged tables with tabletops depicting Mexican village life in colorful cartoon fashion. Brightly colored flags hung from the ceiling, and sombreros of all sizes and colors adorned the walls. The mariachi music was loud, and the wait staff was even louder with uniforms matching the restaurant's décor.

Earlier in the day, Jake and Mikala visited Molly's gravesite, bringing a large bouquet of yellow and white daisies. While the day still held a hint of sadness and a sense of deep loss, together, they could steer through the pain and dock at a place that only held happy memories.

"Do we actually have to eat this shit?" Jake complained for the tenth time.

Mikala frowned and quickly scanned the restaurant. "Shh. Do you want someone to overhear you?"

"Yes!"

"Jake!" Mikala's eyebrows shot up, and she attempted but failed to suppress her laughter. "Behave, for God's sake. Stop complaining, and I'll buy you a beer. Besides, I love this stuff and may eat all of it myself."

Jake's lips pursed in a mock-pout. "Fine. But you owe me two beers for this torture, and then I want real food."

Grinning, Mikala licked the melted cheese off her fingers.

Jake threw napkins in her direction. "Glad your appetite is back, but couldn't it come back with more refined taste buds?"

"Shut up, Super-man, or I swear I'll make you bring me here every single week." Mikala reached for the loaded nachos and stuffed one in her mouth. Her appetite had returned, and she'd gained some of the lost weight. She was happy, healthy, and energetic. Two to three times a week, she ran on a treadmill. Now that she ate with *the hoover* on a daily basis, Mikala made an effort to eat a balanced diet. Jake had a ridiculous appetite and ate enough for three people, but he never gained an ounce of fat.

Having Jake home again was a joy, although at times, like now, he was a giant pain in her ass. He took almost six months to sell his condo in LA and close his practice. A month ago, he shifted some of his more reasonable clients to Jacobson Law and began working with Lester and the witches.

Jake and Lester came to a temporary agreement. He agreed to join the practice as a partner for the time being, filling the space David vacated. Lester agreed to stay on as managing partner until Jake understood all aspects of the firm, and the hellcats Lester fathered were tamed.

Priscilla and Leslie were unaware of Lester's plan to retire. But they were intelligent women who'd never warmed to Jake and never understood their father's interest in him over the years. They vehemently objected to Jake joining the practice and did everything to block him. The witches, however, were no match for Lester who held controlling interest and had the ability to control his girls better than any man on earth.

Lester's grand plans for Jacobson Law didn't stop with Jake. His plans also included Mikala. Shortly after Jake decided to move to Connecticut and join the firm, over high tea, Lester began his campaign. "There's a place for you at the firm, Mikala. Why don't you come to your senses and join us? Jake will be there, and we can be one big happy family," Lester said with a chuckle.

Mikala almost choked on her tea. She set down her cup as she coughed until her eyes watered. Two decades had passed since the last time Lester offered Mikala a job. When she and David graduated law school, married, and passed the Bar, Lester made his first attempt. Mikala wasn't interested in working at Jacobson Law and not stupid enough to be in the vicinity of the witches' cauldrons.

Although much changed in Mikala's life since Lester's initial offer, little changed at Jacobson Law. The firm was a bullet train with a high-pressured boiler room. The witches regularly terrified and tortured interns and associates. They tore off limbs with their teeth and claws and threw various body parts into their cauldron, concocting a brew that sustained them. Mikala sighed and shook her head. "The law isn't for me anymore, Les. I no longer have the drive or desire to be in the courtroom. I'd be a huge disappointment."

Lester's gaze softened. "Nothing you could do would disappoint me. But if you change your mind, a place for you exists at the firm."

Mikala smiled and patted Lester's hand. "Thank you, but I won't change my mind."

She was content with her research job, but she spent much of her time at the community center, leading her own support groups. She also started an online support group for women all around the country who'd experienced loss. Other than being Molly's mama, she gained more satisfaction from her volunteer work than anything else she'd done in her life.

"You should write a book." Sybil, a new friend and volunteer at the community center, had encouraged. "You've survived so much. Your story would inspire others."

Although flattered, Mikala shrugged. "I'm not

special. The world is filled with stories like mine. My suffering is unique to me, but everyone has their own story."

"You don't understand. The suffering doesn't make you special, but surviving does."

Mikala wasn't convinced, but she'd mentioned the idea to Jake, and he agreed with Sybil. With their encouragement, she flirted with the idea and scribbled some thoughts in her journal. Maybe one day she'd do more with the idea, but for the time being, she was content.

Mikala smiled and watched Jake consume mouthful after mouthful of food he supposedly despised. Her life now was better than she dreamed it ever could be two years ago. She, Jake, and Rena made remarkable strides in their recovery.

Three months ago, Rena had returned from an impromptu trip to Las Vegas with Ted— married. "I'm eight weeks pregnant. I told Ted while we were away. Next thing I know, I'm saying *I do* in a beautiful chapel."

Rena showed Mikala pictures of a chapel filled with lilies and white roses. Cascading silk drapes, sparkling crystal chandeliers, marble pillars, and tall candelabras adorned the chapel. Rena and Ted's wedding pictures revealed a glowing bride and an adoring groom. Mikala was thrilled. Rena deserved to be outrageously spoiled and adored for a lifetime.

A week later, Rena put her house on the market.

As Mikala predicted, Rena moved to New York. Seeing Rena pack and drive away was difficult. They'd been through so much together and had resided close to one another for two decades. But Mikala was thrilled

Rena opened her heart to Ted and received what she deserved—a real family of her own.

Mikala wasn't sure if she would have dealt with Rena's move as well as she did if Jake wasn't by her side. She studied the ridiculously hot Latino sitting across the table. He monopolized the loaded nachos and shoveled chip after chip in his mouth. Jake's wavy black hair fell over his forehead, and she reached across the table and pushed it off his face. Despite his grumblings about the food, he made a pig of himself. When Mikala gave the waiter her credit card to settle the bill five minutes ago, Jake hadn't even looked up.

One sure way to get his attention existed. Mikala pulled the plate of nachos from under Jake's nose and toward her.

Jake growled, and he darted his gaze to meet hers. He reached for the plate with both hands.

With a grin, Mikala slapped away his hands. "You've devoured my nachos, most of the tacos, and half of the taquitos. I swear to God, you're a hoover. I thought you said the food was garbage?"

Shrugging, Jake grinned. "Just doing my job and taking care of the rubbish."

Mikala laughed and stood. "Come on, Super-man. We're done here."

Jake's eyebrows shot up. "But what about the fried ice cream? We haven't had any yet. Yesterday, after I ate the green-brown balls you insisted were a vegetable, you said I could have ice cream," he whined as he followed her through the restaurant. "Shouldn't we at least pay the bill since you ate most of it?"

Mikala stopped, put her hands on her hips, and glared. "First, I hardly ate anything. In between lobbing insults about the place, staff, and food, you devoured everything that wasn't nailed down. The check is paid, you oblivious, over-eating, not-so-super, superhero wannabe. And no ice cream for you. You've reached and exceeded your daily allotment of fat, and you've been a pill." Mikala turned and continued walking out of the restaurant to the parking lot with Jake in tow.

"Wait. What do you mean I've been a pill?" Jake asked when they'd made it to Red.

Exasperated, Mikala shook her head and looked toward the heavens. "Out of everything I said, that's what you heard?" She grinned. "A pill is a person who's been so whiny and grumbly, they've been hard to swallow. A massive pill—that's what you've been, Cardona, and you ate my food. So, no. No more anything for you today."

In seconds, Jake's arms circled Mikala's waist, and he whipped her around so her back collided with Red's driver's door.

The breath whooshed out of her. He was fast, and he was big. His six-foot, three-inch hulk dwarfed her by a foot. Mikala's eyes widened, and then she grinned. God how she loved her overgrown man-child.

Jake caged Mikala in between him and the truck. "You hurt my feelings, Mick." He shot her a pout he couldn't sustain more than a few seconds before a grin emerged. "I ate all that food so you wouldn't have to. I did you a favor and protected your stomach lining. Now, apologize"—he stepped farther into her space— "or the next time you somehow get a squirrel, chipmunk, or whatever that possessed rodent was, stuck in your garage, you're on your own."

Mikala glanced at Jake's face, and her breath

stuttered. God, he was hands-down the most gorgeous man she'd ever known, and he had no idea the effect he had on women. He might only be a friend, but she was a woman, and she wasn't blind. She had the ability to appreciate his sexy ass and not lose her mind like most of the female population.

In the restaurant, the majority of the women, and some of the male servers, tripped over themselves to serve Jake. But all the man did was bitch and complain, while swallowing every morsel of food placed in front of them. Everywhere Mikala accompanied Jake, he hypnotized women with his stunning good looks and charm. The sexy Latino persona he exuded was impossible to resist. Mikala, however, was immune. She spent most evenings protecting her beautiful, yet remarkably dense boy, from the female population.

Mikala placed her hands on Jake's muscular chest, and her gaze connected with his. "Here's what's happening, big boy. You'll come running any time I call your name or else you're on your own with the women of this town." She smirked. "I'll no longer be your buffer. Instead, I'll leak a rumor your broken heart has finally healed from a painful break-up, and you're looking for the right woman to spend the rest of your life with."

Jake's eyes widened, and his mouth dropped open. "You wouldn't," he whispered. "You know I'm weak, and sooner or later, I'll fall under one of their spells. I'll have to move again because I'll have a gaggle of women claiming I've promised them my life and future babies."

Although she mustered a herculean effort, Mikala kept a stern face. "Oh, I would. I'll drop a few hints to the right people at the community center. Maybe I'll put up a flyer that says—*Horn Dog in Need of Reform. Be His Savior.*"

Jake quirked an eyebrow. "Horn dog?" He burst out laughing, and she joined him. He backed away holding up his hands. "Okay, okay. You got me. I'll do anything you want. Please, no flyers. That reform campaign sounds ghastly. What are your demands, my queen?"

Mikala glanced down at her right elbow where a bruise formed. She rubbed her elbow and winced. "First, promise not to hurl me against solid metal, brick, or any other hard objects in the future. I'm not invincible like you. Keep man-handling me, and you'll hurt me, Super-man."

In a flash, Jake was in front of her. He flipped their positions, so his back was to the truck, and she stood in front of him. He took her arm in his hand and inspected it. "Sorry, sweetheart." A frown replaced his smile. "I'd never hurt you. Never."

Hearing the remorse in his voice, Mikala darted her gaze to meet his. In his expressive licorice eyes, she saw something she hadn't seen before. She blinked, and her breath caught. Jake had never gazed at her like that before. Adoration? Hope? What were those beautiful eyes telling her? For a few minutes, she was mesmerized by the tenderness in his eyes and the soothing stroke of his thumb over her bruised elbow. Her body melted into Jake's.

Jake's other arm went around her waist, and he held her against his solid, warm body.

She sighed and sunk deeper into Jake's arms, never breaking eye contact. God, being in a man's arms once again was divine. She relished the strength, safety, and intimacy of his embrace. Two years! How had she survived two years without being held in such an intimate and tender manner? She'd forgotten the feeling of being held, comforted, and adored. How could she have forgotten this bliss?

For the briefest of moments, Mikala gave in to her needs and her fantasy of being whole once more. She closed her eyes, laid her head against Jake's hard chest, and savored the sensation of being safe, protected, and not so alone in the world. She took a deep breath and inhaled his spicy, all-male scent. It filled her lungs, swirled in her brain, and intoxicated her. His delicious scent poked at and awakened long-hibernating emotions.

Mikala smiled, snuggling in deeper. She exhaled, and then took one more hit of his heady scent—so soothing and delicious. A shiver of awareness ran up her spine, and before she could lasso her runaway emotions and her traitorous body, her hormones took over, reminding her she was a woman. Mikala was a woman who enjoyed being in the arms of a man, and a woman who was young, healthy, and now—very aroused.

Chapter Seventeen
Terrains and Tour Guides

Mikala gasped, and her eyes flew open. Her heart galloped, and her breathing stuttered. A fine tremor ran through her. Oh, God, what the hell was she doing? She was in Jake's arms! *Jake's arms!* How in the world did she get there?

Her head snapped up, and she searched Jake's gaze before she ripped herself out of his embrace and looked away. She stumbled back several steps. Heat traveled up her neck to her cheeks. Her body and her brain were aflame. She was seconds from self-combusting.

Mikala couldn't think, and her chest constricted, making breathing impossible. She scanned the parking lot, focusing on everything but him. She turned, cursing herself for her moment of weakness, of idiocy, and total delusion. God, what had they done? She took a steadying breath and cleared her throat. She had to get her act together. She'd led them to this weird, foreign, no-go land. Now, her job was to transport them out.

Mikala wished she owned a time-machine so she could undo the mess she'd created by her moment of neediness and weakness. Turning toward Jake, she glanced at her watch, pretending she hadn't just dipped her toe into the forbidden zone. When she could no longer stall, she glanced up.

Jake ran a shaky hand through his hair.

His eyes were dilated, and he appeared just as disoriented as she felt. "I'm sorry. I don't..." Mikala stammered.

Jake exhaled slowly and shook his head. "Micky, it's okay. We..." He reached for her.

Mikala shook her head and stepped out of his reach. She wasn't ready for what just happened, and she didn't have the wherewithal to talk about it—not yet. "The time's ah...almost three. The truck's coming today. We've got to get going." She scooted around Red to the passenger side. Before Jake said a word, she climbed into the truck and busied herself with the seatbelt.

A few minutes passed before the driver's door opened, and Jake started the engine.

Mikala couldn't look at him. She'd stepped over the line, and although nothing happened, she was mortified. Over the last few weeks, Jake had held her hand, kissed her cheek or forehead, and hugged her on occasion—all innocent gestures. Nothing new, and nothing he hadn't done in the past. So, why was this embrace different? Why did his gentle touch, tender eyes, intoxicating scent, and his strong, protective arms affect her so intimately today? And why did she feel bereft the second she pulled away?

In the decades Mikala and Jake had known each other, they never came close to being more than friends. Even in those early college days, before Mikala met David, Jake kept her at arm's length, treating her more like a buddy than a potential girlfriend. His indifference puzzled and irked her. Then David came along, and Mikala fell hard and fast.

In college, once Mikala became more acquainted

with Jake, she was glad she hadn't given him her heart. The man was an absolute man-whore. He was known for being a good lay, but that was the extent of his relationship-building repertoire. Girls who thought they could trap him and change his ways found themselves on the curb with Mikala holding their hands and advising them he wasn't worth it. She'd lied. Her broken boy was more than worth the risk of an aching heart.

Mikala stared out the window and sighed. Having Jake back in her life over the last six months had transformed her life. They talked or texted several times a day. Even when he resided on the Pacific coast, he made time. Once he moved to New Haven, when he wasn't mired in work, they spent most evenings and weekends together. Perhaps, they spent too much time together. After all, things were different now.

Alone. Single. Widowed. Unattached. Did those words really describe her? Mikala didn't like labels, but those adjectives fit. For the first time since she was nineteen, she was without a man. David had been her first and only. The thought of another man never crossed her mind. But with Jake, her life was now filled with color, and even more astonishing, her world was filled with possibilities she never considered.

Mikala was finding her way back to happy. This version of happy was new and different than the one she'd shared with David. Step-by-step, she reached a new milestone and reinvented herself. But at the end of the day, when she lay in the bed she'd shared with David, she felt lonely and sometimes even afraid. She was adrift without David's arms anchoring her and his hard chest pillowing her head as the steady beat of his heart lulled her to sleep. Was she substituting Jake for David?

Closing her eyes, Mikala rested her forehead against the window and searched for a way to smooth over things. The desires Jake awakened were wrong—so wrong. Despite how her traitorous body behaved, Mikala didn't need or want a man. Her man, David, the love of her life, was dead. What she needed was her best friend, Jake. Mikala prayed she hadn't ruined the precious friendship they shared.

"Micky?"

Mikala jolted, hitting her forehead against the window. "Ow." She straightened and rubbed her forehead. "God, by the time this day is over, I'll look like a battered woman. Everyone at the community center will insist I attend the domestic violence support group. Jesus, I can't attend another group!"

Jake's laughter rang out in the truck's cab.

Mikala glared. "If I'm forced to attend another group, I'm making you come with me. Shit! I love my support group and the friends I've made, but I can't take anymore."

"Shit?" Jake smirked. "Did you just curse? I'm so proud of you."

Mikala tried to scowl, but her facial muscles had a mind of their own, and a grin formed. "Shut up, Jake, and drive. We'll be late."

Just like that, the tension in the cab evaporated, the awkwardness dissipated, and they were back on common ground. Jake and Mikala had traveled through the terrain of friendship for decades, and they didn't need a map or a tour guide. She treasured their easy banter and the laughter they so often shared. She never wanted to lose the precious rapport and affection they'd forged through thick and thin.

They arrived at Mikala's house, and the Jenny's Friends truck pulled up behind them. Mikala closed her eyes and gave herself a pep-talk. The time had arrived to let go of Molly's belongings. If she survived the next few hours, she would reach a huge milestone.

Mikala spent the last six months preparing for this moment. With Jake's help, she packed Molly's toys and clothes. She kept a few items she couldn't part with— the blanket she swaddled Molly in when they left the hospital, her christening dress, first pair of shoes, favorite stuffed animal, and a variety of other items Molly adored.

Then Mikala stumbled upon Molly's baby book. The book told the story of Molly's life and her mother's love. The diary wasn't a traditional baby book filled with dates of firsts and pictures, although Molly had one of those books as well. No, this leather-bound journal was filled with letters Mikala wrote from the day she found out she would be a mother. Some letters were written on special events—the day Molly was born, her first Christmas, and every birthday. Other letters were written to memorialize a milestone—the day Molly said her first word. Not mama or dada, Molly's first word was *stop*. She screamed this one word repeatedly while pulling Jake's hair as he blew raspberries on her plump baby belly.

Mikala never shared the contents of the journal with anyone, not even David. The letters were for Molly's eyes only when she grew old enough to understand the words and the depth of a mother's love. Although Molly knew her mama was writing a book and was curious, Mikala hadn't been in a rush to share the letters.

"When do I get my book, Mama?" Molly often asked.

Each time Mikala answered, "Not yet, my love. The time hasn't come yet."

Molly scrunched her little nose. "But when, Mama?"

Mikala smiled, lifted her baby girl onto her lap, and whispered in her ear, "I don't know, beautiful girl. But not right now." She had planned on continuing to write in the book for a very, very long time. She hadn't been sure when she would give it to her child, but she imagined the right time would come, and she would know. Maybe she would've given the book to Molly on her eighteenth birthday or her twenty-first. Perhaps she would've given it to her on the day she got married or the day she discovered she was having a child of her own. But those plans changed in an instant. She should have written the final letter already, but Mikala wasn't ready to bid her baby a final farewell.

Each time Mikala sat, pen in hand, and opened the journal, the words vanished. They vaporized into thin air, and the tears she swore she wouldn't shed flooded her eyes and slid down her face. She'd said goodbye to Molly in every other way. Molly even stopped visiting Mikala's dreams altogether. Perhaps, the day would come when Mikala wrote the final letter. Perhaps the day would never come. One way or another, Mikala refused to be rushed.

"You ready to say goodbye, sweetheart?"

Jake's gentle voice penetrated Mikala's thoughts. Was she ready? Mikala took a deep breath and nodded.

Molly no longer inhabited her room. She'd moved into Mikala's heart and memories where she resided forever. The time had come to share all the beautiful things Molly loved with other little girls in need. She hopped down from Red and waited for Jake.

Jake circled the truck and joined his fingers with Mikala's trembling ones. He opened the front door and directed the workmen to wait in the foyer. Jake led her past the men to the kitchen. Rubbing his stomach, he said, "I'm starving. You promised to feed me real food."

Mikala glanced toward the foyer in confusion. "But the men, I…"

"Stay here, Mick." Jake squeezed her hand. "Cook anything. I promise to eat it." He cupped her cheek with his palm. "Trust me. I've got it, sweetheart. I've got you. Okay?"

Jake wasn't hungry. Her super-man was doing his self-appointed job—protecting and sparing her. For once, Mikala gave in without argument. "Okay, Super-man. Okay." She surveyed the kitchen then walked around aimlessly, opening cabinets and drawers. When she heard the workmen thumping their way down the stairs, she retreated to the backyard and sat in the old tire swing Jake, against Mikala's better judgment, hung for Molly on her fifth birthday. She closed her eyes and pushed off, letting the glide of the swing, and the wind swishing through her hair, soothe her.

Twenty minutes later, the rumble of the Jenny's Friends truck echoed through the tranquil backyard. Then the backdoor creaked and slammed shut. Molly's belongings were gone, and Mikala had survived yet another day. This time, however, Jake was with her,

177

and the future wasn't so bleak.

Jake stood behind Mikala. In silence, he waited for Mikala to glide back to him, and then he pushed the swing.

What started as gentle pushes, with the swing floating through the warm summer air, soothing Mikala's aching heart, and lulling her into a half-doze, soon turned into death-defying acrobatics. Mikala's eyes flew open as Jake shoved the swing with enough force to send it soaring toward the sky. She screeched, and her heart hammered as her hands clenched the ropes tighter. She did her best to keep her ass firmly planted on the tire. "Jake! What are you doing? Stop. I'll fall off, you idiot."

Jake laughed and kept pushing. "Are you talking to me? Did you just call me an idiot? Now, that's not a nice thing to call the man who has your life in his hands, is it?"

"Jake, you lunatic, are you trying to kill me? Stop pushing me so high. I'll break my neck." Although she scolded him, Mikala couldn't keep the smile off her face. The man was a menace. Few people saw this crazy, over-grown man-child side of Jake which made its appearance at the most unexpected times. Mikala loved his wicked sense of humor and playfulness. Jake knew how to relax her and bring a smile to her face when no one else could. But right now, she wanted to kill him.

"You've been mean to me all day." Jake huffed. "Say you're sorry, and I'll consider helping you out of this precarious situation."

Mikala glanced over her shoulder. "Are you serious? You retarded ape. You put me in this situation, you oaf, and if you don't stop, I'll hurl."

The next time the tire swung in Jake's direction, instead of pushing Mikala again, he brought the swing to a grinding halt against his powerful body. "Say you're sorry for calling me names and refusing to buy me ice cream. Add on I'm the world's best friend," he whispered into her ear. "Say it now"—he laughed into her flushed face—"or I'm upping my game. This is fun, and I'm getting a nice upper-body workout."

Turning her head, Mikala grinned. "Okay, okay. I'm sorry."

"And?" He quirked an eyebrow.

Mikala gave him a tender smile and laid a hand against his cheek. "You're the best, the absolute best, Super-man."

Chapter Eighteen
Grow a Set

"Come in." Jake glanced from the thick file he'd been staring at for the last hour. He couldn't focus on a single word on the page.

Teetering on her four-inch black pumps, Leslie entered Jake's office. "I hope I'm not disturbing you."

Even though Leslie was five years older than Jake, she appeared no more than thirty-five. She was an attractive woman who was the center of attention in any room. Her tall, lean, and toned body was always showcased in top-of-the-line designer clothes. Leslie's signature blood-red manicured fingernails, unlined Botoxed features, and sharply arched eyebrows, added to her look-but-don't-touch effect.

Tonight, her ebony hair was styled in an elegant French twist, exhibiting her long neck, high-end diamond choker, and two-carat diamond earrings. Carrying a thick manila folder, she sashayed toward Jake with runway-model precision—head up, shoulders back, hips swaying, and gaze focused on her victim.

Jake stood and rounded the desk, meeting Leslie in the middle of the room. He extended his arm, palm up, and waited for the folder. Jake knew the routine, and he wanted to get this interaction over with before he lost his temper. Unlike Priscilla who was overtly hostile and made Jake's life a living hell since he'd joined the practice, Leslie's tactics were more subversive. Each night for the last week, she'd found an excuse to come to his office. Sometimes she asked for his advice on a case, and other times she miraculously discovered a file Jake's secretary had been searching for.

Jake wasn't a fool. He knew what Leslie was up to, and he wasn't falling for her antics. He had a shitload of work to do, and she wasn't on his to-do list. "What can I do for you, Leslie? I'm exhausted, so let's make this chat quick." He snatched the file out of her hand.

Leslie puckered her lips in a pout. "Jake, you're always in such a rush. Tomorrow is Saturday. Slow down." Turning, she strutted to the couch in the corner of the room, providing a full view of her ass. She leaned against the couch and caressed the brown leather. "Why don't we sit and have a drink? You look stressed."

Jake sighed and prayed for patience. He was tired of her games. He gritted his teeth and shook his head. "I have a lot to do. Perhaps you can tell me what you need."

She shook her head and let out a dramatic sigh as she ran her hands down the sides of the skin-tight navy pencil skirt that stopped five inches above her knees. She'd paired the sprayed-on skirt with a sleeveless silk camisole that was unbuttoned well past her cleavage and displayed her ample breasts encased in a white lace bra. Leslie smiled and walked to the desk. "I have a better idea. I bet you haven't eaten. Work can wait. We'll catch up over dinner and drinks. You look like you could use a night off."

Jake looked away and silently counted to ten, harnessing his rising ire. He really didn't have time for

Leslie's shit tonight. The work was piling up, and another woman filled his thoughts day and night. Still, he needed to keep the peace for Lester's sake. "I don't have time for dinner tonight. Thanks for the offer. Besides, we're having dinner tomorrow, and we'll catch up then. What can I help you with?"

Stepping toward Jake, Leslie snatched the folder out of his hand. She walked to his desk and dropped the file on it. Before he could move, she closed the lid to his laptop and turned. Leslie sat at the edge of Jake's desk. "Tomorrow's a family dinner. Those events are hardly relaxing." Slowly, she slid the tip of her tongue across her upper lip and smiled. "Let's have some fun tonight. If you don't want to go out, fine." She undid the buttons of her shirt. "I know just what we need to relax us both."

Jake hung his head, and his hands fisted by his side. Fuck! He needed to put a stop to the witch's schemes. He'd rather have her hostile and hungry for his blood. No fucking way would he ever lay a hand on either of the Jacobson witches.

Some people called Jake a man-whore, but even man-whores had standards. Besides, he was a reformed man-whore. He'd been only with one woman in the last year and a half—Elle. Jake and Elle's relationship was of the on-and-off variety and revolved around sex.

Glancing up, Jake met Leslie's cold stare. He shook his head. "Stop," he barked. "This little seduction isn't happening. Not now. Not ever. You need to go." Walking to the door, he gripped the handle and wrenched it open.

Leslie's pupils dilated just a fraction, but her smile never wavered. She re-buttoned her shirt and straightened. Walking in an unhurried pace, she stopped in front of him. "You know, Jake, I've watched your career for the last ten years. You're quite talented." She ran her fingers down his tie. "I can see why Lester has kept an eye on you." She cupped his cheek.

Jake's face flushed, and his breathing accelerated. He was through playing nice. He caught Leslie's wrist in a tight hold and yanked away her hand. "That's enough. I'm not interested and never will be. I've been patient with you and Priscilla, but enough is enough. From now on, contact my secretary with any business-related requests, and stay the hell out of my office and out of my way."

Pulling her wrist out of his grasp, Leslie straightened and squared her shoulders. Her icy blue eyes narrowed, and her lips turned into an ugly sneer. "You've made a tactical error tonight I think you'll soon regret." She scrutinized every inch of his body, and then she met his gaze. "While you more than fill David's shoes in the courtroom, you're not David, and you're not a Jacobson. You may think you have everything under control and Lester under your thumb. Trust me when I tell you, that notion is far from the truth. Just remember, you could have had me as an ally." She sauntered out of Jake's office with a small smile pasted on her lips.

Jake slammed the door behind her and locked it. He ran a hand through his hair. Taking a deep breath, he slowly let it out. What had inspired Leslie to make a play? He'd never showed any interest. What had she hoped to gain from all that nonsense? Having Leslie as an ally was not something Jake cared one way or another about. He would have liked to find common ground with the witches and come to a peaceful understanding about the practice. But each day he spent at the firm, he was more convinced an amicable resolution wasn't possible.

Lester was right. The women were excellent attorneys, but they would tear apart each other and the firm if left to their own devices. They lacked leadership skills evidenced by the fact they were strongly disliked by just about every associate and secretary.

Jake was well aware he wasn't a Jacobson, not that Lester cared. Although Lester had promised to be patient and wait until Jake better understood the practice, and Leslie and Priscilla were more accepting of his presence, daily he spoke about retiring. He even mentioned changing the name of the practice to Jacobson, Cardona & Associates. Lester moved too fast.

While Jake had the funds and the clients to buy into the practice fully, and he didn't doubt he possessed the skills to run and grow the firm, the timing was off. He needed time to settle into New Haven and into the new life he was building with Mikala. He had to find a way to slow down Lester. While Jake didn't care for Leslie and Priscilla, he understood their anger and resentment. They saw the writing on the wall, and they were bitter. Perhaps Mikala knew why Lester was in such a rush. She spent hours with him every week, talking on the phone and having tea. Maybe she could get him to open up.

Jake sat in his plush leather desk chair, closed his eyes, and rubbed his face. Fuck, he was tired. He glanced at the crystal desk clock Mikala gave him as a graduation present years ago and yawned. The time was nine-thirty p.m. His brain no longer assimilated the case he'd been reviewing before Leslie's visit. He needed sleep.

Sleep was a wonderful concept that eluded Jake for the last two weeks. Each night, he lay in bed wide awake, reliving the feel of Mikala's body as she leaned into him for those few minutes outside The Purple Armadillo. He recalled the softness of her skin against his thumb as he caressed her bruised elbow and the warmth of her whisky eyes. He'd wrapped his arms around her and relished the feel of her delicate body against his.

Powerful emotions, Jake hadn't experienced before for any woman, appeared out of nowhere. They surged and overwhelmed him. Having Mikala in his arms was magical. She was perfection. Protective and possessive instincts he didn't think were part of his fiber awakened and came to the forefront. He didn't want to let her go. For a brief, life-altering moment, Jake threw caution to the wind and let himself fully enjoy her heady scent and how her soft sighs tugged on his heartstrings. But when they emerged from their fantasy, reality hit hard.

Mikala's eyes widened. Astonishment, confusion, and fear showed in her stiff body and trembling voice. Her expressive eyes mirrored his own muddled emotions. A rapid pulse hammered at her throat, and a tremor ran through her and into him.

Like a dazed schoolboy after his first kiss, he felt stunned and paralyzed. He didn't know what to say or do. He'd behaved like a bumbling idiot.

Jake swiveled in his chair and faced the massive cherry-wood bookcase and credenza that matched his enormous executive desk. He took out the bottle of

Cognac and one of the crystal snifters Lester gave him on his first day at Jacobson Law six weeks ago. Jake poured a generous portion and downed most of the Cognac in one swallow. He grimaced as the potent brew hit the back of his throat and then his stomach. Lester loved this fancy shit and often shared a glass with Jake at the end of the day when all Jake wanted to do was go home and drink a cold beer with Mikala.

Mikala. Jake shook his head and poured a second dose. Lately, when he wasn't thinking about a case, his thoughts wandered to Mikala. Since he moved to New Haven, Jake spent almost all his free time with her, and he didn't want to be anywhere else.

Mikala and Jake had picked up where they left off before the fateful car accident. They finished each other's sentences, teased and taunted one another, and talked for hours without ever running out of things to say. When needed, they sat in comfortable silence. But their relationship had changed. This new development excited and terrified him.

Jake picked up his cell and stood, taking his glass. He walked to the windows that overlooked the meticulously manicured grounds surrounding the Sun-Dial Corporate Towers where Jacobson Law was located on the twenty-third floor. Outside was pitch black. He glided his fingers over the telephone's touch screen. He selected a number he dialed more often than he should and waited.

"Jake," Rena croaked. "Do you have any idea what time it is, man? You're killing me with this newly developed insomnia."

Wincing, he checked his watch. Nine-fifty-five p.m. "It's before midnight. You said never to call you after midnight again or you would do something distasteful to a part of my anatomy I'm rather attached to."

"Ugh. All right." Rena sighed. "I can see I'll have to set some pretty explicit rules. Are these calls, at all hours of the day and night, what I missed all those years you showered Mikala with all your attention and ignored me? 'Cause right now, I miss the good old days."

Ouch. Jake winced again. Rena was right. He'd spent years either keeping her at arm's length or exchanging hurtful barbs. Mikala and David had been his people, and he'd behaved badly. His newly formed friendship with Rena was still in its infancy. Their bond was birthed from necessity but thrived because they learned to let go of the past. Now, they shared a problem and love—Mikala.

While Jake still shared the majority of his problems with Mikala, some things he could no longer discuss. That development, too, was a shift in their relationship. Over the last two weeks, Jake often called Rena with the intention of seeking her advice. But each time they spoke, he couldn't voice his concerns.

"Jake, are you still there?"

He cleared his throat. "Yeah, Rena. I'm here. Sorry about the calls. I know you need your rest. I've got a lot on my mind. Taking out my problems on you isn't fair."

"It's fine. You're good practice for when this baby is born in December." Rena chuckled. "You want to tell me what's going on? You call, and we chat about various issues, but I get the feeling something else is on your mind. Is Mikala okay?"

Jake hesitated, searching for the words to explain how totally fucked he was. He had to voice his concerns. Rena was the right person to talk to. She knew them both, their past, and the road they'd traveled the last two years. A better person to confide in didn't exist.

Over the last two weeks, Jake had driven himself crazy, and Mikala wasn't unaffected. When she thought he wasn't looking, he found her studying him. Last night, he reached for her hand as they left the crowded movie theater, and they were still holding hands ten minutes later when they walked into the local ice-cream shop. He hadn't wanted to let go. He was fucked!

"Jake?" Rena barked. "Are you still there?"

Jake startled and lost his grip on the telephone, which bounced on the carpet. He quickly bent and picked it up.

"Jake, did you just drop the phone? What the fuck's going on?" Rena bellowed. "Are you and Micky okay?"

Jake held the telephone away from his ear. "Easy, Rena. Bring it down a decibel or two. Micky's fine. Everything's fine."

Rena sighed. "For fuck's sake, man. What the hell's going on? I'm aging here. Don't think. Just say it."

Jake rubbed the back of his neck. He was a grown-assed man behaving like a teenaged girl telling her best friend about a new crush. He was disgusted with himself. "She's fucking with my head, Rena. She's always there—smiling, laughing, asking me questions with her gaze I don't know how to answer. I have no idea what we're doing or the lines we're crossing."

Jake rounded his desk and sank into his chair. Taking a deep breath, he let it out. He waited for Rena to say something, but her even breathing was all he heard. He swallowed hard. "I know she's his, Rena, but I can't help myself. I'm certain she's as confused as I am, and I don't know what to do." After a few more seconds of silence, Rena's exasperated voice filled his ears.

"Grow a set, Jake. For fuck's sake, man, just grow a set."

Chapter Nineteen
Cross the Line

Jake knifed upward, releasing the glass he'd held in a death grip. Although Cognac splattered all over his desk and case files, he hardly noticed. "What? What did you say?"

"Grow. A. Set." Rena enunciated each word. "It's about fucking time you got your head out of your ass."

Jake pulled the cell away from his ear and stared. Had the pregnancy hormones affected Rena's ability to process complex situations and hold a civil conversation? So much for calling her to gain clarity. "Want to tell me what the fuck you're getting at?"

Rena sighed. "You and Mikala have been dancing around each other for years. You've loved her, and she's loved you and don't bullshit me with that 'we're just friends' nonsense."

Jake's breath hitched, and he was fairly certain his heart skipped a few beats.

You've loved her, and she's loved you!

Resting his elbows on his desk, he dropped his head into his hands as he absorbed Rena's words. Much like the alcohol, her words raced through his bloodstream and nerve endings, reaching his brain, giving him an initial high, followed by confusion and stuttering of his cognitive function.

After a couple of minutes, he sat up and shook his

head. If Rena believed he and Mikala loved each other...for years, she also may have come to other inaccurate and offensive conclusions. "You're way, way off base here. Micky and I have never been more than friends. She was always faithful to David. We've never—"

"Jake, just shut up," Rena scoffed. "I know she was faithful, but was David? Did he deserve her? I may be many things, but I'm *not* deaf, dumb, or blind. I loved David, but I wasn't *in love*. I saw him clearly—clearer than you and a hell of a lot clearer than Micky."

Jake pushed away from his desk and stood, sending his desk chair crashing into the credenza. Rena knew about David's infidelity? How the fuck did she know? Jake was sure he'd cleaned up the evidence. Jesus! "Stop. Just stop. You don't know what you're talking about. Go back to bed. I'm not discussing David with you. The man's dead. I'm sorry I called."

"She's not his, Jake, not anymore."

Rena's voice rang loud and clear through the phone line, and Jake almost dropped his phone again.

"She *was* his, and we both know he didn't deserve her."

For a minute, silence reigned. Right before Jake disconnected the call, he heard Rena's pleading voice come over the line again. "Just listen, will you? Please?"

Jake wanted to punch something or someone. Instead of responding, he paced as he evened his breathing and lassoed his hammering heart. He couldn't have this conversation, not with Rena or anyone else. For so long, he'd protected Mikala from the ugly truth. Even though David was gone, if she found out her husband had been having a fling with an associate, she'd be crushed.

A year before David's death, Jake had walked in on David getting a blow job from Jessica Harrison, a new associate. David swore he'd never before cheated. But Jake knew better. He read the guilt all over his friend's face. Although Jake wanted to beat the ever-living shit out of David, when David broke down and swore he would end his affair with Jessica, Jake held back. David claimed he loved Mikala and vowed he would never again be unfaithful.

Jake stopped pacing and studied the picture of Molly and Mikala on his desk. He picked up the photo and traced their identical smiles with his finger. God, how he'd loved that little girl, and he would do anything for Mikala—anything. David had known that fact and played Jake like a Stradivarius.

For three months after he walked in on David and Jessica, Jake stayed away from New Haven, claiming he was snowed with work. David disgusted Jake. He even contemplated telling Mikala what an ass she had for a husband.

Then David called, begging for help. He'd attempted to end his relationship with Jessica, but she refused to accept their affair was over. When David informed her he would never leave Mikala, she threatened to go to Lester and claim sexual harassment. Guilt-ridden, he broke down and cried.

Jessica was young and innocent-looking, and the media would have a field day. While Jacobson Law's reputation would take a hit, the firm would survive. Mikala, however, would be humiliated and devastated, Molly would be confused, and their family would be torn apart. Once again, Jake stepped in. He paid off Jessica and relocated her to a more profitable position. Jake shook his head. He had no desire to trudge through this ugly part of the past with Rena.

Rena took a breath and exhaled. "Jake, I'm sorry I was so harsh. But honestly, you know I can't make things sound pretty. I shouldn't have said anything. No good will come from discussing David's proclivities now anyway. The time for that conversation has passed. But I want you to know one thing, and then I swear I'll never bring up this topic again. Jake, do you hear me?"

He rubbed his forehead and sighed. "Go ahead, get it out of your system because you're right about one thing, we're never again revisiting this issue."

"For years I lived on the fringes, watching the three of you act out a drama bound to end in heartbreak and anguish—better than any tragedy Shakespeare ever wrote. I was a part of that play, but I wasn't integral to the triangle the three of you created. In many ways, I was a silent observer—an outsider." Rena sighed. "You spent the last twenty years loving Mikala. You made excuses and covered up for him, and you got him out of messes that would have destroyed them. We don't need to rehash the specifics or justifications. The past isn't important anymore. But Jake." Rena swallowed. "She's not David's anymore. David. *Is.* Dead."

Jake paced back to the window and stared out into the darkness. While Mikala would always love David, she had a big heart. David was her past. Could Jake be her future? His pulse bounded, and his heart beat against his ribs. Was the impossible, possible?

When they were nineteen, Mikala gave herself to David. She'd loved him to a fault. When they were young, she turned a blind eye to David's misadventures and questionable decision-making and continued to do so throughout their marriage. She loved the family he gave her, and she protected it and him with all her might. How could Jake ever compete with that kind of unconditional, blind love, and commitment? Besides, she deserved better.

Jake was shitty with relationships. He'd let himself fall in love once, but Alison Pennington III taught Jake a long-lasting lesson. An intelligent man, he never made the same mistake twice. He didn't want or need that all-consuming love where people sacrificed everything, lost their minds, and lost themselves. Did he? Every relationship he knew where people let themselves be overcome by another was flawed or led to disaster.

Jake's mother loved his father beyond all reason. She made excuse after excuse for Jake's abusing, cheating, morally defective father. Even when his father was arrested for murder, tried and convicted, his mother stood by him. She visited him in the penitentiary on a weekly basis. Three years later, he was stabbed and killed. She mourned him even though, when he was alive, he showed more kindness for his dog than he did for her.

Jake shook his head. He wasn't David, and he sure as hell wasn't his father. Mikala, despite her loyalty to David, wasn't anything like his mother and she wasn't Alison. Could they have a future together?

"Jake," Rena huffed. "Come on, man. I hear your heavy psychopathic breathing. Is that all I'm getting?"

He smiled and scrubbed a hand over his face. "I'm here. Just thinking."

"Okay." She sighed. "Look, don't hate me for speaking my mind and for loving you and Mikala enough to tell you a few hard truths. Someone has to push you out of your comfort zone. The time has come to be brave. Cross the line. Grow a set. Proceed slowly and with caution because she's fragile. She'll fight you each step of the way. Haven't you noticed how she's changed? She's lost her crazy spontaneity, her frenzied energy, and her love of life."

Jake swallowed past the lump in his throat. "Yeah, I've noticed...I notice everything where Micky is concerned." Mikala might think she's fooled everyone, maybe even herself, but he noted her tentative and reserved approach to life. She wasn't living fully. Mikala might be on the path to healing, but she was stalled. She used to live on hyper-speed, taking in as much of life as possible and teaching Molly to do the same.

Now, an eerie stillness surrounded her. Mikala was afraid of moving too fast and testing life. If Jake had to guess, she made the choice to just exist. She accepted whatever life gave her without asking for more. She was probably terrified if she built a new life, one day she may lose everything and everyone precious once more.

Mikala, however, wasn't the only one scared to roll the dice. Jake hadn't put his heart on the line for anyone—not in a long time. But Mikala was the one person in the world he would take a chance with.

Jake's heart beat against his ribcage, readying to take flight. Rena was right. He loved Mikala! For as long as he could remember, he'd loved her so deep and so all-consuming he wondered how he'd survived at all without her. Why had he taken this long to realize the depth of his love for this remarkable woman? He'd compared every other woman who entered his life to her, and every one he'd found lacking because none were Mikala.

Jake raked a shaky hand through his hair. "What if crossing the line means losing her? What if I'm not what she needs or wants?"

Rena chuckled. "Jake, Jake. Haven't you ever heard any of the clichés about love and life? For the most part, they're true. Life's a gamble. There are no guarantees. It's better to have loved and lost than never to have loved at all…and all that shit."

"Been there, done that, Rena. Don't you remember the infamous Ms. Pennington?" He gave a harsh laugh.

"You were a kid, and she was a bitch. You've grown up, I think, and she's on her third marriage. I think you can let go of that fiasco. Listen, I know you're a hotshot attorney. You like to look at all sides of an argument, study things to death, and strategize before you make a decision. You don't like surprises and puzzles you can't figure out. You like to control everything." She took a deep breath and slowly exhaled. "You recognize all those tactics are bullshit when applied to the real world, right? You're a semi-intelligent person, even if you do have a dick." She cackled.

Jake laughed. "When in the hell did you get so smart, oh wise and gracious one? Seriously, is it the hormones?"

"Fuck off, Jake. I've finished a pint of Ben and Jerry's talking to you, and now I have to pee. This kid is wide awake. She's tap dancing on my bladder from all the sugar I mainlined into her system." Rena sighed. "Here's the bottom line, my friend. Mikala needs a strong and honorable man. She deserves a person who is kind and faithful and who appreciates the gift she is– –a man who will love, protect, and cherish her. She needs someone who will make her laugh and live life to its fullest. Are you that man?"

Jake opened his mouth to answer, but Rena wasn't finished.

"Before you answer, do me a favor?"

Jake shrugged. "Sure."

"Close your eyes. Are they closed?"

Jake closed his eyes and smiled. "Yeah. Go on."

"Imagine Micky in the arms of another man. Imagine him holding and kissing her. Hell, for the best effect here, imagine him making love to her. Got that image?" Not waiting for an answer, Rena continued. "Now, answer my question. Are you that someone? Are you an honorable man, Jake?"

Before Jake had time to process Rena's question and formulate an answer, he heard a click. Jake didn't know how long he sat at his desk. When he'd followed Rena's directions, and he imagined Mikala with another man, pressure quickly built in his head until he was certain his head would explode. He never considered Mikala with another man, other than David. Rena's little exercise nearly gave him a stroke, but it also helped him want to grow a set, as she'd so eloquently repeated. He was a planner and a strategizer, but he had no idea how to go about convincing Mikala to let go of the past and trust him enough to build a future.

Mikala was Mikala, and he was Jake. The relationship they were about to explore was brand-new ground, but it wasn't. Neither of them was different, and yet together, they would be something new. They would still be the best of friends, but an exciting world of possibilities now existed. Many people met, fell in love, and built a relationship with a lot less history and a rockier foundation than what they shared.

Jake and Mikala enjoyed what felt like a lifetime of memories. They'd been in each other's lives since they were barely legal to vote and before they could drink. Mikala was the one constant, and the one person he could depend on other than Mateo. Together, they'd endured life-changing transformative events, and they survived. They knew each other's families, and over the last twenty years, borne and protected each other's secrets, fears, and confessions.

But Mikala *didn't* know all Jake's secrets. If she knew, would he lose her? Would she be blinded by pain and anger? Would she blame him for another's mistakes, or would she understand everything he did was for her and Molly?

Shaking his head, he stood then packed his briefcase. Time to get the hell out of the office. He wouldn't find the answers to the questions plaguing him tonight. He needed sleep. Perhaps, overnight he would grow a set, and by morning he'd be a good man—the kind Mikala needed to cross the line.

Chapter Twenty
Let Yourself Fall

"Why the hell do I need so many apples to make a simple pie? I ate two of the required eight apples yesterday, and I had to go out this morning for more. Do you have any idea what the grocery stores look like the day before Thanksgiving?" Mikala continued slicing apples, barely missing shaving the skin off a finger. "Crud! Hold on. This is getting dicey. I have to put you on speaker before I lose a finger." Mikala placed her cell on the counter and, using her elbow, she pushed the hair off her sweaty face. "Did you know that people are bat-shit crazy this time of year? Honestly, I saw two women playing tug-of-war over a can of cranberries. What's wrong with the humans of the world?"

"Oh God." Rena giggled as she listened to the rhythmic *thwack* of Mikala's knife against the chopping board. Although many miles separated them, Rena always found time to catch up. "Please don't make me laugh anymore, or I'll have to pee again. This kiddo is snuggled over my bladder, poking it with its middle finger."

Mikala burst out laughing. "You only have a few more weeks to go, and Ted's treating you like a queen. Don't you have one of those chefs from the cooking channel whipping up a Thanksgiving feast?"

Rena laughed. "Yeah. I'm being pampered, but I deserve it. I'm growing a human, for the love of God. Stop grumbling and concentrate. People's lives are in your hands. Are you still determined to take a homemade pie to the Jacobson family feast tomorrow? I know the witches and their High Priestess probably deserve to be poisoned, but what about Jake and Lester?"

Mikala huffed. "Shut up, Rena. I'll have you know my cooking instructor at the Community Center says I'm the most improved in my class and have potential. Jake even complimented me on the stew I made last night. He ate his entire bowl and asked for seconds."

"Okay, okay. Don't get all defensive. Too bad tomorrow's a holiday, and your realtor probably won't have a showing today. People love the smell of baked goods. The next time you have a showing, you should bake a bunch of cookies or brownies. I bet you get an offer."

"Hey, that's a great idea. But the house has only been on the market a few weeks, and I'm not in a rush to sell." Mikala looked out the kitchen window to the snow-covered backyard and sighed. "I can wait 'til spring. I don't have a plan yet."

"Are you comfortable with your decision to sell, or are you having second thoughts?"

Mikala finished cutting the apples and placed them in a bowl. She washed her hands and grabbed the kitchen towel. "No second thoughts. Selling the house wasn't a hard decision." Late one night, as she'd walked from room to room turning off lights and locking doors, Mikala realized she only utilized fifty percent of the house. Her cleaning lady saw more of the house than she did on a regular basis.

Mikala and David had purchased the spacious four-bedroom home with the intent of having a large family. But that dream wasn't meant to be. After three miscarriages, Molly was their little miracle. Once, the house was filled with David, Rena, Jake, and Molly's friends. Now, much of the time, the house was under-utilized and unappreciated.

For Mikala, the house was no longer a home but only a place to lay her head at night. Although many wonderful memories were made in this big house, they were overshadowed by the avalanche of tragedy that hit her family. Mikala sighed. "The for-sale sign is a daily reminder I have to move on without David and Molly, and I'm not sure yet where I want to live."

"What does Jake say about the whole thing?"

Mikala let out a long breath. "Jake is really supportive, but he's forcing me to make my own decisions and refuses to give me his opinion. Sometimes, I wish he would tell me if I'm making the right decisions." She walked around the kitchen gathering sugar, flour, cinnamon, nutmeg, and salt for the next phase of her baking.

"I'm glad you have Jake. So, things are going well with you two?"

Measuring cup in hand, Mikala paused. Were things going well? That question was good. Although she could talk to Rena about anything, she wasn't prepared to discuss her feelings about Jake. She needed time to analyze and understand what was happening between them. "Everything is…fine." Mikala hesitated. "Everything is okay…good…I guess. He's Jake. Why do you ask?"

"Fine? Okay? Good? Seriously?" Rena scoffed. "Why do you people think I'm an idiot? Want to tell me what's going on, Micky? You and I have been friends for a long time. I know something is troubling you. I've been waiting for you to tell me for a while now, but I'm through waiting. Stop bullshitting me." Rena huffed. "I'm pregnant. That means my hands are swollen, and I haven't seen my feet in a few months. Being pregnant doesn't mean anything is wrong with my hearing or my brain. Spill."

Mikala finished measuring the flour into the metal baking bowl and wiped her shaking hands on a dish towel. Was she that transparent? Over the last few weeks, she'd done her best to keep all conversations with Rena as light as possible, focusing on the baby and the upcoming holidays. She hadn't wanted to face Rena's interrogation without having a few prepared answers. Right now, she had more questions than answers.

Mikala took a deep breath. In order to throw Rena off the trail, she had to get her act together and be more convincing. Rena was a bloodhound and wasn't easily thwarted. Mikala cleared her throat. "Honestly, Rena, everything is fine. I have nothing to tell." Although she did her best to sound calm and blasé, Mikala was certain the tremble in her voice gave her away.

Then the mixing bowl filled with flour and sugar clattered to the ground, showering the kitchen in white powder and sugary granules. "Oh, darn it! Look what you've made me do." Mikala surveyed the mess, and her eyes filled with tears. "All the dry ingredients are on the floor, cabinets, and counters. Damn it! What a disaster. I'll need hours to clean up this mess, and now I have to start from the beginning."

"Hey, it's okay," Rena soothed. "You should see how many things land on the floor when I waddle around the kitchen these days. Take a deep breath, Micky."

"I can't do this. I just can't. I don't know how." She swiped at the tears trailing down her cheeks and sniffed. "Starting from the beginning again is too hard. I really don't think I can."

"Micky, stop," Rena commanded. "Breathe before you give yourself an aneurism. Leave the mess, grab a cup of coffee, and sit. The cleaning and pie can wait. We need to chat, girlfriend."

Mikala shook her head. She didn't know where to start. Over the last few months, the time she and Jake spent together had been wonderfully confusing. She treasured every minute, even if he was insane at times. But she didn't know how to describe what she felt or feared. While her emotions were a jumbled mess, Jake appeared content and comfortable with their relationship.

Although most weekdays Mikala only saw Jake for a quiet dinner, their weekends were a buzz of activity. He had an endless list of things to do, and he planned all their weekend outings. None of their excursions included staying home, visiting a museum, sitting on the beach, or strolling through the botanical gardens. His idea of fun, when the weather was warm, was a fifteen-mile bike ride across Connecticut and hiking the Giant Steps Trail at East Rock Park. He'd also insisted they go rock climbing, apple picking, and walking through a haunted house that almost gave Mikala a stroke.

Mikala smiled. Jake certainly kept her active and entertained. She'd laughed more in the last two months than she had in two years. She was happy, joyous even, and when he was around, she wasn't so scared of the future. He gave her a reason to dream and hope. But each of those happy, hopeful dreams included Jake. Those rose-colored dreams scared her to death.

Mikala dried her eyes, blew her nose, and poured herself a cup of coffee. She grabbed the phone and sat at the kitchen table, waiting for Rena to begin lecturing her.

"Talk to me, Micky. I'm here, and you're safe. You know you'll never hear a word of judgment from me. You can trust me."

Her stomach clenched. Rena would make her talk. Maybe the time had come to share her troubling thoughts with someone. She trusted Rena. Perhaps Rena could help her sort out her conflicting emotions. Mikala cleared her throat. "Jake and me…we're changing. Our relationship is evolving."

Mikala was a forty-one-year-old woman—about to be forty-two. She wasn't a young, inexperienced girl, but she'd only been with one man. Compared to other women her age, her inexperience was laughable. But even if she had a long string of relationships, she still would be freaked out. What she felt went way beyond friendship, and Jake was her best friend! At times, when she was in his presence, she was paralyzed by the swell of emotions that engulfed her. She needed Rena's wisdom.

"Changing? Evolving? For the good or the bad?"

"I don't know." Mikala's heart pounded. "I'm not sure," she whispered.

"Bullshit, girlfriend!" Rena scoffed. "You're terrified to admit what's in your heart. I get it. But deep inside, you know how he makes you feel. Say the words, Micky. Lightning bolts will not rain down from the sky and strike you."

Rena was a pain in the ass. How had Mikala forgotten that fact? She wouldn't let her get away with half-truths. Deep down, Mikala knew how she felt. Each time she saw Jake, a smile stretched across her face, and she was helpless to stop it. Her super-man was always a kind and generous man with a great sense of humor and a big heart. But now she saw him with new eyes. He was still all those wonderful things, but he was also smart, savvy, and sexy as hell. His intense gaze and smoldering black eyes, known to turn a witness into a pile of goo on the stand, warmed her to her core and, at times, rendered her speechless.

Over the last few weeks, Jake slowly advanced their relationship. Mikala recognized he gave her time to adjust to the new them. He never asked more than she was willing to give, and he treated their fragile, budding romance with reverence. Often, he held her hand and caressed it with his thumb. Sometimes, as they watched television, she laid her head in the crook of his arm or on his chest and listened to the beat of his heart. Although she longed to feel his lips against hers, at the end of each day, all she felt was the whisper of his kiss on her cheek or forehead.

"I think I'm falling for him, Rena." Mikala sighed. "I didn't plan on it. One minute, he was a friend and the next, he was more. I'm afraid of screwing up the friendship we built over the years." She closed her eyes. "I haven't felt this off balance, this confused, and...well"—she took in a shaky deep breath and released it—"this *good* in a long time. I don't know what to do." Relief washed over Mikala. Saying the words out loud and sharing her fears was freeing.

The women were quiet for a few moments—each lost in their own thoughts.

"You know, Mikala, when you lost Molly and then David, I didn't think you would ever recover. I couldn't imagine how anyone could survive that double blow. Your recovery hasn't been easy, and I don't think you'll ever be the person you were before their deaths, but that's okay. Even without tragedy, over time, people mature and evolve. Life isn't static, and none of us are exempt from change—good and bad. You've learned that lesson the very hard way."

Mikala opened her eyes and stared into her coffee. "I know I have to move on. The thing is, everything is changing all at once...again. You moved away. Jake moved here. I'm selling the house and then...well, then there's Jake." Phone in hand, she stood and paced the kitchen. "I'm afraid, terrified actually—of doing the wrong thing and of losing anyone else. If Jake and I jump into this relationship, and we don't work out, I'll lose him, and Rena..." Mikala stopped pacing and stared into the backyard where the tire swing glided back and forth in the breeze. "I can't lose one more person," she whispered.

"Oh, Micky, sweetheart, you've been through so much. I understand your fears, but you can't let them rule you. You can't let fear stop you from fully living once more. You deserve to be happy. You encouraged me to let in Ted, put the past behind me, and leap. Even though I was terrified of giving myself to anyone, I did, and I built a new life. My life is very different now in every way, but I couldn't be happier. The time has come for you to be happy."

Mikala shook her head. "But we're talking about Jake. Jake! My friend. David's friend. How can what I feel for him be right?"

Rena sighed. "The more important question is how can what you feel for Jake be wrong? Why do you think you're not entitled to your feelings? You and David loved each other. Moving on and starting something new and good doesn't negate the love you shared with David. Stop coming up with excuses not to be happy."

Mikala swallowed past the boulder in her throat. "God, Rena, I wish life was that easy. For the most part, when I'm with Jake, I feel no awkwardness or pretense. We fall into step with one another. We naturally fit. But at night when he's gone, and I'm left alone with my thoughts, in the dark…" She sank into the kitchen chair, recognizing what she was about to say made little sense, and wondered if Rena would understand.

"Yes, go on," Rena encouraged.

"I feel like I'm cheating on David. I feel like I'm somehow soiling what we shared—his memory." Mikala shook her head. "I'm not stupid. I know he's gone, and I have nothing to feel guilty about. I understand I'm no longer married, and I'm not really cheating, but that's how I feel." Rena was quiet for a minute.

Rena cleared her throat. "Micky, you're entitled to your feelings. I've never walked in your shoes, and I won't tell you how you should or shouldn't feel. But give this relationship a chance. You and Jake are unattached. Just see where life takes you. Let go, and let yourself live. Let yourself fall, knowing he will be there to catch you."

Mikala's eyes filled with tears. "What if I'm making a terrible mistake and I lose him altogether?"

"What if this relationship is the most beautiful gift you've been given and you allow it to slip through your fingers? Don't you think he has the same fears? Don't you think he's terrified of losing his best friend—the only family he has?"

Mikala hadn't considered how Jake felt, but as she absorbed Rena's words, she recognized she'd been selfish. The time she and Jake spent apart after David died, had been agonizing for both of them. They rarely spoke about the painful past, but when they did, they promised they would never hurt one another in that way again. Of course, Jake must have the same concerns. This change in their relationship was new ground for him too. "I hadn't thought about how Jake was feeling. When we're together, he doesn't appear to have a care in the world."

Rena chuckled. "Trust me, looks can be deceiving. Don't worry. I can't imagine, after everything you both have lived through, either of you would be so careless as to destroy the precious bond you have. You tried that nonsense once, and the separation nearly killed you both. I know you two have fancy degrees attesting to your intelligence. I'm certain you'll put that IQ to work and not make the same mistake twice."

Mikala smiled. Rena certainly had a unique way of communicating. "Now what?"

"Lord, do I have to tell you people everything?" Rena huffed. "Now, stop blubbering, go make pie, and then take a walk on the wild side. You've got a hot superhero by the balls. Let yourself fall, you ridiculous woman. He'll catch you in his big strong arms, and you'll fly off into the sunset together. That's it. I'm done. I've got to pee."

"Okay." Mikala wiped her face with a kitchen towel.

"You good?"

"Yeah, Rena. I'm good, and I get it. Happy Thanksgiving, my friend."

"Be happy, Micky. For fuck's sake, just live and be happy."

Chapter Twenty-One
An Expedition into the Jungle

Let yourself fall. Just live and be happy.

Rena's words were simple. They made sense and easily rolled off the tongue. Mikala hoped her friend was right. She prayed one day she would be brave enough to fall, live, and be happy. For now, though, Mikala surveyed the kitchen and shook her head. The place was a wreck, and she still had a lot to do. Jake would be home with pizza and beer before long. He'd called earlier in the day, asking for updates on the great baking experiment.

"Don't ask." She forced a dramatic sigh. "If I produce anything, I'm test driving a pie on you."

Jake chuckled. "Thanks for the warning. Since I'm the guinea pig for dessert, I'll bring dinner. I'm willing to put my stomach through only so much jeopardy in one day."

Mikala spent the rest of the afternoon baking. Then, she tackled the kitchen as she replayed the conversation with Rena. Talking to Rena relieved her anxiety. She'd been worried about making the wrong decision. But, in truth, the decision was simple. She wanted Jake in her life, and she wanted to be happy. The easiest decision to make right now was not to make any decision. She would take Rena's advice. Mikala would live day-by-day and trust in herself, and in Jake, not to hurt each other.

After cleaning the kitchen and showering off the apple pie ingredients, she settled into the easy chair in the family room with a mug of warm cider. The time was perfect to call home. Thanksgiving at the Cummings' house was a production with many guests. Calling a day ahead guaranteed she'd speak to her parents without too many distractions.

Dani answered the telephone. After a brief conversation, she handed the phone to Mikala's mother.

Mikala spoke briefly with Sandra and told her all about her pie-making efforts. They even laughed about the mess Mikala created in the kitchen. Over the last six months, Lester used every opportunity he could to lecture Mikala on family and respect for her parents. His arguments were persuasive and heartfelt.

"You know what the good book states, don't you?" Lester admonished her, usually at their weekly high-tea or over dinner and drinks. "It says honor your mother and father. No waivers are written in small print at the bottom of the Ten Commandments. They don't say to honor them only if they are good parents or only if you like them. The Commandments are blanket statements, girl. You don't know how long you'll have your parents in your life. Haven't you learned anything? Make up with your mother so you won't have any regrets."

Grudgingly, and only to get Les off her back, Mikala promised to call and speak to her mother weekly. Each time, she made an effort to find some common ground. While Mikala still harbored some hurt and resentment, their conversations had become less stilted and uncomfortable. Mikala was grateful Lester pushed her to begin healing old wounds. Life was unpredictable and too short to hold grudges.

Mikala finished chatting with her mother, and as Joe's frail voice filled her ears, Mikala stood and walked to the kitchen.

"Happy Thanksgiving, my girl," Joe said.

"Hi, Dad. How are you feeling?"

"Fine. Fine. Tell your old dad how his baby girl is doing. How are you spending the holiday?" he asked with a deep sigh.

Although her father sounded happy to hear from her, something was off. Mikala noted a fragility in his voice she hadn't heard two days prior. She'd learned her father had a heart attack after Molly's death. He never fully recovered. Over the last three months, Dani's husband, Jason, ran the farm while Joe took more and more to his recliner. "I'm fine, Dad. Jake and I are having dinner at the Jacobson's." Mikala frowned. "But never mind that. How are you? You sound tired. What's going on?"

"Oh, I'm fine, Mikala. Just fine." Joe yawned. "Just a little tired, that's all. Nothing a nap won't cure. Your dad isn't a young man anymore."

Mikala ignored Joe's deflecting techniques. "Didn't you have a doctor's appointment yesterday? What did he say?"

"He said my family nags me too much, and I should tell all of you to leave me alone," Joe grumbled. "Micky, stop worrying, for Pete's sake. It's Thanksgiving. Give yourself the day off."

Mikala chewed on her bottom lip. Over the last month, each time she spoke to her father, she hung up feeling more and more uneasy. "Dad, you would tell me if something was wrong, wouldn't you?"

Joe exhaled. "Of course, of course. But now I've got to get to dinner. Your mother's hollering. Happy Thanksgiving, my girl. I love you, and every day I am thankful for you."

Mikala swallowed hard. "I love you, too, Dad. Take care of yourself." Something was wrong. The whole family still treated her as if she were made of crystal. She hated being kept in the dark about her father's condition. The lack of information added to her anxiety. Her parents were aging, but she wasn't ready to lose them. Maybe a visit home at Christmas would give her the answers she needed.

As tears filled Mikala's eyes, she heard the creak of the garage door. Jake was home. He knew the garage door code and had a key to the house. Soon, he would make his way from the garage, to the mudroom, and into the kitchen. Mikala took a deep breath and blinked to keep the tears at bay, but she failed.

Life was so unfair. She'd experienced enough sorrow for a lifetime. Right now, she should be baking with Molly or trying to anyway. She should be enjoying a glass of wine with David as they discussed Christmas plans. She shouldn't be standing in her kitchen wondering if by next year, she would be without another person she loved.

Turning toward the mudroom, Mikala swiped at the tears escaping down her cheeks. Lord, she was a mess. After a long day at work, poor Jake didn't deserve her emotional meltdown. Mikala grabbed a paper towel and blew her nose. She wrestled with her emotions and did her best to shake off her morbid thoughts.

"Hey there, Chef Mikala." Jake walked into the

kitchen with a cocky grin, balancing a pizza box in one hand and a six-pack of beer in the other. "Something smells fantastic in here. Hope the pie tastes great, or you and I will be spending some time with your usual frozen friends."

Mikala gave him a watery smile and grabbed the pizza box. She set it on the kitchen island. "Hi, Jake."

Jake set the beer next to the pizza and turned. His smile faded. "What's wrong, sweetheart? You've been crying." He ran his thumb over her damp cheek and cupped the side of her face.

When Mikala's eyes filled again, she closed them. She took a deep breath and slowly let it out. She turned her head into Jake's hand and reveled in the feel of his calloused thumb caressing her cheek.

"Hey, now. What's going on?"

Mikala opened her eyes, ready to tell him about her conversation with her father, but once her gaze met his, the words vanished. Jake studied her with such tenderness, her heart ached, and she longed to feel his arms around her—comforting and protecting her.

Jake slid his hand from her cheek, down her arm, and to her hand. His gaze never left hers as he tugged her close.

Mikala's breath hitched, and she remembered Rena's words—*let yourself fall*. This moment was pivotal. She could continue holding back, fighting herself and him, or she could let go. Mikala's heart pounded, and she trembled. She wanted to give in. She needed to give in. Every emotion Mikala had been holding in check for months, rose to the surface, and gained strength. The dam she'd carefully erected gave way.

She didn't want to wake up, trudge through the day, and go to sleep every night by herself. Mikala longed to be held, comforted, and loved. She wanted to share her days and nights with someone who she could trust and love and someone who would always catch her when she fell. Damn it, but she wanted her world to right itself.

David was gone forever, but Jake stood in front of her, offering a new and exciting future. Mikala wasted time and energy on self-doubt when she could have beauty. Jake wouldn't wait forever. She had to prove to him and to herself, she was bruised but not broken.

Letting out a shuddering breath, Mikala fell into the warmth of Jake's embrace. She didn't fight him. She closed her eyes, laid her head against his heart, and wrapped her arms around his waist. She breathed him in.

Jake's arms circled her. One hand worked its way through her hair, to the back of her head, as his other arm banded around her back. He buried his nose in her hair and inhaled, and then exhaled, matching his breathing to hers.

In Jake's arms, Mikala loosened the reins on her emotions and held on to Jake. She buried her face in his chest and took deep breaths, letting them out slowly. No matter how much she wanted to leave the past behind, hiccups would happen—days that tried her and reminded her of all she'd lost. Today was one of those days. The holidays would be hard for a while, and she had to allow herself some grace. The conversation she had with Rena, topped by the conversation with her father, pushed Mikala into emotional overload. But Jake held her in his arms and held her together.

Jake rocked her back and forth. He kissed the top of her head. "I've got you, baby. I've got you," he whispered.

The word *baby* coming from Jake's lips ripped away what was left of Mikala's resistance. A long time had passed since any man had given her a pet name. David used to call her darling. Now, she was *Jake's* baby. She loved that name. Mikala felt cherished and precious. She'd traveled a long distance, and her weary body and soul finally found refuge in Jake's arms. Her heart rejoiced as her stomach did a somersault. She and Jake were really happening.

When Mikala's tears dried, she calmed. She pulled away and blew her nose. Certain she looked like a wreck, she didn't care. The day's activities and emotional tsunami wiped out Mikala. She glanced up to see Jake smiling. Heat crept up her chest, her neck, and to her face. Suddenly, she was embarrassed, unsure, and felt more than a little vulnerable.

Jake pulled out a kitchen chair and sat. He tugged Mikala onto his lap. "Better?" He wiped her cheek with his thumb. "Want to tell me what those tears were about?"

Mikala nodded, and then glanced away, unsure of where to start. Words eluded her.

"Mikala." Jake kissed the top of her head. "Look at me, baby."

Baby. Mikala's heart leaped once more. Their relationship had definitely changed. They forged ahead into unknown territory—an expedition into the jungle without a tour guide. Mikala took a shuddering breath and raised her head. "I'm sorry. I'm an emotional wreck because of the holiday and the memories it evokes." She sniffed and wiped under her eyes with her hands. "I spoke to Dad, and I don't think he's well. My brain went to the possibility of losing him." Mikala shook her head. "I'm being ridiculous."

Jake rubbed her back. "You're not being ridiculous. I think you're too hard on yourself. You've been worried about him for a while. Why don't you spend Christmas with your family?"

Mikala's eyes widened. "You're a mind reader. That's exactly what I thought I'd do. You wouldn't mind being on your own?"

"I'll miss you, but I'm a grown man. I'll be fine. Besides, I have Lester and the witches." Jake smiled and quirked an eyebrow. "Anything else bothering you?"

Mikala took a deep breath and looked away. They had to discuss what was happening between them, didn't they? She started up from his lap.

"Just say the words."

Mikala swallowed. "I'm afraid, Jake," she whispered. "Our relationship is changing, and I'm scared to death."

Jake took her hand and raised it to his lips. "There, saying the words and admitting your feelings wasn't so hard, was it? Thank you."

Mikala met his gaze and frowned. "For what?"

Jake pulled her deeper into his arms and squeezed. "For being brave. For letting an us exist. You're trembling. I know you're terrified, and to be honest, so am I. But you and I, *we* fit. In my arms is where you belong. Don't you feel it? We have something special."

Mikala's arms snaked around Jake's waist, anchoring herself as she let the words roll off her lips.

"Yes," she whispered. She laid her head on his chest and listened to his racing heartbeat. "I do feel it. But if we don't work, I'll lose you again, and, Jake, I can't…"

Jake kissed the top of her head. "Shh, sweetheart. I can't lose you either. But I have faith in us. Just give us a chance."

Rena was right. Jake wasn't unaffected. He had as much to lose as she did. He asked her to be brave, put her heart on the line, and believe in them. Mikala wanted to very badly.

Jake rested his chin against the top of her head. "You're not alone in this adventure, Micky. Here's the thing I want you to remember. I trust you, and I swear, you can trust me. I promise you, no matter what happens between us, no matter how our relationship evolves, you'll always be my family, and I'll always be your super-man."

Mikala let Jake's words sink in. Through thick and thin, he'd always been her super-man. Even when they were separated, part of her knew he'd come back. If she gave her fragile heart to anyone, who better to trust than the one man she'd always trusted and loved? The time had come to take a leap of faith—right into Super-man's arms.

Chapter Twenty-Two
Milestones and Mishaps

"Catch me, Daddy, catch me." Molly giggled as she ran from her father as fast as her little legs could carry her across the warm sand. Her blue eyes sparkled with mischief, and her auburn curls danced around her shoulders as her giggles filled the air.

"I'll get you, Butterfly, and when I do, I'll tickle you all over until I get the kiss you promised me." David grinned and sprinted after his daughter. He grabbed her around the waist, and she shrieked. He tossed her into the air, caught her in his arms, and covered her face with kisses. "I love you, my butterfly," he said, smiling into his daughter's face.

"I love you, my daddy," Molly sang back.

Mikala smiled and hugged the pillow closer. She nestled deep under the covers and sighed. She loved watching her baby girl and David playing on the beach. Molly was the same carefree little girl, full of mischief and life. David was more relaxed and carefree than he'd been in a long time.

An annoying buzzing disturbed Mikala's slumber. Frowning, she pulled a pillow over her head, wanting to stay with Molly and David. They were visiting her together, a rare treat. But staying with Molly and David wasn't an option. The buzzing persisted, and the spell broke.

Mikala relented. As she emerged from sleep, she left David and Molly stretched out on the beach, enjoying the warm summer day. She turned her head toward the noise and cracked open an eyelid. Her cell vibrated on the nightstand. Surrendering to the day, Mikala rolled over, grabbed the phone, and answered the call. "Hello," she croaked.

"Good morning, sunshine."

Jake's very caffeinated and energetic voice filled her ears. Mikala closed her eyes and groaned. She cleared her throat. "Go away, Jake. I'm sleeping."

"Micky, baby, it's almost noon. You need to wake up. We're supposed to be at the Jacobsons' in two hours."

Mikala's eyes popped open, and she bolted upright. "Noon? Oh my God! How could I have slept so late?" She threw off the covers and pushed away the hair covering her face. "I was so tired. You kept me up ridiculously late. I never sleep this late. I've got things to do—maybe bake another pie or find someone to sell me one. Fuck, I have no idea what to wear!"

"Did you just say fuck?" Jake chuckled. "I'm so proud of you."

"Shut up and get over here." Mikala put the phone on speaker and threw it on the bed beside her. She gathered her wild hair and used the hair-tie she kept on the nightstand to tame it into a messy bun. "You didn't taste the pie I made last night, and I need to know whether it's edible or not."

Mikala stood and righted her bedside clock. She always placed the clock face down before she slept, as any light, even the slight glow from the clock, kept her up. She froze and blinked a few times, studying the clock. "Jake Santiago Cardona! It's ten-fifteen, you ass. What the hell? Are you trying to kill me? I hate you. Go away."

Jake's delighted laughter filled her ears. Mikala grabbed the phone and disconnected the call. The man infuriated her. She ran a hand over her face and walked to the bathroom. She couldn't fall back to sleep now. Instead, she washed her face, brushed her teeth, and slipped on the ridiculously comfortable, yet hideous, purple bear-claw slippers Rena sent last week as a birthday present. Tomorrow, she would turn forty-two.

While some women hated their birthday and lied about their age, Mikala was the exact opposite. Birthdays were a celebration of life, and she, more than most people, understood if you weren't celebrating a birthday, you were dead. Mikala glanced at her feet and smiled. She opened her bedroom door. Although she was the only one living in the house, she felt safer with the door shut.

The minute Mikala opened the door, the smell of freshly brewed coffee hit her nose. *Jake*. He had to be responsible for that delicious scent. No one else had a key to her house, and burglars didn't stop to brew their victims coffee before they ransacked the place. Mikala breathed in the heavenly aroma and sighed. How long had the idiot been in her house, and why was he there?

Mikala padded down the stairs in her clawed feet, festive Christmas trees and reindeer sleep shorts, and red tank. She didn't think twice about her attire. Over the years, Jake had seen her in plenty of swimsuits that displayed much more than her preferred sleeping attire. She strolled into the kitchen and found Jake arranging a huge bouquet of stargazer lilies and lavender roses in one of her crystal vases. Mikala froze.

The kitchen island was covered in food—sliced fruit, bagels, croissants, cheeses, jams, quiche, and even smoked salmon. The small kitchen table was set for two, complete with orange juice and coffee. On the counter sat a small chocolate cake with the words *Happy Birthday, Micky,* written in white flowing letters.

Mikala gasped. Jake remembered her birthday. Why was she shocked? Jake never celebrated her birthday on the day she was actually born. He said doing so lacked the element of surprise. Even when they'd been apart, he'd sent her a birthday greeting through Rena. Today, he'd gone all out.

"Happy birthday, baby." He walked to her with a big smile.

The man towered over Mikala in jeans that hugged his thighs just right and a gray Irish fisherman's sweater.

He surveyed her from head to toe. Under his appreciative stare, Mikala reddened.

She tugged at her tank that had ridden up to expose a ribbon of her belly. God, Jake looked like he could devour her. He'd never looked at her that way before, and although she felt exposed, in his eyes, she also felt beautiful—maybe even sexy.

"Hello, beautiful," Jake said in a husky voice. "Love the outfit—especially the slippers. Rena?"

Mikala nodded.

Jake cupped her face in both his hands. He lowered his head and touched his lips to hers.

His lips were soft, and he kissed her in the gentlest, most tender of ways. Mikala's eyes widened, and her breath stuttered. Her hands flew to his wrists, and she held on as he slowly and tentatively kissed her. He led the way, and she followed. Mikala's heart hammered, and her head swam. Her eyes fluttered closed as she gave herself over to the kiss and to Jake. She wrapped her arms around his neck and returned his kiss.

Last night, they'd stayed up laughing and talking. They agreed to take life day by day and just enjoy each other. Mikala told Jake about Rena's advice to let go and live.

"She sort of told me the same thing, sweetheart, but she also told me to grow a set," Jake admitted with a chuckle.

Mikala and Jake ended the night with a hug. He'd kissed her cheek and promised to see her in the morning.

This kiss, however, was no peck on the cheek. Jake made his intentions clear and staked a claim. He was through being just friends. Forgetting all her fears and inhibitions, Mikala sighed and melted into Jake. His lips were firm on hers as he took turns nibbling on her upper and lower lips, and then he deepened the kiss. He took his time. The kiss was an exploratory introduction and a promise of a delicious future.

Mikala fought to reconcile what was happening. She questioned whether she should be kissing Jake at this point in their fragile new relationship. But her heart shushed her over-analytical brain and urged her to enjoy every second in Jake's arms. He awakened long-forgotten feelings that had been buried under tragedy. Being in his arms, with his lips caressing hers, felt perfect.

Jake broke away and kissed her nose and forehead. He gathered her close.

She snuggled against his chest and caught her breath. She breathed in his delicious spicy scent, and a sense of peace stole over her. She'd imagined their first kiss and worried it would be awkward and uncomfortable. She feared Jake wouldn't find her desirable and would realize they should have stayed friends. But as he held her close, her body molded to his, Mikala felt the evidence of Jake's attraction, and her pulse raced.

Jake wasn't David. Mikala had worried she wouldn't enjoy another man's touch or kiss, especially from someone who'd been firmly placed in the friend category for decades. But the second Jake's lips touched hers, her concerns vaporized. She was definitely attracted to Jake.

David and Jake couldn't be compared. They were very different people. Each was special in their own way. David's memory did not compete for space in her mind or heart. For twenty years, she'd been blessed with David, and now, she was blessed with Jake. She wasn't ready for anything more than Jake's embrace and kisses, but he wasn't asking for more. They were in no rush.

Mikala lifted her head and smiled. This first kiss was a big turning point. Every day from now on, as their relationship grew, they would share new milestones and mishaps. Today, this kiss, thank God, was not a misstep. Their first kiss was perfection. "Hi," she whispered.

"Hi, baby. You good?"

Mikala grinned. "Yeah, Super-man. I'm good. I'm very good."

After another brief kiss, Jake dragged her to the

table and insisted on serving her. They enjoyed the wide variety of treats, and then he delved into one of the pies.

Mikala held her breath as Jake forked a large piece into his mouth, chewed, and swallowed.

He grinned and shook his head. "Micky, I know you love Lester, and perhaps we can take him a slice, but this ambrosia is too good for the coven."

"Yes!" Mikala pumped her fist in the air. Ecstatic her pie was edible, she grabbed Jake's shoulders, pulled him toward her, and quickly kissed him on the lips. Then she ran upstairs to get ready for the day.

As Jake cleaned the kitchen and changed in the downstairs bathroom, Mikala took her time dressing for dinner. Thanksgiving in Ohio was informal, but she knew the drill at the Jacobson household. The food would be fantastic, and the atmosphere unpredictable— a crapshoot. Some years, everyone drank enough to be civil. In other years, the alcohol produced the opposite effect. However, when Molly was old enough to understand, Lester made sure civility reigned.

The last two years had been difficult for Mikala. After Molly's death, she and David ignored the holidays completely. David took enough drugs to sleep away the holidays, while Mikala spent the time crying in Rena's arms. After David died, Mikala refused to see anyone during the holidays. She ate little and evaded calls from friends and family.

This year, however, no matter what the witches said or did, they couldn't ruin the day. Mikala had Super-man. Over breakfast, they'd discussed how to behave around the family. Mikala didn't want to flaunt their relationship, and she worried about hurting Lester.

"Micky, we have nothing to be ashamed of," Jake insisted. "If we attempt to hide our relationship, we'll appear as if we are doing something wrong. I don't believe we are. Besides, I think Lester will give us his blessing."

Mikala wasn't sure about Lester, and she wanted an opportunity to talk to him herself. Jake agreed to distract the witches and their mother while she spoke to Lester after the feast was consumed.

Forty-five minutes later, Mikala descended the steps dressed in a three-quarter sleeve, wine-colored silk sheath dress and matching pumps. The dress had a rounded neckline and a slim fit that clung to her body. She'd been careful with her makeup, and her auburn hair cascaded around her shoulders in waves.

Jake stood at the bottom of the stairs tracking her every step.

He was handsome in black dress slacks and a black turtleneck sweater that matched his thick, wavy black hair and dark eyes. Once more, Mikala warmed under his smoldering stare.

"Beautiful," he said when she reached the landing. "You're breathtaking." Jake held her in the circle of his arms and touched his lips to hers.

Mikala ran her hands up his chest, over his shoulders, and to his back. She relished in his firm muscles and towering strength. In his arms, she felt safe and secure. Dixie was right. At this moment, dressed as he was, Jake was the epitome of tall, dark, and delicious. The man had no idea how beautiful *he* was and the havoc he wreaked on the female population when he focused his penetrating gaze and devastating smile on them. Mikala gazed into his eyes and smiled.

"Thank you, Super-man. So are you."

"One more thing before we go." Jake reached into the pocket of his slacks and pulled out a small blue jewelry box. "Happy birthday, baby." He smiled and opened the box.

Mikala gasped. She covered her mouth with her hand. Nestled in blue velvet was a shimmering, dainty butterfly pendant in rose gold. Glittering diamond accents outlined looping butterfly wings. Suspended, slightly askew, on a matching chain, the tiny creature shimmered and danced.

She traced the butterfly's wings with her finger. "My butterfly," Mikala whispered. She closed her eyes and breathed in through her nose as she held the tears at bay. God, the man knew her better than she knew herself. She opened her eyes and cradled Jake's cheek in the palm of her hand. "I don't deserve you, Super-man. You always know exactly what I need when I need it. The necklace is perfect—just like you. Thank you, sweetheart." She stood on tip-toes and touched her lips to his. She rested her cheek against his and thanked God for allowing her this new start. Mikala prayed the bliss she experienced at this moment would last, and last, and last.

Chapter Twenty-Three
A Single Second of Happiness

Jake drove Mikala to the Gentle Winds Cemetery in contented silence. When they arrived, Mikala gathered the lavender roses she'd picked out of the bouquet Jake brought and walked to Molly's headstone while Jake waited in Red. She needed a few minutes on her own.

"Hi, Butterfly." Mikala brushed the snow off Molly's headstone. "Happy Thanksgiving, my darling. I hope you and Daddy are having fun in heaven. I miss you, sweet girl. I thank God every day you were in my life." Laying the flowers in the glistening snow, Mikala said a silent prayer. She closed her eyes and raised her face to the sky. A slight wind blew, caressing her cheeks, and for the briefest of moments, the sun peeked out from between the clouds. Mikala smiled. Her baby was with her—in her heart and in her soul.

"I'm well, Molly," she whispered. "Uncle Jake is good, too, and he is taking care of me. Rest, my darling. Your mama is fine, and she loves you." Mikala walked back to Red and climbed into the warm cab.

Jake captured her hand and brought it to his lips for a tender kiss. He continued holding her hand as he silently drove to David's grave. When he parked Red, he squeezed her hand.

Mikala turned her head. Jake raised an eyebrow,

and she shook her head. She needed to say her final goodbye to David alone.

Carrying a small bouquet of flowers, Mikala stopped in front of David's grave and laid them down. Her heart was full. She had so much to say, but she didn't know where to start. She'd visited his grave every few months and on special occasions. Each time Mikala stood in front of David's grave, she searched for the words to bid him goodbye and to forgive him for leaving her. But words eluded her.

Anger no longer burdened Mikala. The guilt, too, was almost gone. But many unanswered questions still haunted her. David had held all the answers. *What really happened the day of the accident? Why couldn't you talk to me? Why did you take your own life?*

Mikala took a deep breath and let it out slowly. One day, she hoped she would find closure and accept the past as it was—unresolved. Molly was gone, and no explanations would ever bring her back. Her support group friends told her to give herself time. When she was ready to move forward, she would. Forcing herself to let go of the past wouldn't work.

"Hi, David," she whispered. "I miss you. I saw you this morning playing with Molly, and I was so happy you were in heaven taking care of and loving each other. Part of me was jealous. I long to feel your arms around me and to hear her sweet giggles." Mikala bent her head and closed her eyes. "I'm thankful, David. I'm thankful for all the joy you brought into my life and all the love we shared."

Mikala opened her eyes and looked over her shoulder to where Jake waited in Red, and then she turned back. "My life has changed so much, but I'm good. I…" She swiped at the tears that made their way down her cheeks. "Jake's good to me, David. I need you to understand. You're not here anymore, and I'm lonely without you and Molly. I hope you know I loved you with all of my heart, and nothing will ever change that fact. The time has come for me to let you go and build a new life."

After pulling off her gloves, she studied her left hand. She'd never removed her wedding band. It hugged her ring finger and sparkled. Could she take off the ring, leave everything she'd shared with David in the past, and move forward? With trembling fingers wrapped around the ring, she caressed the smooth band, feeling the warmth it radiated. Memories of the day David had slid the band down her finger, in front of all their family and friends, flooded her.

Once the ring was in place, David brought her hand to his lips and kissed it. "Always and forever, my darling," he said, as he gazed into her eyes.

He'd promised her a lifetime of his love, and he'd kept his promise. He'd loved her his entire life, but their time together had been way too short.

Mikala dropped her fingers from the ring. She just couldn't take off her ring. She had Jake, but she still couldn't be without David. She wasn't being fair to Jake, but the time hadn't come to say her final goodbye—not yet. Kissing the tips of her fingers, she touched the headstone. "Be well, my darling. Be well."

Head lowered and shoulders slumped, Mikala walked to Red. She climbed into the truck and warmed her hands in front of the heating vents. Feeling guilty and torn, she kept her gaze downcast. She hadn't said goodbye to David. How could she start something new with Jake?

Jake tugged at Mikala's left hand. He brought her hand to his mouth and kissed the back, stroking his fingers over her wedding band.

Mikala gasped and snapped up her head. Her gaze connected with his.

"Micky, stop beating up yourself. I understand. I'm not pushing. One day at a time, baby. All I'm asking is for a chance. That's all."

Mikala shook her head. "I'm sorry. I don't want to hurt you, but I can't say good-bye—not yet. I feel so guilty. I'm not being fair to you, but—"

Jake shook his head. "Shh, now. Don't be so hard on yourself." He stroked her cheek with the back of his hand. "You have nothing to feel guilty about. I know what I'm doing. You're not hurting me, and you'll never lose me. Let's enjoy the day and be thankful for what we have. We shouldn't waste time defining our relationship or setting unnecessary rules, boundaries, and timelines. Okay?"

For a long moment, Mikala studied him. She remembered the joy and the overwhelming feeling of rightness that flooded her when he'd kissed her. Rena was right. She deserved to be happy. Sighing, Mikala nodded. Right now, today, they had to be thankful they had each other. They were survivors, and together, they bloomed. Apart, they would shrivel and die.

Thirty minutes later, Jake and Mikala sat in the Jacobson family room. Cocktail in hand, Mikala admired the beautifully decorated Christmas tree and enjoyed a roaring fire. Leslie, Priscilla, and Sylvia were still sober and on their best behavior.

Leslie studied every move Mikala and Jake made.

Each time Jake smiled in Mikala's direction or laid an arm across the back of the loveseat they shared, Leslie's scowl deepened.

Under Leslie's scrutiny, Mikala squirmed. Leslie was a great white shark, and she was her helpless prey.

When Leslie stepped out of the room to take a call, Jake pulled Mikala closer and whispered in her ear. "Stop fidgeting and just enjoy the evening. Don't let her intimidate you. Remember, we're not doing anything wrong. We deserve to be happy. Breathe, baby, breathe."

Mikala glanced at Jake's face, and his smile reassured her. She touched the delicate butterfly at the base of her throat and exhaled. Rena would kick her ass for letting Leslie and the rest of the coven intimidate her. Mikala nodded and smiled.

As predicted, the Jacobsons' long-time cook, Erma, outdid herself. The Thanksgiving feast was beautifully displayed and delicious. Wine and conversation flowed. For the most part, conversation remained light and civil. But when the topic of Jacobson Law came up, the atmosphere deteriorated and became charged.

Although the coven refused dessert, Lester, Jake, and Mikala enjoyed the apple pie Mikala made, along with an assortment of delectable treats Erma presented. The minute dinner was consumed, Sylvia and Priscilla excused themselves.

As planned, Jake engaged Leslie in a conversation about a recent case.

While Jake and Leslie took their coffee back to the family room, Lester invited Mikala to his office to see a rare book he'd acquired.

Mikala sat in one of the two over-stuffed brown

leather chairs facing the fire, and Lester joined her. She studied her lap and smoothed her hands over her dress as she searched for the right words to tell him her news. She didn't want him to think she'd forgotten David. "Nothing is wrong, Les. In fact, something good has happened." Mikala licked her lips and raised her head. "It's just that this development is new and a bit surprising and I, well—"

"Spit it out. I'm an old man, Mikala. Surprises don't have the effect they used to." He smiled.

Mikala swallowed, took a deep breath, and let it out. She straightened and met his gaze. "You know how much I loved David. He and Molly were my world— my everything. But..." She stood and walked to the mantle which held a series of crystal picture frames portraying each of the Jacobson children as well as a family photo of Mikala, David, and Molly. As she spoke, she traced David and Molly's faces with her finger. "I'll never stop loving him. He and Molly will always have a place in my heart. When I lost them, I was devastated." She cleared her throat. "For a long time, I didn't want to live. But you, Rena, and Jake didn't give up on me, and I began to heal."

She turned and met Lester's piercing blue-eyed gaze. "Now, more than ever, I want to live. I've met someone. He's good to me, Lester. He cares and shows me how much in a million different ways." Mikala walked back to the chair and sat. She turned and reached for Lester's hands. "Les, he makes me feel alive again. When we're together, I smile and even laugh, although at times I want to throw something at his head." She shook her head and laughed. "He's a good man. He's strong and honest with a kind and generous heart."

Mikala released Lester's hands and sighed. She glanced back at the mantle where David's smiling eyes stared back. "I've known him forever, and yet, we've only just met. Our relationship is new, and yet, it isn't. I don't know where this journey will lead, but I have to travel the road." She glanced back at Lester, and their gazes connected once more. "I have to see if he's more than just my super-man," she whispered.

"Well, it's about damn time Jake got his shit together," Lester bellowed, slapping his knee and chuckling.

Mikala's eyes widened. "What?"

"You heard me, girl. I told that boy months ago to get his elbow out of his ass and make his move."

Mikala shook her head. "You knew? About Jake and me? I didn't even know about us until very recently."

Lester grinned. "Mikala, you and that boy have had a thing for each other for as long as I can remember."

Mikala's cheeks heated. She opened her mouth but seeing Lester's upraised hand, she closed it.

"No, let me speak my mind. I know you loved my boy, and I'm not implying you were unfaithful to David in any way. On some level, you and Jake have always been connected. That boy would move heaven and earth for you, and I have a feeling you would do the same for him."

Lester stood and took Mikala's hands in his, pulling her to her feet. He studied her and swallowed hard. "The day David married you was one of the happiest days of my life. You were a good and faithful wife. But he's gone now." Lester cleared his throat. "I see how you've suffered the last two years, and if you think I would begrudge you a second of happiness, you don't know me. You deserve to be happy."

Unshed tears burned Mikala's eyes, and she blinked to keep them at bay. Having Lester's blessing made all the difference in the world. He'd stood by her side, making sure she wanted for nothing. When she cried, he'd held her, and when words failed her, in silence, he'd walked by her side. She loved him as much as she loved her own father. "Thank you, Les." She smiled and squeezed his hands.

"Don't let anything stop you from being happy. I think we both know life is unpredictable. I'm not telling you to forget David and Molly. I know that's not possible." Lester paused and glanced at the mantel before his gaze met hers again. "You have a great big survivor's heart—one that can love deeply and forgive much. Remember that fact, dear girl."

A few minutes later, Mikala hugged Lester and walked out of his office, feeling more optimistic about the future than she had in a long time. She wanted to find Jake and head home. She'd been a nervous wreck since they arrived, but now all doubt was replaced with a growing excitement for the future. As Mikala approached the family room, she was surprised to hear Jake's voice raised.

"Mikala and I are none of your concern. Stay away from her, and stay the hell out of my personal life. I won't tell you again."

"Come on, Jake." Leslie scoffed. "I can't believe you're falling for her. Honestly, I have no idea what hold Mikala has over the men in this family."

At the mention of her name, Mikala froze at the

entrance of the family room. Leslie and Jake faced away as they traded barbs back and forth. Mikala frowned.

"What's wrong with all of you? She's an adult, but all of you treat her like a fragile porcelain doll to be protected and pampered." Leslie sneered. "Don't you ever get tired of playing the superhero just so her little heart doesn't break? Don't you want a real woman who can handle anything thrown her way without bursting into tears every two minutes?"

Jake's hand fisted by his side. "Shut the fuck up, Leslie. You have no idea what you're talking about."

Mikala scanned Jake's flushed face, noting his tightened jaw and knitted eyebrows. In all the years she'd known him, she'd never seen him quite this angry.

"I don't know what I'm talking about?" Leslie mocked. "Who do you think paid off David's gambling debts, guarded his secrets, and kept his ass out of jail? You think you did that all by yourself?" She tilted her head to the side. "Who do you think dealt with the police and the insurance company after the accident? You think Lester was capable of tackling the mess on his own after wonder boy fucked up in the biggest way possible? David didn't just need you, Super-man. He needed an entire fleet of superheroes to keep his life on track and his antics out of the media."

Gambling debts? Jail? What was Leslie talking about? Mikala slapped a hand over her mouth, stifling a gasp.

For a minute, silence reigned. Then Leslie took a breath and sighed. "You know what, Jake? You're a bigger fool than my brother ever was. He didn't deserve any better than the witless farm-girl he married. He was a loser, a lousy attorney, and a drunk who chased anything in a skirt. Worst of all, he was a fuck-up who killed his own kid. What's your excuse?"

Swaying, Mikala collapsed against the wall. Her heart stuttered, missing a beat. A roaring filled her ears as a deep stabbing pain erupted in her belly, and she folded over. "No, no."

Chapter Twenty-Four
A Heartbeat. A Breath.

"No! Oh God, no."

Jake turned to the sound of Mikala's agonized moan. When he saw Mikala bent over and gasping, he stilled, his heart racing, and his gut churned. He rushed toward her huddled figure at the entrance of the family room and wrapped his arms around her just as her legs gave out. Gathering her trembling form in his arms, he carried her to the sofa and sat with her in his lap.

Glancing at Mikala's pale, tear-streaked face, Jake clamped his jaw, his heart breaking. She'd heard every vile word Leslie spewed, and she fractured once more before his eyes. Pain and devastation ravaged Mikala's sweet face. He'd always known one day the truth would be unearthed, but he hadn't adequately prepared for its crushing blow. "Mikala, sweetheart, easy now. I've got you."

"M-Molly? H-he, he killed Molly? What? Why? I...no...Oh, God. No!"

Jake held her closer, absorbing the quakes that shook her small frame. "Shh, baby, shh. You'll be okay, Micky. I'm here."

Mikala's wild gaze met his.

Whatever she saw in his eyes—the truth maybe—made her struggle to free herself from his embrace. Jake relaxed his hold. He couldn't protect her from the ugly truth any longer. The words were out, polluting her memories of her husband and her comprehension of what happened to her child. Although he was her superhero, he lacked the power to roll back time and change the unchangeable. He'd failed her.

Mikala's legs trembled. Her body shook, and her breathing was labored.

Jake stood at her back. He longed to take them back to earlier in the day when their world was filled with possibilities.

"M-Molly...D-David? I...I don't understand. I..." She surveyed the room, focusing on Leslie's pale face. She swallowed hard. "Tell me," she choked.

Leslie licked her lips and shook her head. She lowered her gaze.

"Tell me!" Mikala fisted her hands. "She was my child. He was my husband. You didn't have any trouble speaking your mind a moment ago—making up shit about your brother. Why are you silent now? What are you hiding? Tell me!"

"What the hell is going on here?" Lester bellowed as he strode into the room. His head swiveled between Leslie, Jake, and Mikala. "Mikala, what is it? What's wrong?"

Mikala turned and glared at Lester. "Someone, explain what David did to our child. What did he do to my baby?"

Lester froze. His features paled, and the hand holding his cane shook. He swayed.

Leslie rushed toward him.

He motioned her away, gripped his cane, and steadied himself.

"Tell me, damn it, about the accident, the police,

his gambling, and his women. I need to know everything. I *deserve* to know the truth." Mikala turned toward Jake. Narrowing her eyes, she focused once again on his face. "Do you know what she's talking about? Do you?" She screamed.

Jake swallowed past the boulder in his throat and ran a hand through his hair. He wished he could honestly deny having any knowledge of the fucking mess about to destroy the only woman he'd ever loved. He would do anything to spare Mikala, but he wouldn't lie. Not now. The truth was out, and she wouldn't rest until she knew everything. But the truth would wreck her and any future he hoped to build. Jake couldn't save either of them. With every beat of his heart, pain reverberated in his chest. Losing Mikala would end him.

He surveyed the room. Agony radiated from Mikala. Priscilla and Sylvia had just walked in. Confusion and shock dominated their expressions. Lester trembled and wheezed. And Leslie? She stood motionless. Her face, like her heart, was hard and cold as granite.

The Jacobson lair wasn't the place to dismantle Mikala's world. Uttering the words she demanded to hear with the coven witnessing her pain, confusion, and humiliation would be inhumane. Jake wanted to shield her from their judgmental eyes and knowing looks.

Lester, too, wouldn't tolerate rehashing the story. He was on the verge of unraveling. This situation was Jake's worst nightmare. He nodded. "Yes, Micky, I know. Let's go home and talk there. I promise I'll tell you everything I know."

Mikala shook her head. "No! I'm not going

anywhere. Stop stalling."

"Micky, this isn't…"

Mikala dug both hands in her hair. "For God's sake, Jake, just talk to me. Speak the truth. Tell me what she said was all lies."

Jake's heart hammered. He reached to steady her, but she stepped away. Distrust and betrayal filled her gaze. He couldn't bear to witness her pain, and like a coward, he looked away. His stomach churned, and bile rose up his throat.

"Look at me, Jake."

Jake took a deep breath and slid his gaze to meet hers.

Mikala wrapped her arms around herself. "I'm dying here. You can do nothing to save me," she whispered. "Just don't lie anymore. I trusted you. I trusted all of you." She glanced at Lester, and then back to Jake. "*You* were supposed to be my family."

God, what was he supposed to say? Jake dropped his head in his hands. He'd kept the facts from her to protect her. The truth *wouldn't* set her or him free. On the contrary, the truth would tie her down and drag her in to the depths of hell. Reasoning with Mikala now was futile. In her shocked state, she wouldn't accept any of his justifications. No place to run and take shelter existed. Even from the grave, David wreaked havoc, and Jake still cleaned up after him.

Mikala was in the midst of a powerful storm—unanchored and alone. Jake had shattered her trust. Although he'd promised he would always catch her, he'd left her open and vulnerable. If he could just get her home, he would try to repair the damage.

He scrubbed at his eyes and shoved his hands

through his hair. He raised his gaze and met hers. "I am your family, Micky. I'm sorry, sweetheart," he choked. "Please come with me. Let me take you home. I swear I'll tell you everything I know."

"For the love of God, what's wrong with all of you?" Leslie's voice cut through the room. "She has a right to know." She took a step toward Mikala. "David was on his cell-phone. That's why he lost control of the car."

Leslie's words dropped like a nuclear bomb, tainting the air and sucking the oxygen from the room. For a second, time stood still, and everyone's breathing and heartbeat ceased.

Priscilla and Sylvia gasped.

Mikala froze, and her face drained of color.

Fuck! Jake's hands fisted, and he ground his teeth. He wanted to murder Leslie. Why was she behaving so callously? What good could come from being a heartless bitch? He put an arm around Mikala's waist and pulled her close.

She leaned into him.

"Leslie, stop," Lester barked. "That's quite enough. This matter has nothing to do with you."

Leslie's mouth opened and closed, and she shook her head. "You think David's actions didn't affect me? Are you kidding? Stop putting him on a pedestal. Wonder-boy wasn't so wonderful. You know he was a fuck-up. Now, she knows it. The time has come to face the truth about her husband."

Crimson infused Lester's face, and rage poured off him.

Jake was confident, if Lester could, he would throttle his daughter.

"Get out," Lester hissed. "All of you...leave! You've done enough damage."

For a few seconds, Leslie faced off with her father. She squared her shoulders and straightened her spine. But under Lester's glower, she capitulated.

The women paraded out of the room. Sylvia leaned on Priscilla as tears streamed down the older woman's cheeks.

Ragged breaths heaved Lester's chest. Even with the aid of his cane, he swayed as he turned to Mikala. "Mikala."

Mikala remained quiet.

"Micky?" Lester repeated.

She slowly turned her head and glanced at Lester. Her eyes were wide and unfocused.

"I'm sorry you had to hear the truth this way. I should have said something a long time ago, but I just couldn't. I..." Lester stumbled to the nearest chair. His big frame deflated, and then crumpled.

"But the accident...," Mikala whispered. She shook her head and glanced at Jake. "The day was rainy. The police said he... I don't understand?"

Jake sighed. The day had completely unraveled. Nothing remained to give thanks for. Life was remarkably fragile. In a blink of an eye, a heartbeat, a breath—Molly's life was snuffed out, and no amount of truth-telling would bring her back. Mikala had worked hard to accept David and Molly's deaths. Today, she relived the trauma of their loss all over again, and now he had to reveal added hard truths about her husband and their marriage.

Guiding Mikala to the couch, Jake forced her to sit. He took her ice-cold hands in his. Forgetting Lester,

Jake focused on Mikala and searched for the right combination of words that would do the least damage. None existed. He cleared his throat. "David made a mistake—a terrible decision. For a second, he took his gaze off the road to look at his phone, and he lost control of the car."

Jake waited for Mikala to digest his words. He needed her to understand David's actions weren't intentional or premeditated. He didn't kill Molly as Leslie had so ruthlessly stated. David wasn't a monster. Like all humans, he was fallible. He made a terrible error in judgment—the kind that obliterated one precious life and devastated many others.

People made mistakes every day. Some mistakes were unintentional while others were due to pure carelessness or negligence. David's action was a common occurrence. Hell, on occasion, Jake glanced at his phone while driving. Before Molly's death, he didn't stop to consider the full consequences of his actions. He believed he was a cautious and vigilant driver. But for David and thousands of other people each year, that same action led to disaster.

Shaking her head, Mikala pulled her hands from his. "No, you're wrong." She turned to Lester. "David would never look at his telephone while driving, especially when Molly was with him. He knew better. He wouldn't be so reckless. In fact, we talked about how people who couldn't keep their hands off their phones shouldn't have a driver's license. He swore to me, no matter how busy work got, nothing was more important than his family. He wouldn't. He…"

"Micky, David loved you and Molly more than anything. You're right, he did know better, as do most people. But for a few seconds, he had a lapse in judgment. That slip was enough for the accident to happen. The crash *was* an accident," Jake pleaded, hoping to convince them both.

Mikala swallowed hard. "No matter how many times I begged him to discuss it, he maintained he couldn't remember the accident. How do you know?"

Jake dropped his head. He rubbed at the tight muscles of his neck and shoulders, took a fortifying breath, and met her gaze. "Once he woke in the hospital, he remembered everything, and he fell apart. He loved you and Molly so much, and he was ravaged by guilt."

Mikala twisted her fingers in her lap. "Why didn't he tell me? Over and over again, I begged him to talk to me."

Jake shook his head. "He couldn't face you, sweetheart. He couldn't forgive himself. He was overcome with grief and self-loathing. The night he told me, he was drunk and distraught. He—" He fought the lump in his throat and wiped his wet cheeks with the back of his hand.

"But you knew. All this time, you knew." She pounded her chest with a fist. "*I* had a right to know how my child died. You knew I was going insane trying to understand how she died. I couldn't close my eyes without imagining her last moments. I was there when she took her first breath, but I wasn't when she took her last." Tears streamed down Mikala's cheeks.

Attempting to soothe her, Jake reached for Mikala.

But she pushed him away. "Don't touch me. Don't try to comfort me. Not now. It's too late—too damn late to do the right thing." She glared at him.

Jake flinched.

"Just answer one thing. How could you? I *needed* to understand Molly's final hours to find closure. But David, you, and Lester denied me that truth. You saw my agony and the sheer torture I was in. How could you not comfort me then? What kind of friend...family were you?"

Jake's breath halted. He could no longer witness her pain or hear her accusations. He dropped his head in his hands and let the tears flow. She had every right to her feelings, but couldn't she see she was tearing him apart? By the time this conversation was over, neither of them would be left standing. He deserved every spear she launched. Neither he nor David deserved better. But David took the easy way out —the coward's way. No such option existed for him.

Taking a deep breath, he rubbed his wet cheeks, and straightened. "I learned the facts about the accident a few days before David took his life. He was spiraling—every day getting worse and worse. He drowned himself in liquor. You were a shell—a ghost. You barely breathed. When he told me, I was floored— a complete wreck. His confessions brought me to my knees." He slid his gaze to hers. "But, Micky, baby, you were barely surviving. I couldn't lay any more on you. I did what I thought was right. I made sure Rena was with you, and I dragged him to therapy. Then after his death..."

Jake stood and paced. Although he was physically and emotionally exhausted, he couldn't sit still. His mouth was dry, and his heart was hammering out of his chest. "When David died, you completely broke down. I was beside myself. Was that the right time to tell you?

What good would telling you have done? You were already ruined." Jake dug both hands in his hair and pulled. He stopped pacing and turned toward Mikala. "I blamed myself for his death. I couldn't lose you, too. Revealing how Molly died and why David killed himself wouldn't bring them back and wouldn't change anything."

Mikala sprang from the couch. "What the hell do you mean knowing the truth wouldn't change anything?" she shouted. "Don't you see? *I* blamed myself for his death. I thought I didn't do enough. I thought I wasn't patient enough, and I pushed him too far." She shook her head. "You don't get it. Knowing *would* have changed so much. Knowing *changes* everything. Everything."

She turned her gaze on Lester. "But Jake wasn't the only one who lied, was he? You knew the truth way before he did, and you said nothing. You and Leslie dealt with the police and the insurance company. You and your bitch of a daughter covered up everything. You protected your son and the precious Jacobson name. I suppose that's what a father does"—she laughed—"but what about Molly? What about justice for Molly? The man she called daddy—the man who was supposed to protect her with his life, acted recklessly. I thought more of you. I…"

"Stop," Lester bellowed. Leaning on his cane, he stood. "You stop right now, girl, before you say much more you'll regret. I know you're in shock, and you're hurting. Yes, I loved my boy. Loving isn't a crime. After the accident, he lived in his own, self-imposed jail. He'd already tried and convicted himself to a lifetime of hell. No further action was necessary. But I didn't say anything and didn't burden you with the awful truth because I, like Jake, wanted to protect you. I couldn't do anything to save Molly or David, but I could spare you from more pain."

Shaking his head, Lester took an unsteady step toward Mikala, but she stepped back. He dropped his head. "I did my best for my boy. My best wasn't good enough. I lost Molly. I lost him. I-I *couldn't* lose you," he confessed. "Don't you know you're *everything* to me, girl? I love you."

Lester was pasty white. His lower lip quivered, and he hunched over and trembled. Leslie's unforgivable antics and Mikala's pain had taken their toll. Any minute now, the old man would collapse, and Mikala would have yet another tragedy she would blame herself for. Jake had to make her see past her misery. "Mikala." Jake grabbed her arm. "I know you're hurting, but we *will* continue this conversation at home." He squeezed her arm and nodded in Lester's direction. "Look."

Mikala opened her mouth and then stopped. She dropped her head and took a deep breath.

Jake studied Mikala and waited for Lester's words to take root. *I love you.* While some people threw those three little words around like beads at a Mardi Gras parade, in over twenty years of knowing Lester, Jake rarely heard them coming from his lips. Like precious stones, those three words, were invaluable, and Mikala knew the value of love.

Mikala raised her head and walked to Lester. She cupped his face in her hands, and with her thumb, she wiped the tears making their way down his cheeks. Then she folded him in her embrace, and he wrapped his arms around her. Together, they cried.

Jake joined them, and he, too, wept for the child they would never see grow into a woman, and for the man who took her life, and then his own.

Chapter Twenty-Five
The Center of His World

Attempting to unknot the muscles in his neck and shoulders, Jake stretched his arms above his head, twisted his neck from side to side, and rolled his shoulders forward and backward. Mikala's couch was more like a loveseat—the older, lumpier variety. He ran a hand over his face and sighed. The night had been a long one with no sleep and no escape from his thoughts. He needed coffee.

Last night he'd driven Mikala home from the Jacobsons' in silence. The minute he put the car in Park, he received his marching orders.

"Go home, Jake. I can't take any more tonight. I'm wrung out. I can't say or hear another word."

He wanted to argue, but the resolute look in her eyes, and the set of her jaw told him he'd lose. He sat in the car until she went into the house, and then he continued his vigil until her bedroom light turned off. Jake drove two miles before making a U-turn and driving back to her house. He sat in the truck for another two hours rehashing the night.

Using his key, he let himself inside. He couldn't leave her, and when her sobs echoed through the house, he was certain he made the right decision. For the rest of the night, he'd stayed awake, punishing himself with the sound of her heart-wrenching cries.

As the coffee brewed, Jake cleaned up in the guest bathroom. He found a new toothbrush and used it, and then he splashed cold water on his face. Studying his image in the bathroom mirror, he confirmed he looked just as shitty as he felt. He ran a hand through his messy hair, and then he exited the bathroom and walked right into Mikala. "Jesus," he grunted, steadying her before she fell. "I'm sorry, baby."

Mikala pulled out of Jake's arms and stared.

Her eyes were red with dark circles underneath them, and her beautiful face was pale and drawn.

"What are you doing here, Jake?" She wrapped her white fleece robe with navy and red stars around her and headed for the kitchen.

Jake followed. Mikala had the hideous robe since they were in college. It was tattered and torn in places. No matter how many others he'd bought her over the years, she refused to give up her safety blanket.

Mikala poured herself a mug of coffee and walked to the family room.

He poured his own mug and followed.

She sat on the couch with her knees to her chest.

Planting himself in the easy chair across from her, Jake drank his coffee. He wouldn't rush her. Instead, he steeled himself for the conversation to come. When she was ready, he would share everything he knew and hope she forgave him.

Jake had used the long night to come to grips with the fact he'd fucked up. Since college, he saved David from mess after mess. While Jake, Rena, and Mikala matured and embraced the cloak of adulthood, David never did. Instead of dealing with work and family pressure, he drank and gambled.

At first, David kept the drinking and gambling to a minimum. He wasn't careless. Those vices were ways of blowing off steam. His harrowing work life and destructive coping mechanisms stayed separate from the perfection that was his home life. But a year before he died, he took on a big case, and the pressure intensified. He became reckless and lost more and more money gambling online. He also drank more than he should—at home, in the office, and at parties.

Jake lent him funds to cover his debts and suggested he seek help for all his addictions. No matter how often he begged David to get help and talk to Mikala, he refused.

"She and Molly are the only things I've ever done right. I won't taint them. They are my perfect world in a perfect storm. Besides, I'm done fucking up. I swear I am," David had promised, time and time again.

Jake sighed and shook his head. Why the fuck had he covered up for him for so long? Maybe he should have let David drown, or maybe he should have told Mikala about his gambling and women. But would she have believed him? Would she have stayed with David anyway—trying to fix him like Jake's mother did with his father? Would she have walked away and started a new life with someone else?

Jake didn't know, and he hadn't wanted to find out. Mikala chose David and loved him as he was. Jake loved her enough to give her anything she wanted— even if what she wanted was a fantasy. But had he protected Mikala, Molly, and David, or had he ruined them?

Mikala cleared her throat and continued staring into her coffee mug. "Start talking, Jake."

He hesitated. He didn't know where to begin.

"Gambling? Women? Debt? Don't make excuses or give explanations. Just say the words. I need to know everything. You can't protect me from the reality that was my world." She glanced up and met his gaze. "For once in my life, I want someone to be straight with me. I don't want to be coddled. I'm a grown woman. I was married for thirteen years and had a child. Yet, my marriage was based on lies."

Jake straightened, rested his elbows on his knees, and focused on her. "I'll tell you everything I know, but I want you to know your marriage and David's love were real. He loved you and Molly with all his heart. He—"

"Stop it, Jake." Mikala sighed. "Stop defending him. Haven't you covered up for him and deceived me in the process enough?" She unfolded her legs and straightened. With a shaky hand, she set the mug on the coffee table. "Don't you see, Super-man, the time for defending and protecting is over?"

Jake studied her. He wondered how much she already knew but refused to admit to herself. After all, she'd known David since he was nineteen. She knew his moods and his reckless, sometimes impulsive, behavior. She'd slept next to the man for two decades. Surely, she sensed the trouble he was in?

He cleared his throat. "Over the last year of his life, David was under a great deal of pressure. He had an Internet-gambling habit that started as a stress reliever but escalated." Jake shook his head. "He became irresponsible and lost more than he could afford. I lent him money a few times, and apparently, he also went to Leslie."

Mikala frowned. "I had no clue. How was that possible? When he died, we had a substantial amount of money in our joint checking and saving accounts." She shook her head. "I guess I never paid much attention to those accounts. He paid all the bills, and I mainly used credit cards."

Jake shrugged and gazed into her bleak eyes. "He didn't want you to know about his gambling. He was ashamed. But he didn't always lose. Sometimes, he did well. Maybe he had a winning streak before Molly died. He was too distraught after her death to ever touch his computer."

She nodded. "The women? How many and how often?"

He hung his head. Other than Molly's death, this truth would be the hardest betrayal for Mikala to hear. No way existed to soften the blow. Right at this moment, he hated David. Jake raised his head and met her gaze. "I only know of one woman for certain, an associate at the firm. I caught them together. He swore he'd given into temptation just one time, and he deeply regretted his behavior."

Mikala stiffened, narrowing her eyes. "You thought cheating, even if it was a one-time event, was acceptable? Was that belief some kind of man-code?" She scoffed. "Fucking around is okay as long as the little woman doesn't find out?"

As her agitation grew, color filled Mikala's cheeks, and her voice rose. Jake raked a hand through his hair. How could she think he approved of David's behavior? She knew him better than that. Didn't she? "No, of course not. I was furious. I cut off all contact. Do you remember that period of time when I didn't visit for three months—about six months before the accident? I kept my distance. But—"

"But you didn't see fit to tell me." Mikala stabbed a finger in her chest. "*You* protected him. *You* condoned his actions by not saying anything. In my eyes, you're just as guilty. Just tell me why. Why would you deceive me? Why didn't you warn me? After all we've shared, why did he mean more than me?"

Jake flinched. Jesus, no one was more important than Mikala. David may have been his brother, and yes, he'd loved him, but Mikala was everything. Jake realized she'd been the center of his world since the day their gazes first connected across the green during the first day of orientation. How could he make her understand how precious she was?

He rose and walked to the mantel where all the family pictures were displayed. He studied Mikala and David's wedding picture and then the picture of the four friends on the day of their college graduation. They stood with their arms around one another—Mikala flanked by him and David and Rena next to David. Their smiles were wide and innocent. Their eyes shone with excitement and the thrill of accomplishment. How he longed to go back to that time. How he wished he had the ability to rewrite history.

Turning, he studied her. He swallowed hard. "Micky, I've loved you for as long as I can remember—first as a friend, then as family, and then more. Looking back, I don't know when my feelings turned into more. Maybe I've loved you from the beginning, and I was too young and too uncertain of who I was and what I wanted to clearly see how much you meant to me. So, no, he didn't mean more."

For a second, Jake closed his eyes and took a deep breath, and then he released it. He opened his eyes and refocused on her. "I would have done anything for you, and that fact hasn't changed. I would lie, cheat, steal, and kill to keep you happy. Don't you get that? You chose *him*. You loved *him*. I gave you the him you wanted and the him you needed."

Tears ran down Mikala's face. She opened her mouth but closed it when Jake shook his head.

"Just listen. Try to hear me, baby."

Mikala swallowed and nodded. She swiped the tears off her cheek.

"You built a family for us all. You gave me something I never had. Each of us played a role. You loved, Rena nurtured, I protected, and David was our child. That life worked for us. That's who we were. The problem was, David never grew up—even when Molly came along."

Jake walked to the couch and sat next to Mikala. He picked up her hands and kissed the back of them. "Yes, I am guilty. I'm guilty of loving you, Molly, and David to a fault."

He squeezed her hands in his and held on. His next words would be hard for her to hear. He didn't want to hurt her, but the words had to be said. "Mikala, sweetheart, you, too, are guilty of loving too much—if that can even be considered a crime. You loved David and made excuses for him. You tolerated and condoned his behavior when we were in college, and you continued to turn a blind eye through your marriage."

Mikala snatched her hands away. Redness spread up her neck to her face, and her breathing accelerated. "Are you saying David's behavior—his infidelity, gambling, drinking, whatever—was my fault? What exactly are you insinuating?"

Jake widened his eyes. "Jesus. Please Micky, I know you're hurting, and I'm so damn sorry. Please hear me. I'm not blaming you. David is the only one to blame for his actions. He made his choices and so did we."

Mikala looked away. "He was my husband, my lover, and the man who held my heart. I loved and trusted him." She ran a hand through her hair. "He wasn't perfect, but neither was I." She shook her head slowly. "He was under so much pressure," she whispered. "I wanted to be his safe harbor. I never thought he would cheat. I was so blind and I..." She wrapped her arms around her middle. "I was so, so stupid."

Jake cupped her face. "No, you weren't stupid. You opened your heart, and you loved him with everything you had. We both made mistakes."

Mikala's gaze connected with his. "I kept calling you super-man, and the title went to your head. Did you think you could protect me forever?"

He dropped his hands. Had he wanted to protect her? Sure, he had. His job was to protect the woman he loved, and he'd failed. He rubbed at the ache in his chest. He didn't want to lie to Mikala ever again. Looking away, he kept silent.

She sighed. "I don't know what's real and what's a lie anymore. I feel like such a fool." She scooted to the corner of the couch. Pulling up her knees to her chest, she wrapped her arms around them and laid her cheek against her knees as she studied Jake. "I don't know what we're doing here, Jake. You've been taking care of me for years. Is that what our relationship is based on? Am I your long-term, fix-it project? Because your work here is done. I'm no longer a damsel in distress."

He shook his head. "Haven't you heard anything I've said? Don't you know how I feel about you? I love you, Micky."

Mikala closed her eyes. "Nothing in my world makes sense."

He sighed. He longed to gather her in his arms, but she'd already shut down. "I know you're hurt, angry, and confused, but don't shut me out," he pleaded. "Let me help you. I am still your family, as you are mine. I am still your super-man."

Opening her eyes, Mikala shifted her gaze to the mantel. "Family? Look around, Jake. They're all gone. The people we called family no longer exist. They no longer inhabit this house. Perhaps they never existed." She glanced back at him. "Maybe we just made them up." Uncurling, she rose. "I'm going home. I'm returning to my roots to figure out who I am and how my life got this screwed up. I'm going back to the family I had before I had you."

Every cell in Jake's body reacted to the profound sadness that dominated Mikala's features and the fatigue engraved on her face. He was compelled to follow her, fight her demons, and take away her pain. Yet, he was powerless because, this time, he was the one who needed a superhero to help him fight his way out of the mess he'd created.

Six Months

February

Chapter Twenty-Six
A Thirty-Year Head Start

Mikala tiptoed through the silent condo, making every effort not to wake Rena, Ted, and baby Ariana. Ariana had fussed much of the night and quieted only two hours ago. Although Mikala was awake and offered to take the baby, Ari only settled when she was in Rena's arms. Rena, who was normally a short-tempered bitch when she banked less than seven hours of sleep, possessed endless patience and energy for the baby.

Even littered with baby gear, Rena and Ted's palatial condo was exquisite. Located in the Upper East Side, the luxury condo, decorated in soft creams, golds, and earth tones, spread across the entire seventeenth floor. Floor-to-ceiling windows in every room and three fabulous balconies revealed a mesmerizing three-hundred-and-sixty-degree aerial view of Central Park, the Hudson River, and the George Washington Bridge.

Although sunlight usually flooded the condo, the curtains were drawn. Mikala padded in the dark, out of the wing containing the master bedroom, nursery, and five guest bedrooms. She shut the door behind her, hoping noise wouldn't infiltrate the brief respite Ariana afforded her exhausted parents. Blindly, she tiptoed around furniture and into the kitchen until she found and flipped the light switch. Blinking against the light and the shine coming off the stainless-steel appliances and marble countertops, Mikala brewed coffee.

The kitchen was a chef's dream. But the twin, oversized Viking refrigerators, two dishwashers, and professional, six-burner stove intimidated the hell out of Mikala. Although her cooking skills had improved, she had no idea what to do with half of the appliances. Why did anyone need six burners?

She poured a large mug of coffee and walked to the family room. This wing of the condo had an open floor plan. The kitchen flowed into a breakfast nook and spacious family room. Placing her coffee on a nearby table, she reached for her cell and searched for the app that controlled all the gadgets and gizmos in the condo. When she'd arrived two weeks ago, Ted downloaded the app and gave her a one-hour, expedited course on how to control the curtains, lights, music, and temperature in the entire house. The app did many other things, but when Mikala's eyes rolled to the back of her head, Rena had put an end to the lesson.

After a few failed attempts, Mikala pushed the right combination of buttons, and the heavy curtains parted. Covered in a pristine layer of shiny white snow, Manhattan came into view. At five-thirty a.m., the sun rose, stretched, and pushed the moon out of the way, taking its rightful position in the heavens.

Mikala loved this time of the morning when New York and all its inhabitants awoke, although some people had yet to shut their eyes. In the two weeks she'd stayed at Rena's, she never tired of the view from the condo. Even in freezing weather, joggers left their footprints around Central Park. Taxis and cars clogged the streets and bridges, and people bustled about, heading toward the shelter of the under-ground subway stations.

New York was remarkably different from Connecticut. Yet, Rena fit in well. The home she'd built with Ted was a far cry from her one-bedroom loft in New Haven or humble Brooklyn dwelling. But Rena hadn't changed. She still maintained her Brooklyn *charm*. Not even the baby altered her colorful vocabulary. Still outspoken, brash, and abrasive, she'd learned to spell out her expletives and made everyone else do the same in Ari's presence.

Mikala settled in one of the plush chairs that provided the best view of the park. Tomorrow, she would return to Connecticut. She'd stayed away for ten weeks, spending the first eight weeks in Ohio with her family. But the second anniversary of David's death and Molly's birthday were in a few days. The time had come to go back to reality and face Jake.

Two days after Thanksgiving, Mikala had left for Ohio. Jake insisted on driving her to the airport, and the thirty-minute ride was silent and uncomfortable. He promised to take care of the house, her mail, and more importantly, he promised to give her space.

"Just don't shut me out, Micky," he pleaded the night before she left. "I'll give you all the space you need, but promise to keep in touch."

Mikala hung her head. She wanted to go radio silent, punish him, and hurt him as she was hurting. But she couldn't. "I'll try, Jake," she murmured.

I have loved you my entire life. Jake's declaration of love, as well as every other word they'd said to each other Thanksgiving Day and the day after, filled her thoughts. While her ten-week retreat from her normal life had been what she needed to gain perspective, she still lacked clarity where Jake was concerned.

When Mikala arrived in Ohio, she was physically and emotionally exhausted. Joe briefly questioned her sudden appearance, as well as her pale complexion and the dark circles prevalent under her eyes. But he was too sick to conduct a full interrogation. High blood pressure, diabetes, and heart failure ravaged his health, and Mikala spent hours with him at various doctors. With a new drug regimen and a strict diet plan, he improved.

Late one evening while Joe slept, Mikala sat in the family room, holding a mug of cocoa and staring absently into the fire.

Sandra walked in and without a word, she removed the mug and replaced it with a glass of brandy. She sat in the rocking recliner next to Mikala and pulled an afghan onto her lap.

Mikala nodded but remained silent.

"I know I'm not your first choice for a heart-to-heart, but I love you." Sandra shifted and plucked at the afghan. "I'm here for you, my child. You can tell me anything, and I'll listen."

Mikala continued to stare into the hearth. Sandra was the last person she could open up to. Although their relationship had improved over the last year, she couldn't remember the last time they had a meaningful conversation.

Sandra sighed. "I know you don't think I'll understand. You believe we're too different to ever have anything in common, but give me a chance. I'm seventy-two—thirty years older than you. Do you know what that means?"

Mikala raised an eyebrow. "That you think you

know better, can tell me how I should behave, how I should feel, and what I should do?" she answered in an acidic tone, sounding like a bitch.

With a sad smile, Sandra shook her head. "No, I've had a thirty-year head start on the joy and pain life dishes out. I've had thirty more years of loving and losing and thirty more years of laughing and crying. Despite my years, I'm not an expert on life. God knows I've made enough mistakes for twenty people. But I am your mother. I am the woman who gave birth to you, reared you, and loved you for forty-two years. I'm the woman who knows you much more than you believe."

Mikala took a sip of her brandy and sighed. She appreciated Sandra's historic effort to actually mother her. But her actions were too little, too late. Mikala wanted to get through this visit without a confrontation, but if Sandra wanted to play the doting mother, she would put her in her place. She squared her shoulders. "I appreciate the offer, Mom, but we *don't* have anything in common. What have you ever lost? You grew up with a silver spoon in your mouth, and Dad gave you everything you ever wanted. We've never talked, because we have nothing to say to one another. You've never understood me or approved of me."

Sandra set down her glass. Her shoulders sagged. "Oh, Mikala, you couldn't be more wrong. I was tough on you, because when you were a child, you scared the dickens out of me. You were a rambunctious, carefree child. I saw myself in you—my younger, wilder self."

Taking a deep breath, she cleared her throat and stared into the fire. "I *know* all about loss. My story is long, but I'll spare you all the details." She swallowed hard. "You see, when I was fifteen, I got pregnant. My parents banished me to Tennessee where I lived with my Aunt until the baby was born. I was forced to give up my child—a beautiful baby boy." Sandra sniffed. "Upon returning home, daily I received lessons on how a well-bred girl should behave. Daddy was very proficient with his belt."

Mikala gasped, and her mouth hung open. She'd known very little about her mother's childhood. Sandra had said she was raised on a big estate in Kentucky, but her parents died before she met and married Joe. Mikala really didn't know her mother at all. They were both mothers who'd lost their babies, but at least Mikala had precious memories of the years she'd shared with Molly. She wondered if Sandra ever thought of her lost baby boy. "I didn't know. You and Dad said…"

Sandra glanced at Mikala. "I know what we said. It's the story I wanted you to know. I didn't want to explain to you girls why you had grandparents who refused to acknowledge your existence. I was dead to my family and they to me."

Mikala frowned and shook her head. "I don't understand."

Sandra nodded and turned back to the fire. "You see, my daddy's belt wasn't as effective as he thought. When I was eighteen, I fell in love with a young man named Joseph Riley Cummings. His daddy brought him to a horse show in Kentucky. I attended that same show with Daddy—a rare day my mother let me out of her sight."

Smiling, Sandra rocked back and forth. "Joe dazzled me. For me, it was love at first sight. The specifics aren't important. The day I told my parents I was marrying him, my father threatened to disown me.

My mother tried to talk some sense into me and have me reconsider my actions. But I knew what I wanted, and I didn't care what I had to do to have him. I left, turned my back on my family, my friends, and everything and everyone I knew. They did the same."

Mikala studied her mother. She was overcome with sadness. Sandra had been so young when she lost everyone she loved. She must have loved Joe very much, and that love and devotion had withstood the test of time. Still, the loss of a child, as well as the loss of her parents and friends, must have shaped Sandra's view of the world and impacted her parenting style. So many of her mother's actions made sense now. "What happened? Did you ever contact your parents? Did you ever see them again?"

"Of course. Despite what they'd said and done, I loved them. I contacted them on many occasions, but they never relented. Every now and then, I would see them from a distance, but they never acknowledged me or my family." Sandra turned to Mikala and pierced her with her whisky-colored gaze.

Mikala now understood that her mother's eyes— identical to her own—had seen much more of life than she'd attributed to them.

"Mikala, both of my parents died bitter and alone. Despite my many attempts at reconciliation, they never forgave me. They never knew their grandchildren. If they could have seen the beautiful life Joe and I built, and the beautiful children we had…" Sandra closed her eyes. For a few seconds, she remained quiet. Then she opened her eyes and glanced at Mikala. "Now you know my story. I still mourn for the little boy I never got to hold. I understand loss and starting from scratch, and I understand, all too well, the fear and uncertainty that accompanies losing everything that matters."

Sandra smiled. "Just because our stories are different doesn't mean we cannot understand one another. Despite those differences, we can share in one another's grief and help carry one another's burdens."

For a few beats, Mikala held her mother's gaze and then looked away. She'd wasted so many years blaming Sandra for treating her harshly. She never tried to understand her. Sandra was influenced by her beginnings, and she did the best she could to parent Mikala. She gave up her entire world for Joe and the family they made. Mikala wished they had this conversation earlier. They wasted so many years. She cleared her throat. "I'm sorry, Mom. I'm sorry for your pain and your loss. I wish I'd known."

"Oh, Mikala. Thank you, sweetheart." Sandra touched Mikala's cheek with the tips of her fingers. "Losing my family and friends was hard. Giving away my child devastated me. But I made my peace with all my losses a long time ago. I feel sorry for your grandparents. They lived a lifetime shunning me and hating your father. They could have had you, Dani, Joe, and me. They missed out on a loving family because they chose anger and resentment over us. They were mired in the past forever, and they could never move forward."

Mikala's eyes filled with tears, and something inside her gave way. Maybe Sandra would understand. Perhaps, she could help her make sense of the past and the emotions holding her hostage. She needed to unburden her soul. "I can't forgive him, Mom. I've tried, but I can't," she whispered. "He had this whole other life I didn't know about—other women, drinking, and gambling. But even if I could get past those indiscretions…" Mikala took a stuttering breath and wiped her face just in time for more tears to slide down her cheeks. She turned her tortured gaze toward Sandra and forced the words out on a sob. "He killed my baby—my butterfly."

Sandra moved and knelt in front of her daughter. She took her in her arms. "Talk to me," she whispered in Mikala's ear. "Tell your mama everything you've been holding inside."

As she spoke, Mikala held on to Sandra. At first, the words dribbled out. But soon Mikala sunk into the comfort of her mother's embrace, and the words poured out. "David might have been driving that day, but I, too, was to blame. I knew he was stressed. I saw him glued to his phone, day and night. I witnessed him drinking too much. I didn't say or do enough."

Mikala wiped her eyes and slid out of her chair to sit next to Sandra on the carpet. "On Thanksgiving Day, I went to visit David and Molly. I stood in front of his grave, and I'd almost reached acceptance. That same day, my world exploded again, and I lost the hard-won peace I'd achieved. Nothing I knew about my marriage was real. Now, I can't forgive him, and I can't forgive myself."

Swallowing hard, Mikala shook her head. "That day—the day of the accident…" She paused. "I had this awful feeling. I should have listened to my gut. If I had, Molly would be alive. David wouldn't have died." She hung her head. Exhausted. Defeated.

Sandra and Mikala sat in silence, staring into the fire as it crackled and warmed their faces. After a few minutes, Sandra took Mikala's hand in hers. "You know, as far as I know, angels don't walk the earth—people do. Good people make terrible decisions. Making poor choices doesn't make them bad people. Their actions just make them human." Sandra sighed. "We have no choice, as those left behind, but to find forgiveness...for our loved ones and for ourselves. We, too, are not perfect. Even when we know better, *all* humans make bad decisions. Dig deep. Work hard, Mikala. Learn to forgive, or you'll be the one making a terrible mistake."

Clutching her mother's hand, Mikala let the memories of Molly's death, David's suicide, Leslie's words, and Jake's confessions wash over her—each memory a tsunami. When she was certain she would drown under the waves of grief and betrayal, she felt the strength of her mother's hand pulling her above the surface. Then, she was reminded she wasn't alone, and she was a damn good swimmer. Each stroke brought her closer to the life vest called forgiveness.

Chapter Twenty-Seven
Mountains to Scale

Recalling that pivotal conversation still brought tears to Mikala's eyes. She took a deep breath and scanned Rena's family room for a box of tissues. Finding none, she went to the kitchen for a paper towel. Mikala splashed cold water on her face, blew her nose, and retrieved her mug from the family room. More coffee was in order. She had to get her act together before Rena woke up.

Six weeks had passed since Mikala and her mother bared their souls and shared their secrets. Their relationship blossomed, and they talked daily. That initial conversation was also key in setting Mikala firmly on the road to self-discovery and recovery. She'd learned much about the latitude of the human heart and its limitless ability to love, heal, and forgive. Now, she knew what she wanted from life.

When she arrived in Ohio, Mikala had called Rena. She gave her an abbreviated version of what occurred at Thanksgiving. But since Ari's birth, Mikala refused to discuss anything that wasn't baby related. She didn't want to taint the excitement of Ariana's birth and the holidays with her problems. For two weeks, Rena tolerated Mikala's reluctance to discuss what happened, but now Rena was ripe for a confrontation. The only reason Mikala got away with her avoidance behavior was the baby.

Ted had been instrumental in diverting Rena's attention. Whenever he noticed Mikala squirm under Rena's scrutiny, his gaze softened, and he handled his wife in ways Mikala never witnessed before. When Ted was in the room, Rena forgot everyone but the baby. One word or one look from Ted, and Rena was silly putty—soft and pliable. Their relationship was beautiful to watch.

When the door leading to the bedrooms creaked open, Mikala startled.

Rena stumbled into the kitchen carrying Ari. Rena's crimson hair was wild, and her eyes were half-closed. "Here, take her fussy a-s-s before I give her up for adoption." Rena slid Ariana in Mikala's arms. "I have to fix her a bottle, and I'm in desperate need of caffeine."

Cuddling Ariana in her arms, she lifted the baby to her face and breathed in her addictive baby scent. "Hey, sweet girl. You gave your mommy h-e-l-l last night. Good for you. I hear she likes a challenge."

Rena glared. "Stop inhaling my child like she's a warm baguette. If you're hungry, make some toast."

Smiling, Mikala caressed Ari's pudgy cheek with her finger. "I'm memorizing her delicious smell for the future. I'll miss you guys so much."

Rena scoffed and raised an eyebrow. "Is that why you've been crying? 'Cause you'll miss us?"

Her smile faded. She sighed and shook her head. She saw the writing on the wall. Rena was sleep deprived, caffeine deficient, and short tempered. No escape was possible.

Rena measured baby formula into a clean bottle.

"You know, Micky, I've been a saint for two weeks. I've kept my mouth shut, let you live in your head, and do your ridiculous moping. Two weeks! I think that's a record." She turned and faced Mikala. "I hope you have on your big-girl panties because you and I are talking out this mess today—before your disappearing act tomorrow."

Mikala took in Rena's no-nonsense stance—hands on hips, gaze focused on Mikala, and jaw stubbornly set. While she had every intention of talking to Rena, a part of her was irritated at the confrontation. Rena wasn't completely out of the loop. Mikala was certain each time she'd refused Jake's call, he'd called Rena.

Settling Ariana against her shoulder, Mikala sighed. "I didn't think I had to say a word. I thought by now Jake filled you in on every little detail of my life. Have you guys formulated a how-to-fix-Mikala plan yet? 'Cause you might have wasted your time."

Rena's gaze flashed, and she shook her head. "Now see here, girlfriend. I haven't had a full mug of java yet, and you've made the mistake of throwing attitude my way. I popped out that kid six weeks ago, and my hormones are all over the map. You must have a death wish."

She grabbed the baby bottle, shook it, and thrust it at Mikala. "Take this. That bottle is for Ari, although right now, I'm tempted to fix one for you as well."

Mikala's stomach clenched. This conversation wouldn't be pretty. She'd pushed Rena too far. She opened her mouth.

"Uh-uh," Rena warned, jutting out a hip and placing her hands on her hips. "Do not say another word. Stay as silent as you've been for two weeks. Feed my child. We'll talk when I've mainlined some caffeine and have transformed into a human."

"But I think—"

"Don't think, Micky." Rena shook her head. "I love you, but you overuse that over-educated brain of yours. For the love of God, go out there, and sit the f-u-c-k down. I'll be there in a second with coffee for both of us to sort out your s-h-i-t before you f-u-c-k up your life. Honestly, can't you and Jake do anything right yourselves?"

Shaking her head, Mikala went to the breakfast nook. She regretted being sharp with Rena. By her silence and now her words, she'd hurt her friend. Thank God Rena had tough skin and a big heart. She sat and fed the baby. Mikala used the last two weeks to reflect on the past and the future. While she couldn't quite say she'd found closure, she was close. She'd reached acceptance, and she was close in her journey to achieving the peace and forgiveness her mother talked about.

On a whim, Mikala had taken Molly's baby book to Ohio. She started composing her final letter. Although penning each word tortured her, pouring out her heart to Molly was also cathartic. Word by word and tear by tear, as she let Molly go, she inched closer and closer to forgiving David.

Rena didn't know any of these facts, and that situation was Mikala's fault. Mikala had packed all the love, compassion, and strength she received from her family and friends and took them with her on her journey of self-reflection. But ultimately, she'd scaled the mountain on her own. She now understood the road to healing the heart was a deeply personal pilgrimage.

"You want to put down that bottle, or are you planning to drown my child in formula? The kid's asleep, and you're watering her ear."

Mikala jumped. She glanced at Ari, who was fast asleep, blowing milk bubbles with her rosy lips. Although Ari had a bit of formula on her chin and cheeks, she wasn't in danger of drowning. Mikala wiped the baby's chubby cheeks. She patted her back until she was rewarded with a healthy burp and carried her to the bassinet near the windows overlooking Central Park. She turned to Rena. "I'm sorry. I didn't mean to freeze you out, and I didn't mean to snap. Please forgive me."

Rena pulled out a chair and sat. She snorted and shook her head. "Girl, don't be ridiculous. No apology is needed. About time your mean streak kicked in." She grinned. "Now sit your ass down and talk. We've only got a couple of hours, before that child starts screeching, and Ted wakes up foraging for food. Give me the abbreviated version of your life since Thanksgiving."

Mikala breathed out in relief. She didn't deserve Rena. She sat across from Rena and reached for her coffee. Mikala started speaking, telling Rena how her heart skipped a beat when she heard Leslie talk about David's gambling, drinking, and women, and how she wanted her heart to cease beating when Leslie added, *"He was a fuck-up who killed his own kid."*

Rena stayed silent, but she reached for Mikala's hand.

The women held tight to one another as Mikala described her trip to Ohio, the love and acceptance she found in her mother's arms, and her personal journey of reflection and recovery.

Rena smiled. "I'm proud of you, sister. You've been through hell and back. But look at you, standing on your own, so strong and beautiful. When Ari grows up, she'll have my beauty, of course, and Ted's weird toes, but I hope she'll have your strength."

Mikala wiped her cheeks. "Thank you. But I think she'll be fine in that department. Her mama has the strength of an eighteen-wheeler." She smiled and settled into the chair, enjoying the last sips of her coffee. Her cell vibrated in her pocket. She knew who the message was from and what the message would say. She pulled her cell out of her pocket and glanced at it.

—Good morning, baby. Remember I love you.—

For the last ten weeks, every morning and every evening, Jake sent the same text. Some days she responded with,

Good morning or *Goodnight.*

Other days, she held back. Still, his messages never failed to come and never failed to cause her heart to ache.

Mikala was no longer angry with Jake. She understood why he kept silent on the true cause of Molly's accident. A right time to tell her hadn't occurred. In truth, had she been in his position, she wasn't sure she would have acted differently. But David's infidelity and gambling? Mikala wasn't certain how she would have reacted had she been informed.

Jake vowed he was protecting her and giving her what he thought she wanted. While she understood protecting her was his way of loving her, she was deeply troubled by his actions. Was she so weak in his eyes he thought the only way to love her was to shield her from reality? Often, Mikala recalled Leslie's words.

"All of you treat her like a porcelain doll. Don't you ever get tired of playing the superhero and cleaning up after David?"

Mikala skated her thumb over Jake's message. They had a lot to talk about. She wasn't a victim or an object of pity. She wasn't delicate or incapable of handling all life threw at her. Hadn't she proven that fact over and over again? If Jake's love was based on his mistaken perception she needed shielding, she didn't want it.

Weeks of reflection helped Mikala see she needed to forgive David and herself for the mistakes they made. She was ready to rebuild her life and be happy. But she wouldn't make the same mistake twice. She wanted to love and be loved as an equal. She needed to trust the person she gave her heart to, and she wasn't sure she could trust Jake. The possibility of saying good-bye to Jake tortured Mikala. But if she had to, she would set him free from the obligation of being her superhero.

"You ready to talk about Jake now?"

Rena broke into her thoughts in a soft voice. Mikala glanced at Rena. She was ready. Maybe Mama Rena could shed some light on Jake's behavior. Mikala cleared her throat. "I've always loved Jake, but I'm also in love with him. Do you understand?"

Rena smiled and nodded. "How does he feel about you?"

Mikala blushed. "Before I left, he told me he loved me. Every morning when I open my eyes, and every night before I close them, he reminds me." She smiled and tapped the screen of her cell.

"But?" Rena quirked an eyebrow. "Do you doubt him?"

Mikala shook her head. "No, I don't doubt he loves me, but I worry about the way he loves me. After all these years, I'm not sure I can trust him."

Rena frowned. "I'm not following."

Sitting straighter, Mikala glanced at her wedding band. "Jake said he covered up for David all these years, because I chose David and loved David. He said he gave me the David I wanted, and while I understand his logic, I can't dive into another relationship where I am not told the truth under the guise of love. I think he sees me as weak and incapable of handling the truth, and that's not acceptable, nor is it reality."

Rena shook her head. "Mikala, you were crazy in love with David. From the very first time you laid eyes on him, you were blind to everything he was. Don't you remember all the conversations you and I had before you married him and all the messes he used to get in? You had to send Jake to clean up his shit on a regular basis."

Mikala pushed the hair off her face. "Of course I remember, but we were in college, and he was young. His wild ways were his way of dealing with the stress Lester put on him. I know you'll say he never learned to deal with Lester, his sisters, or his job. I get it, and you're right, but he wasn't perfect, and neither was I."

"Oh, Micky. Listen to me." Rena laid her hand on top of Mikala's. "I'm not criticizing you, and I don't think you're weak. Neither does Jake. You know what my grandma always said? 'Happiness is a choice. It's an illusion we create for ourselves.' "

She stood and walked to the window. "When I was

young, I had no idea what that old woman talked about. Now, I understand. In order to be happy, we tell ourselves all kinds of little lies. Our spouses are perfect. They don't look at other women because they only have eyes for us. Our relationship is strong and has no flaws. We don't keep secrets from one another. We trust each other implicitly." She turned, shook her head, and smiled. "You know all that is bullshit, right? Those little white lies just make us feel better, that's all."

Mikala studied her hands. "I realize I'm partly responsible for the mess in my marriage. I should have been more vigilant, held David more accountable, and made him stop drinking. I take responsibility for my behavior. The mistakes I made in my marriage have nothing to do with Jake's responsibility, and his accountability, as my friend. He should have told me about David's gambling and women. I should have been informed and given a chance to act as I saw fit. But he decided to protect me. He determined I was too weak to know the truth."

Rena took a deep breath and sighed. "Micky, look at me. Jake loved you. I loved you. You're an intelligent woman who created her own illusion of happiness. Despite the evidence right in front of your eyes, you chose to marry David and stay married. You accepted him as he was. *We* understood that you loved him—his fine points and his flaws. For better or worse, *we* took our cues from you. If you chose to continuously hide your head in the sand, did you expect us to pull it out against your will? Where would that have left us?"

Studying her wedding band, Mikala shook her head. Had she lied to herself all the years she'd been married? She'd loved David to a fault, but had he loved her? At this point, did the truth even matter? By refusing to see David for who he really was, she'd put her friends in a terrible position.

Now, the time had come to make peace with the past, find closure and forgiveness, and heal old wounds. But she had to learn from her mistakes, just as Jake did. No longer would she be viewed as weak and helpless, and no longer would she live in a fantasy world. She deserved to live a full life. She only hoped Jake was ready to embrace the new-and-improved her, because if he couldn't, they wouldn't have a future together.

Chapter Twenty-Eight
Let Me Love Her

Jake gripped his cell with such force, it was a miracle the device didn't shatter. Mikala made him lose what was left of his sanity. Ten weeks! He hadn't heard her voice in ten weeks, and now that she was coming home, she wouldn't let him pick her up. Why the fuck was she being difficult?

He missed her so damn much. That he hadn't taken a flight to Ohio or New York to retrieve her weeks ago was a testament to his self-control. But he promised to give her time and space, and he had. Now, she was out of both. Jake was ready to grovel or fight for his woman. *His* woman. Not David's. Jake used the ten weeks to come to grips with the fact, if he wanted Mikala, he had to get his head out of his ass and grow a set. He had to fight for Mikala, even if that meant fighting David's ghost, David's memory, his legacy, and the hold he had over them.

Mikala had been David's for a reason. Jake gave her to him on a silver platter. He never made a play for her—not when she was single and could have been his, and not when she was David's. But she wasn't David's any longer.

Jake never felt he was good enough. She was goodness and light. He was nothing like Mikala—not even close. He was a boy from the hood. Jake was transported to Yale, to a new life far from the ruins of his old, but nothing could erase where he came from. No matter how hard he worked, what he created, or how much he earned, he was who he was. But now, he realized his feelings of inadequacy were unfounded. Long ago, Mikala accepted him for who he was. She knew where and what he came from, and she didn't judge him. He let his insecurities stand in the way of him loving Mikala the way he should have. But he was done with that nonsense.

For the last hour, Jake text-argued with Mikala. He wasn't sure who was winning the texting war, but his fingers ached, and he saw double. The day had been busy and stressful, and the time was nearing midnight. He ran out of time and energy. He had to change strategy.

—Baby, I'm exhausted. I haven't slept a full night since you left, and I've been in court all day. Answer your phone when it rings, or I swear I'll call Rena followed by Ted.—

Jake, no.

—Your choice. Pick up your phone, or I put plan B into action.—

Smiling, Jake grabbed a bottle of water from his refrigerator and walked to his bedroom. All was fair in love and war. Mikala left him no choice. He had to play dirty. He recognized they had a lot to talk about, but they couldn't work out things if she was in another state and wouldn't communicate.

Jake understood Mikala's world had been rocked once again. What he struggled with was the fact she didn't want anything to do with him and wouldn't accept his help. He was her super-man, and he didn't want their relationship to change. Jake wanted Mikala to trust him with everything in her world. He would move heaven and earth to fix their relationship.

As the days passed, Jake realized Leslie did them a favor. While she acted in a jealous rage, maliciously and with no regard for Mikala's feelings, she also gave them the opportunity to face the past and remove the veil of secrets and lies. Despite the uncertainty of where he stood with Mikala, for the first time in a hell of a long time, he breathed easy.

Jake piled pillows against the headboard and climbed into bed. He rubbed his eyes, and then dialed Mikala.

Mikala answered on the first ring. "Hello."

Her breathy voice filled Jake's ears. He closed his eyes and smiled. There she was—his Micky. God, he missed hearing her voice. Not seeing her for so long was difficult, but not hearing her voice tortured him. Once more, she'd banished him from her world. He deserved her anger. He had a lot of explaining to do and so much to make up for.

"Jake? Are you there?"

"Yeah, baby. I'm here. I am so damn glad to hear your voice. You have no idea how much I've missed you. No idea at all."

For a few seconds, except for the sound of Mikala's breathing, silence prevailed. Then she sniffled. Fuck, she was crying. He hated when she cried, especially when he couldn't wrap his arms around her and comfort her. Jake hung his head. "Micky, please don't cry," he whispered. "I'm so damn sorry." He swallowed hard. "I'm sorry for all of it. We will be okay. I promise."

Mikala sniffled again. "I'm okay, Jake. I'm so happy to hear your voice. I've missed you, too."

Jake smiled. Mikala missed him. Thank God. Was she ready to listen? "Let me pick you up. Please."

Mikala sighed. "We have a lot to talk about, Jake."

He nodded. "Yes, we do. What time do you get in?"

Silence reigned.

"I'm taking the train tomorrow morning."

Jake stretched and opened the drawer of the nightstand. He shuffled through it until he found a pad of paper and a pen. "I'll be there. What time do you arrive?"

Mikala cleared her throat. "Let's meet for dinner instead. How about I meet you at Bella's at six-thirty?"

Bella's? Was Mikala avoiding being alone with him? Jake frowned. "What's going on? Want to tell me why you won't let me pick you up, or why we're meeting at a restaurant instead of your house or mine?"

"I think meeting in public is best. We need to talk."

He rubbed his head and took a breath, letting it out slowly. Patience. He needed patience. "Yes, I know we need to have a serious conversation. I'm ready to talk, but I don't understand—"

"Jake. Stop," Mikala choked. "Can't we just do this meeting my way? Please?"

He snaked a hand through his hair. "I thought that's exactly what we've been doing for the last ten weeks. I don't understand, but since I don't have a choice, I'll be—"

"I love you," Mikala whispered.

Jake froze. His mouth hung open, and his heart picked up speed. He had to be sure he heard her right, and his brain wasn't playing cruel tricks. "What did you just say?"

"I love you," she reaffirmed.

As his heart pounded a bruising beat against his sternum, he stilled, and his breath stuttered. *Jesus*. God. She loved him! After all the shit he'd done, she loved him. Jake closed his eyes, and his chin hit his chest. He told Mikala he loved her before she left, and he texted those words daily. This moment was the first time she said those words. Through the years, she'd told him she loved him, but that love was an expression of their deep friendship. Now, right at this instant, he was in heaven…and he was in hell.

Jake swallowed past the boulder in his throat. Could Mikala actually love him? Could she love him with her entire heart as she'd loved David? Why did the woman have to be so many miles away when she said those words for the first time? If he could just see her eyes and feel her heart beat against his, Jake would allow her words to take root, and he wouldn't doubt his ears. He cleared his throat. "I love you, too, Mikala. I love you with all my heart."

After a few seconds of silence, she said, *"Bella's*, Jake. Please do as I ask. Meeting at *Bella's* is important to me."

"Okay, baby. Whatever you want. I'll be there." He disconnected the call and lay back on the pillows with a wide grin. Mikala was coming home. She said the words he dreamed of hearing from her sweet lips. Down deep, he was a romantic, and he believed love really *could* conquer all—maybe not all the time, but it sure as hell would this time. He would meet her at *Bella's* right after he did what he should have done a long time ago. He had to have a talk with David.

Jake slept in the next morning and woke up at eight-thirty a.m. feeling more rested and more positive about the future than he had in two months. He couldn't remember the last time he enjoyed the luxury of a full night of sleep, let alone sleeping in. He rolled toward the nightstand and grabbed his cell with the intention of texting Mikala to see if she'd gotten on the train safely, but his woman had him beat. He opened his message app and read,

On the train. All is well. See you tonight.

Mikala knew him better than anyone else on this earth. He smiled and sat up. He sent his daily greeting.

—Good morning, Micky. I love you and can't wait to see you tonight.—

Jake had plenty to do before his dinner with Mikala. At noon, he was having lunch with Lester at the Hartford Country Club. He thought long and hard about his upcoming conversation, and he was comfortable with his decision. While Jake loved Lester, and he owed him much, Jacobson Law was not where he belonged. He didn't like the high-pressured, cutthroat atmosphere, and he didn't like the type of law they practiced. The practice belonged to Lester and the witches. Jake was not David, and he could not take his place. Although Lester denied Jake was David's stand-in, in many ways, Jake was the son Lester dreamed David could have been.

Then came the matter of the witches. Over the last few months, Leslie did her best to avoid him, while Priscilla did the opposite. Shortly after the holidays, Priscilla asked him to lunch. She apologized for her behavior and asked his advice on how she could improve her relationship with the associates and paralegals. Surprisingly, Priscilla took his advice and distanced herself from Leslie. At first, her behavior was suspect, but slowly, the associates and staff showed signs of trusting her. Her reputation was changing for the better.

Jake drove to the country club and gave Red's keys to the valet. Several times in the past, he'd met Lester at the club for lunch and dinner. Each time he entered the ostentatious restaurant, he liked it less. Jake didn't understand why Lester frequented this place. From the overly shiny wood flooring to the vaulted ceilings and dazzling chandeliers, everything about the club screamed money.

As they ate, Jake kept conversation light. After the waiter removed their lunch plates and poured coffee, he cleared his throat. "Lester, I've been doing a lot of thinking over the past few months, and I've reached a decision I want to discuss." He took a swig of his coffee and scalded his mouth. He grabbed his water to put out the fire and hoped he hadn't burned away a layer of skin. Taking a deep breath, he met Lester's stare. Jake shifted in his seat like a nervous teenager about to tell his father he crashed the new car. Fuck, he was an adult. Why did Lester have this effect on him? "Les," Jake started once more.

"Son, I'll put you out of your misery before you fall off that chair and embarrass us both. When are you leaving?"

Jake stilled and studied Lester. He knew? Was there anything the man didn't know?

"I'm sorry, Les." He hung his head. "I'm sorry to disappoint you. You've done so much for me. You've been there whenever I needed you. I can't continue at the practice. I've tried, but I don't feel right. Being there, sitting in his office, and doing his job…Well, this arrangement isn't right for me, Leslie, Priscilla, or"— Jake glanced up and shook his head—"you. I'm not David, the son you had, or the son you wanted."

Lester sighed. "No, Jake, you're not my son, but I love you like you were. I always will." He patted Jake's back. "You could never disappoint me. You do what you need to, and I'll stand by you."

Once Jake cleared the hurdle of telling Lester of his decision, they spent several hours discussing Jake's future and his recommendations for Jacobson Law. By the time he left for the cemetery, a heavy weight lifted from his shoulders. He had no regrets. He was carving out a new future. If he and Mikala could successfully build a life together, they needed to leave the past behind and start fresh.

Mikala's house was already on the market, and she had several offers. Other than Lester and her memories, nothing tied her to Connecticut. Jake believed change was in order. He only hoped once he told her of his plans, she would be on board. If she wasn't, he would do what she wanted. Nothing mattered as much as she did.

Jake drove Red through the gates of the cemetery. He passed the children's section and drove toward the Jacobson family plot. Parking, he walked to David's grave. The second anniversary of David's death was the next day. While he would accompany Mikala if she wanted, he needed time alone with David. Jake shifted from foot to foot. He took a deep breath, let it out, and gazed at the sky.

Although the sun was bright, the air was crisp, and a slight breeze tousled his hair. He shivered, stuck his hands in his pockets, and hung his head. "I love her, David. I suppose you knew, but I didn't." Jake recalled one of the last conversations he had with David. He'd been lecturing him about how much Mikala needed him and how he had to get his act together.

David suddenly grabbed his arm. "You don't understand. I'm done. There's nothing more I can give. It's your turn now, Super-man. She needs *you*."

At the time, Jake thought David's strange ramblings were due to his depression and possibly the drugs and alcohol he'd sustained himself on. Now, he knew better.

Jake focused on the headstone. "She knows everything, and she's hurting. You hurt her by your actions, and I hurt her by my inaction. For years, we both fucked up. Yesterday, a beautiful thing happened." Jake smiled. "She told me she loved me. Man, you know how that feels. You know how those words, coming from her lips, wrap around your heart and squeeze. I've never felt anything quite so beautiful and perfect. Her love is a gift I'll fight to keep."

Slowly, Jake shook his head. "David, brother, I need you to let her go. Let me love her." He swallowed passed the lump in his throat. "Let me love her the way she deserves to be loved. You and Molly are gone. The life we shared is over. Mikala and I were left with only memories—good and bad. If you release us, we can build something new—something strong and good. After all I've done for you, I only ask one thing. Let her go so she can come to me free from the past."

Chapter Twenty-Nine
Don't Screw This Up

Jake pulled Red in front of *Bella's* twenty minutes early. He scanned the parking lot but didn't see Mikala's car. Taking a deep breath, he closed his eyes and rested his head against the headrest. Today had been one hell of a day, and the day wasn't over yet. Over lunch, he'd told Lester of his plans not only for his career, but also for him and Mikala. Lester didn't even blink.

"Slow down, Jake. Give her time to adjust. Don't steamroll her into making decisions she's not ready to make. She'll be gun-shy," Lester warned. "She loves you, and you love her. I've never seen two people so connected and right for each other but so talented in screwing up their lives. You've got your work cut out for you, boy. Don't screw this up."

Jake opened his eyes and silently repeated Lester's words. Deep in thought, he stepped out of the truck and walked, head down, to the front door. As he reached for the door, another's hand covered his. Jake glanced up and found Mikala's warm whisky eyes focused on him. A smile formed on his lips and spread across his face.

He couldn't take his gaze off her beautiful face. A blush rose on her cheeks and a hesitant smile formed on her full lips. Her auburn curls fell around her face and cascaded down her shoulders and back in wave after thick wave. Although only ten weeks had passed since he last saw her, the time apart felt like ten years.

"Hi, Jake," she whispered.

"Hi, baby." Jake couldn't hold back. Never taking his gaze off her, he gently pulled her toward him.

Mikala hesitated for only a second, and then she slid into his arms, sighing and sagging against him. She laid her head against his chest and slipped her hands inside his open leather jacket. Her arms went around him, and her hands fisted his shirt, holding on tight.

When Mikala trembled, Jake lost what little control he had. He crushed her to him and breathed in her vanilla smell. He memorized and relished her scent. Thank God Mikala was home.

Without invitation, Lester's words popped into Jake's head— *Slow down. Don't screw this up.* Fuck Lester and his fatherly warning. Jake was nervous enough, he didn't need Lester's ominous words running amuck in his head and distracting him. He understood the stakes were especially high tonight, but he had no intention of leaving the restaurant without Mikala in his arms and life—forever.

Breaking the embrace, Jake tenderly kissed Mikala's forehead. Without a word, he grabbed her hand, kissed the back of it, and opened the door. Once they were seated, he studied the wine list and ordered a bottle of her favorite Pinot Noir. Handing the wine list to the waiter, he glanced up to find Mikala studying him.

Mikala looked away and picked up her water glass. She took a sip, and then put down the glass. She placed the napkin on her lap and straightened the silverware.

Jake waited. He wouldn't rush her. He wouldn't

steamroll her.

Clearing her throat, she met his gaze. "I've had a lot of time to think. Going home, and then visiting Rena helped me reflect on the past and understand what I want. When I'm with you"—she looked down once more—"when I'm alone with you, I lose myself in you—in us. That's why we're here. We have serious issues to discuss." Taking a deep breath, she reached for his hand. "I love you, Jake. I never thought I would say those words to another man, but I have no doubt in my mind or in my heart. I love you."

Every time Mikala said those words, Jake's heart squeezed, and his lungs seized until he could barely breathe. The woman took away his breath with her beauty and grace and now with her honesty. Jake smiled and entwined his fingers through hers. "You know I love you too. You are everything to me. I—"

"I *do* know," she interrupted with a firm voice and a steady gaze. She squeezed his fingers and sighed. "What troubles me is *how* you love me and maybe even how I love you."

How he loved her? Jake frowned. He loved her with his whole heart. How could she question his love? Hadn't he showed her the depth of his devotion all these years?

Mikala cleared her throat. "The last time I fell in love, I fell and fell. I didn't bother to look where I was going or how hard the landing would be. For twenty years, I closed my eyes and kept them shut. I can't go through life with rose-colored glasses. I must do things differently. My brain must rein in my wayward heart and set parameters so my heart doesn't get crushed again. Do you understand?"

Jake nodded.

Mikala released his hand and feathered her fingers across his cheek.

He caught her fingers and brought them to his mouth for a tender kiss. He wanted to promise he would never hurt her again. Although he was human and would make mistakes, she didn't need to protect her heart. But he was determined to hear her out. Then he would make promises he would live the rest of his life keeping.

"On the very first day we met, I called you my super-man. You took that title to heart." She smiled. "Since then, you've done everything in your power to protect me from…well, everything. You believed your job was to make my world perfect. If I encountered any bumps, you did your damnedest to fix every bruise. My happiness has been a heavy burden to carry all these years."

Jake shook his head. "Micky, making you happy has never been a burden. It's been an honor."

Looking down, she swallowed hard, and then she glanced at him. "Oh, Super-man, my super-man." Her eyes glistened with unshed tears. "With you in my life, I've always felt safe and loved. But I relied on you too much, and that's not fair. Jake, you can't be solely responsible for my happiness, and you can't protect me from life."

The conversation ceased when the waiter returned with the wine. Once they placed their orders and he left, Jake took a drink and glanced at Mikala. "Sweetheart, I'm not sure what you're asking. I can't stop loving you, caring about you, or protecting you. How can you ask that of me?"

Mikala took a healthy swallow of her wine and put down her glass. "I'm not asking you to stop loving me, just as I couldn't stop loving you. I need you to understand you can't protect me from everything, and that's okay. I'm an adult not a child. Even if I were a child, you couldn't fully protect me. You and I, better than most, know life is unpredictable and fragile."

As the waiter served their salads and refreshed their water and wine, silence reigned.

She stared at her salad and pushed around the greens. Occasionally, she went through the motions of chewing and swallowing.

Jake had much to explain and even more to apologize for, but this time was Mikala's. He bit his tongue and focused on her every word.

Laying down her fork, she sat straighter. "Look, here's the issue. Contrary to popular belief, I'm *not* weak or fragile. Yes, I closed my eyes and refused to see things I should have in my marriage. I made excuses for David. I *allowed* myself to be lied to, cheated on, and manipulated by people I loved." Mikala shook her head. "I wasn't a victim of circumstance. I made mistakes, but I've learned my lesson. I am responsible for my own happiness, but happiness has to be based in reality. I won't turn a blind eye, and I won't tolerate being deceived again...about anything. I'd rather be told the truth—even if the truth hurts."

For a few seconds, Jake looked away, unable to see the self-recrimination and disappointment in her eyes. When he slid his gaze back, he forced himself to *see* Mikala. He studied the strong, beautiful woman who sat before him, and he clearly saw the pain and distrust he'd inflicted. David was responsible for his actions during their marriage, but Jake was also guilty. Lies of omission, even white ones, had a destructive force. They destroyed relationships and rocked the strongest of foundations.

He squared his shoulders and cleared his throat. He wanted his next words to sink in. She needed to understand how fucking sorry he was. "You're the strongest woman I know. I never meant to hurt you or take away your power. Although my actions were always rooted in love, I was wrong. I should have told you about David—his gambling and infidelity. I should have told you how out of control his drinking was. You had a right to know about the accident. I can only ask for your forgiveness. I'm sorry."

Mikala reached for his hand once more. "David's actions were not your fault. I understand you would never knowingly hurt me. I want to put the past behind me…behind us. I want to create a new life, but I can't be in another relationship in which everything I thought to be true isn't." Narrowing her eyes, Mikala withdrew her hand. "I want a partner not a caretaker. You say I'm your family, and you are mine. If that's true, we have to trust one another, lean on one another, and share everything…equally. Otherwise we won't work. Be honest with yourself and me. If you can't give me what I'm asking…" she swallowed hard. "Set me free."

Jake sat in silence as the waiter cleared their salads and served their main course. The food sat untouched as he studied the woman he loved and assimilated the ultimatum she issued.

She'd opened her heart, bared her soul, and made herself vulnerable. If he didn't want to lose her, he had to do the same. He trusted Mikala, and he never wanted anyone as much as he wanted her. She was everything—his forever. In order to forge a future, he would give her his past for safekeeping.

Taking a deep breath in, he let it out slowly. "When I was a kid, I watched my mother work herself into the ground, trying to make enough money to keep food on the table as well as pay off the outrageous debts my father left. Do you know, I can't remember my mother's smile? As a kid, I thought something was wrong with her face, and she couldn't smile."

Smiling, he shook his head. "Now I know she had nothing to smile about—so heavy were her burdens. She loved a man who was a criminal—a murderer. I couldn't understand that type of blind devotion. The man was a shitty husband and the worst type of father. He didn't protect his family. Instead, he planted us right in the heart of violence and mayhem. Still, my mother closed her eyes to all his sins. She loved him, and when he was incarcerated, she pined for him."

Jake studied the water droplets as they slid down the outside of his water glass. "Every day when she left the shitty apartment we lived in to go to one of her many jobs, I wondered if she would come home alive. When she died, Mateo became my only family. Then, my mother's burdens became Mateo's, and I clung to him."

Glancing up to make sure he still had Mikala's attention, Jake pushed a hand through his hair. "When I understood how Mateo spent his days and nights, each night I lay in bed, cowering under the sheets and listening to the shouting and the occasional gunshots in the street." For a few seconds, Jake paused as he fought the panic that occasionally gripped him when he thought of those terrifying days. He cleared his throat. "I felt powerless. And when Mateo came home, I was so relieved he was still alive, I promised I would do whatever I could to make him proud."

Pushing away his plate, he picked up his wine glass and drained it. "Back then, I couldn't do anything to change our lives. I couldn't help my family or protect them from harm. Now, things are different. *You* are my only family. Part of me recoils at the thought of standing by and watching you hurt. I'll always want to protect you, shield you from any pain, make you happy, and make you smile."

A soft smile touched Mikala's lips, and her eyes filled with tears.

Shrugging, Jake smiled. "I'm hardwired that way. But I don't think you're weak, and I'm not trying to take over your life—I only want to share it. I love you, and I was compelled to protect your happiness for as long as I could. I can see my reasoning was flawed." He reached across the table and linked his fingers with hers. "I'm sorry for hurting you. Please give us another chance. I don't want to lose you. Take a chance on me…on us. I promise, I won't let you down again."

As tears trickled down her cheeks, Mikala dropped her head. She wiped them away with her napkin and raised her head.

Jake's gaze met hers. In her eyes, he saw love, forgiveness, and absolution.

"On one condition, Jake," she whispered.

"Anything, baby." He kissed the back of her hand. "Anything."

Mikala smiled. "Will you still be my super-man? An updated version perhaps?"

Jake let out a relieved breath. His heart was full. It overflowed with love for the strong, brave, and beautiful woman across from him. Even if she'd walked away, he could never stop being her super-man. He was humbled and grateful as hell he wouldn't have to live without her. "Always, sweetheart. I will always be your super-man."

Chapter Thirty
I'm Yours

Mikala woke to the sound of sleet pelting the windows. If she hadn't looked at the bedside clock, she wouldn't have guessed the time was almost eight a.m. Apparently, the sun decided to rotate to the other side of the globe for the day. She stretched and reached for her cell. She found Jake's daily greeting.

—Good morning, baby. Remember I love you.—

She smiled and returned his message.

Good morning, Super-man. I love you too. Have a good day, and I'll see you later.

A few seconds later, her cell vibrated.

—Are you sure you don't want me to come with you today? The weather is terrible. I could stay in the car and keep it warm for you.—

Some things would never change, and she wasn't sure that was a bad thing after all.

I'll be fine, sweetheart. Go to work. See you tonight.

After they'd left *Bella's* the night before, Jake drove Mikala back to her house, and they sat in the family room in front of the fireplace for several hours. She curled into his side and stared into the fire. "I'm ready to say goodbye to Molly and David. I'm ready to close that book so I can begin a new one with you— free from the past. I've travelled a long road, and the journey from devastation to recovery almost killed me. I wouldn't have survived without you." She touched her lips to his. "But I have to take this final step on my own. Okay?"

Jake nodded and kissed the top of her head. "I've already said my goodbyes to David. He and I had a long chat. I have my closure. Do what you need to find yours."

They'd talked deep into the night, held each other, and exchanged deep, passionate kisses that made her crave more. She was just about ready to give herself completely to him.

As Mikala showered and dressed in the warmest sweater and jeans she owned, she listened to the weather report. Although the sleet would stop in the next hour, unfortunately, the good people of Connecticut would be treated to a full-fledged blizzard beginning mid-afternoon.

Undaunted, Mikala grabbed Molly's baby book and the bouquets of daisies and roses she'd picked up the day before, and then she headed for the car. The roads were slick, but she didn't have far to go.

First, she drove to David's grave. While part of her couldn't believe how quickly two years had passed, in many ways, they were the longest two years of her life. She parked the SUV under the old oak tree. Its branches were heavy with ice. The sleet had all but stopped, and the cemetery was eerily quiet—the calm before a big storm.

Mikala picked her way to David's grave. After saying a prayer, she placed the roses on the frozen ground. She took a deep breath and blew it out, watching as her warm breath vaporized into the frigid air. Although she knew what she wanted to say, pushing the words out was harder than she'd anticipated. "David, I forgive you. I know all your secrets now. Well, that's probably not true. If I had to guess, I probably know just a little of what your life was like in those last few years. But knowing more won't change the facts. Still, I forgive you."

Closing her eyes, Mikala recalled David's beautiful blue eyes, so like their daughter's, and his engaging smile. She hadn't seen his smile in a long time, and she struggled to recall it. Flipping through the photo album in her mind, she recalled their graduation picture, wedding picture, and the photo of the three of them—David, Molly, and herself—at Molly's first birthday party. "This is how I'll remember you. This is how I'll remember us," she whispered. "I have to let go of all the hurt, lies, and betrayal so I can survive and thrive. I have to forgive you, and I have to forgive me."

Mikala opened her eyes and removed her gloves. She studied her left hand and focused on the diamond-encrusted platinum band David had slid on her finger on their wedding day. She took a fortifying breath and eased it off. Mikala flexed her fingers. The loss of her ring and its weight on her finger was strange.

The ring signified the love she and David had shared, and it had reassured her they belonged to each other. But she no longer belonged to him. Their story was over, and she couldn't wear the ring any longer. The time had come to say goodbye forever. The happy memories of the life they'd shared were burned into her mind and heart. Taking off the ring and leaving it with David was the only way she knew to mark the end of their story.

With shaking fingers, Mikala brought the wedding band to her lips, kissed it, and then placed the ring on top of the headstone. "I loved you, David, the best way I knew how, and I know you did the same for me and Molly. I'm saying goodbye to you and to us—what we were to one another, and the beauty we found in loving Molly. I'm letting you go, and I need you to let me go, too."

Mikala wiped the tears sliding down her cheeks. "Rest in peace, David. I'm fine. Jake and I are together now. We love one another, and we take care of each other. When you see our butterfly, tell her, Mama and Uncle Jake love her."

Turning, she walked to her car without looking back. Mikala climbed into her car and cranked up the heat as high as it would go. She closed her eyes and reveled in the peace that warmed her from the inside out. She'd read all about the power of forgiveness and how those who forgave found peace. Holding on to anger, resentment, and wounded pride took a lot of energy and blocked the ability to give and receive love.

Sighing in contentment, Mikala opened her eyes. She straightened, gripped the steering wheel, and drove to Molly's grave. Today was Molly's eighth birthday, and she was ready to say her final farewell. She wondered what Molly would've look like all grown up. She was five and half when she died, a baby, and that's the image Mikala would always have of her little girl.

Parking, she glanced at the baby book. Picking up the book, she held it to her chest. Molly would never read all the love letters she'd written, but she would hear the final letter Mikala spent weeks writing. Stepping out of the car, Mikala carried the bouquet of yellow and white daisies and the baby book. After today, she would lay this book in Molly's baby trunk, alongside her birth certificate, footprints, a lock of her auburn curls from her first haircut, the hand-stitched, pink and white dress she'd worn home from the hospital, and so many other treasured memories.

Mikala placed the daisies on the butterfly headstone and knelt by her daughter's grave. She didn't feel the cold or hear the crunch of ice and snow as she settled on the frozen ground. "Hi, Butterfly. Happy birthday, baby girl. I wish I could see you now—all grown up, and probably missing a few teeth."

She opened the baby book to the right page. So many empty pages remained that would stay pristine. That fact hit Mikala squarely in the chest each time she opened the book. Molly's life was cut way too short. She could have filled the world with her beauty, joy, and brilliance for many, many years. But Mikala's hopes and dreams for Molly weren't meant to be. She cleared her throat and read.

Dear Molly,

The day I found out I was pregnant was the happiest day of my life, and when I held you in my arms for the first time, my heart soared. Before you, I was unsure why I was put on this earth. With you, the purpose of my life became abundantly clear. The second you moved in my belly and in my soul, I knew my job was to watch over your precious life, give you wings to fly, and watch you soar. Nothing in my life was more important. You completed me in a way I didn't know possible.

Butterfly, you filled my life with love and joy beyond anything I could have ever imagined. I never took a day with you for granted, but I thought you would be in my life for a long, long time. I thought I would pass before you because that's the way life was meant to be. Mothers are supposed to go to heaven way before their babies and watch over them from above. But that wasn't our story was it, my sweet?

Every day, Molly, every single day I had with you was a gift. But I am greedy. I wish I had more. No amount of time, I realize now, would have ever been enough. So, I am grateful for the seconds, minutes, hours, days, and years I had you in my life. But Molly, I wanted to walk you to your first day of kindergarten. I wanted to help you dress for your first date and shop with you for the perfect prom dress. I dreamed of the day I applauded and screamed, "That's my baby!" as you walked across the stage to receive your high school and college diplomas.

Then, there is your wedding day. Oh God, how I wanted to be there! We would have scoured the city, no—the world, for a dress half as beautiful as you, and still, we would have settled. When I close my eyes, I can see you smiling and glowing as you walk down the aisle on your father's arm. I am a sobbing mess, but my tears are joyous.

Molly, I had so many wishes and dreams for you. I wanted to give you the world, but you were snatched from my arms when you were just a baby. I spent two years angry at myself, your daddy, and the world. I've let that anger go now. I've learned to live without you and daddy, and I've learned to forgive.

You, my angel, are the one who taught me to live again, even when I saw no reason to. Your innocent, forgiving heart, and your loving ways showed me the way into the light and urged me to forgive. How is it I was the one who was supposed to watch over you and teach you the ways of the world, but instead you took me by the hand and led me out of the darkness? Our lives weren't supposed to be this way, but I am grateful for your loving vigilance. I wouldn't have survived without you.

This letter is the last I will write. It is the only one you've heard. But that doesn't matter. The letters that fill the pages, and those that would have been written, all carry the same message. Your mama loves you with every fiber of her being. No matter where I go, no matter what I do, I will never forget you. You will always have a special place in my heart. I am comforted by my belief, one day I will see your beautiful face once more. Then, I will hold you, kiss you, and rock you as I long to do now. Until then, my darling, my heart, be well. Rest in peace.

All my love,

Your mama.

Mikala fished a tissue from her coat pocket and wiped her eyes and nose. She tilted her head toward heaven and closed her eyes, waiting for Molly to come. For a few seconds, the sun's rays warmed Mikala's face followed by the riffling of the wind through her hair. She smiled and sighed. "Thank you, Butterfly." She stood and walked to the car. Opening the door, she paused and looked over her shoulder. "Goodbye, baby girl."

Driving back to the house was dicey, and Mikala was glad she had a short distance to travel. She didn't regret coming out in the storm. She'd accomplished what she'd come out to do. As she approached the house, she saw Red parked in the driveway. Shaking her head, she smiled. Super-man couldn't stay away, and she was glad he hadn't. She needed to feel his strong arms around her and hear the steady beat of his heart—a reassurance of life.

Mikala strode through the garage door and into the kitchen. She came to a dead stop. Bags of groceries littered the counters and floor. Had the man robbed a grocery store? Jake stood in front of the refrigerator, lost in a sea of yellow plastic grocery bags, scratching the back of his head, and appearing befuddled.

"Sweetheart, what are you doing here?" she asked as she surveyed the kitchen. "And why do we have enough groceries to feed a small continent?"

Jake glanced up with a lopsided grin. "Haven't you heard? A glorious blizzard is on the way."

Mikala remembered what a child her man was. Her boy from the hood had never experienced a true snowstorm until he moved to Connecticut. That first winter and every winter to follow, he was intolerable. He whined until someone went out in the freezing storm to play and build snowmen, igloos, and one time, even a snow-boat. His fascination and love of all things winter never faded. The man should have been a polar bear.

"I went to two supermarkets and a liquor store to get everything we needed. The storm is supposed to be a biggie." He rubbed his hands together. "I was even tackled by a woman and her four kids. We fought over a loaf of bread. She and her brood won."

Shaking her head, she rummaged through the closest bag. "Ah-huh. But Jake, I think you may have gone overboard a bit. Where will we put all of this stuff? And why do we need three boxes of pancake mix?"

Jake shrugged. "Don't know. I've put away all the perishables, but the rest is a mystery to me." He picked his way to where she stood and took two bottles of mustard out of her hands, placing them on the counter. Hooking an arm around her waist, Jake pulled Mikala to him. "Never mind my shopping escapades. Tell me, how are you doing?"

Mikala nuzzled her face into his neck and breathed him in. Sighing, she let her body collapse into his. She laid her head on his chest and listened to the galloping of his heart. "I'm good now that I'm in your arms."

Placing a finger under her chin, Jake urged Mikala to meet his gaze. He studied her face for a few minutes then bent and captured her mouth in a kiss.

Mikala sighed and shifted. She wrapped her arms around his neck and returned his kiss, giving herself over to it completely.

As the snow fell steadily throughout the day, Mikala cooked, and Jake entertained her. After dinner, she cuddled with him in front of the fireplace with one of the twelve bottles of wine Jake purchased. The lights were dim, and the only sound in the room was their breathing and the crackling of the fire. The world was at peace as was Mikala.

She'd spent the afternoon stealing glances at Jake and reflecting on her feelings. She was ready to take their relationship to the next level. He had been patient and never pushed her. But all afternoon, they'd both found excuses to touch and kiss each other. She didn't doubt Jake wanted her. When he held her close, his body was unable to keep secrets.

Mikala also craved Jake. She wanted to feel the glide of his hands down her body and the caress of his lips on her breasts. She longed to be devoured by this man, and she wanted to satiate his hunger as well. But she understood she had to make the first move and show him she was ready.

Pulling out of his arms, she placed her wine glass on the coffee table. She took his glass out of his hand and set it next to hers.

Jake lifted an eyebrow and a smile played on his lips.

Giving herself a mental pep-talk, Mikala licked her lips. Before she could chicken out, she shifted until she straddled him.

Inhaling deeply, Jake hesitated for a second and gazed into her eyes. Then his arms came around her. One of his hands grasped and squeezed her hip, and the other slid up her back and into her hair. He guided her head down to his and took her mouth in a passionate kiss.

Mikala's mind went blank. She forgot her nervousness. She forgot everything other than the feel, the taste, and the smell of him.

When he pulled away, he kept their faces close. "Look at me, beautiful. Open your eyes."

Mikala's eyes fluttered open, and she tried to focus. God, Super-man could kiss! His kisses had a tendency of making her forget her own name. She wondered how good his other superpowers were.

"Baby, focus." Jake chuckled.

Mikala blinked.

He ran his thumb across her lower lip. "Is this what you want? Are you sure?"

She blinked once more and focused on Jake's onyx eyes. She pressed herself closer, slid her hands up his chest to his shoulders, and rested her forehead against his. "I've waited a long time for you, my love. I'm sure. Take me, I'm yours."

Chapter Thirty-One
Monarch

Jake held Mikala's hand as they hiked the rocky trail toward the *Sierra Chincua* Butterfly Sanctuary. The day was warm, and the monarchs flew low, settling to the ground in search of moisture. Tall pine and fir trees lined the trail, dripping with butterflies. If the altitude didn't take Jake's and Mikala's breath away, the delicate creatures swarming around them did. The monarchs sailed through the warm March air, showing off their vibrant colors and grace.

For ten days, Jake had pleaded with Mikala to take this trip to Mexico. Finally, she agreed to leave New Haven once again. After all the traveling she did over the holidays, she wanted to stay put, and Mexico wasn't a favorite destination. However, when he told her why they were going, her resistance dissipated. The next day she bought them hiking shoes and started packing. Jake hoped by the end of their stay in Mexico, Mikala would be ready to make the decision to leave New Haven for good.

For five days the blizzard had raged, leaving a heavy blanket of glistening snow covering most of the Northeast. While schools and businesses closed, Mikala and Jake's world narrowed, leaving them in their own happy bubble.

Every night, Jake fell asleep with Mikala's head on

his chest, and her arms and legs thrown over him—claiming him. Often, he awoke earlier than she and watched as scenes from her dreams skated across the features of her face. When he could wait no longer, he rained tender kisses over her face, nose, chin, mouth, and then worked his way down her sexy body, coaxing her out of slumber.

Making love to Mikala for the first time was one of the most profound experiences of his life. Each time she gave herself to him, he was reminded of the miracle of the love they shared. He couldn't get enough of her, and he was certain he never would.

The blizzard afforded them the time to reconnect and catch up on the decisions they'd made. Mikala told him about her time in Ohio and with Rena. Late one evening, Jake revealed his decision to leave Jacobson Law. Although she was surprised, Mikala understood his reasoning. But as he shared the details of his conversation with Lester, he noted her rising agitation.

Mikala chewed on her lower lip, and her brow furrowed. "What will you do now?"

Jake took her hands in his. "The question is, what will *we* do now?"

Her head quirked to the side. "We?"

"Micky, I don't plan to live apart from you ever again. Hell, one day, when you're ready, I'll ask you to marry me." Jake smiled at her surprised gasp and gave her a soft kiss. "Baby, what did you think was going on here?"

Eyes wide, she searched his face. "But…"

He placed a finger over her lips. "No but's. This isn't a friends-with-benefits relationship. I love you, and *I* will make you my wife one day. I know you're not ready yet, and that's why you don't see me on one knee right now. One day, woman, you will. That's a promise. Okay?"

Mikala's eyes filled with tears, and she nodded. "What do you want to do now, Jake?"

"I can easily start my own practice here, but that's not what I would prefer." Jake took a deep breath. "I want us to consider starting someplace new where we can make new memories and set down roots. New York maybe. The area's close enough for us to visit here, and Rena's there. We have our choice of the city or the suburbs."

Mikala's mouth hung open. For a few seconds, she gazed in his eyes. "You're really serious, Aren't you? You think we should leave New Haven?"

He took her hands in his and squeezed. "Take your time. Think about it. I won't leave without you. That option is not even on the table. The decision to go or to stay has to be both of ours. I won't push you into something you aren't ready to do. Lester has no problem with a flexible timetable, and I'm in no hurry."

A month had passed since that conversation. Although the topic came up many times, Jake didn't push. He and Lester became embroiled in a case that took all their days and many nights, and Mikala was busy with projects of her own. Miraculously, the case wrapped up in time for them to travel because in a few weeks, the monarchs would migrate across the country once more. Mikala and Jake would have missed their chance to experience their beauty.

Jake and Mikala had landed in Mexico two days earlier, and Jake hired José, a tour guide, to accompany them from Mexico City to Angangueo, and then to the

Sierra Chincua Sanctuary. Many trains, planes, and automobiles later, and they were now climbing the trail approximately ten thousand feet above sea level. The air was thin, and their progress was slow.

They'd been hiking for three hours, taking breaks every half-hour, when José brought them to a stop at a lookout. "Let's take a break and have lunch. We are almost to the top." He handed Jake bottles of water, sandwiches, and fruit from his backpack.

Jake turned to Mikala. "How are you doing, baby?"

The smile that transformed her face as one majestic monarch after another landed on her head, shoulders, and hips, fluttered its wings, and then took off, told him all he needed to know.

Arms out-stretched and face raised to the sky, she slowly spun in a circle "This place is magical. Molly would've loved it."

Jake sat on a bench and pulled her beside him. He handed her a sandwich and a bottle of water. "Yes, Molly's eyes would be huge just like yours are right now. I told her one day she and I would run away here together. Now we are experiencing these enchanting creatures for her."

Mikala nodded and gazed at the butterfly-covered pines. After a few minutes, she began eating. When she finished her sandwich, she sat back and tilted her head to the sky. "I'm glad we came on this trip. We've both been so busy lately. We've hardly had time to say two words to each other."

He squeezed Mikala's shoulder. "I'm sorry. I thought that damn case would never end."

Sitting up, she met his gaze. "It's okay. I have something to tell you, though."

"Oh?"

She took another drink from the water bottle and cleared her throat. "Right before we came, I accepted an offer on the house. I close in six weeks."

Jake grinned. The woman never failed to surprise him. He didn't think Mikala would ever accept an offer. She'd received several good offers, but each time, she turned them down. She insisted the right buyer hadn't come yet, and she would know the second they landed on her doorstep. Even her realtor, whom he knew well, lost hope and begged Jake to intervene more than once. Each time, Jake refused. He maintained Mikala would make a decision when the right time and buyer came along. "What made this buyer the right one?"

Mikala grinned. "Well, this young couple, with twin five-year-old boys, saw the for-sale sign and knocked on my door. My realtor was not happy I let them in without her. Something about that family tugged at my heartstrings. The kids were little monsters. They ran amuck all through the house as their parents walked around as if their little darlings weren't about to tear apart the place." She shook her head and laughed. "The kids brought the house to life with their screaming and stomping. When they made an offer, I didn't hesitate."

"I'm happy for you, and I'm glad you waited until you found the right family for that beautiful house, even if the kids are possessed." He pulled her toward him and gave her a quick kiss and hug.

José stood from the rock he sat on and met Jake's gaze.

Jake shook his head.

José nodded and sat.

For the last few days, Mikala had been preoccupied. His Mikala had more to say, but she'd speak when she was good and ready. Taking a swig of his water, Jake studied the ground.

Mikala cleared her throat. "I've been thinking a lot about moving."

Jake's heart rate took flight. He took a deep breath and let it out slowly. Whatever decision she made, he would support her. No matter what came out of her mouth, he would not let his disappointment show. Raising his head, Jake gazed at her.

Her eyes sparkled, and her body vibrated with excitement. The grin that covered her face told the story. Mikala had made a decision that would make them both happy. Thank Fuck! "Before you burst, tell me, baby." He chuckled.

"Well, I think moving to New York is a good idea." She sighed. "Nothing is left for me in New Haven except Lester. I can take the train and visit him anytime."

Jake nodded. He was ready to sweep her off her feet and kiss her until they both had to come up for air. But he would hear her out—then he would kiss his woman silly.

"I talked to Rena and, as you can imagine, she thinks you walk on water since you came up with this idea." She smirked.

Jake threw back his head and laughed. "Baby, I've always walked on water. It's just taken you and Rena a bit longer to agree with the rest of the female population."

She attempted a glare but failed. "Shut up, Jake. You're off the market for good. No more female admirers."

"Hey." He held up his hands. "I'm not complaining, but you'll have to protect me everywhere I go. I blame the pheromones."

Mikala gazed heavenward. "Will you let me finish?"

"Sorry, beautiful. Go ahead. I'm listening."

"Well." Mikala licked her lips. "Rena and I have this crazy idea."

"Yeah, like that's new." Jake snorted.

She punched his arm. "Stop that. This conversation is serious. We want to start a non-profit organization dedicated to the needs of grieving children and their families. We would provide grief-support services to people who are coping with grief. We could also provide support for schools and communities who have experienced trauma or loss."

Jake's mouth hung open, and he stared. God, she was brilliant. Not only was she willing to move and start over, but more importantly, she took everything she'd experienced and every lesson she'd learned over the past two years and planned to build something that would help many. This new venture would give her something of her own she could be proud of.

"Uh…okay, stop staring." Mikala wrung her hands. "I know our plans are lofty, and we'll need a ton of fundraising and networking, but Ted and Rena have some connections, and Lester said he would help."

Jake shook his head. "You told Lester about this plan?"

"Yes." She nodded and chewed on her lower lip. "I'm sorry I didn't share it with you first. I wanted to be sure my idea wasn't crazy, and I—"

Jake grabbed Mikala and pulled her in his arms. He gave her a resounding kiss.

Breathless, Mikala pulled away and met his gaze. "Guess you like the idea?"

"I love the idea. But Lester, Ted, and Rena aren't the only ones with connections. You remember all those filthy rich-and-famous assholes I represented for years, right?" He rubbed his palms together as a smile spread across his face. "Well, I'm calling in each and every one of my favors. Funding, will *not* be a problem."

Mikala grinned. "Yes!" she yelled, doing a fist pump.

He pulled her into his embrace again. "I'm proud of you. The concept is fantastic. I know the organization will be a great success." He cupped her face in his hands and kissed her long and deep.

José cleared his throat and smiled. "Sorry, folks, but we must go. The summit is only about another thirty minutes."

Jake threw away their trash, and they followed José. At first, the trail was easy except for a few rocks and tree roots. As they neared the end, the terrain became steep. They hiked the remainder of the trail single file with Jose´ in the lead, Mikala following him, and Jake in the rear.

The trail came to an abrupt end into a roped-off area covered in pine needles. The trees were tall and thick, obscuring the intensity of the sun, and the clearing was cool. Shafts of sunlight came through the branches giving the illusion of walking into a cathedral. The cool and peaceful atmosphere tempted the butterflies to come out for a dance. And they did. The monarchs were everywhere—hanging from pines, clumping on branches, and filling the air with their unique whirring sound—music to the ears, a balm to the soul.

"Oh my God, Jake. Is this place real?" Mikala whispered.

"I've never seen anything like it, and I've been to some pretty amazing places. But this…" Jake shook his head. He held her in his arms—her back to his front. They stood in the middle of the clearing surrounded by thousands of miraculous monarchs, swaying to the music they made.

Mikala closed her eyes and laid her head back against Jake. As butterflies landed on her face, tickling her nose and chin, she smiled. "This is heaven." She sighed. "This is where our butterfly is." Tears slid down her cheeks, and the moisture attracted the butterflies.

"Yeah, baby. I think you're right," Jake whispered in her ear.

Except for the sounds of nature, silence reigned. With Mikala in his embrace, Jake swayed. In this miraculous place, he was finally at peace, and he was certain Mikala was, as well.

As if reading his thoughts, she opened her eyes and turned in Jake's embrace. "Monarch."

Jake glanced down and met Mikala's sparkling eyes. "Hmm?"

"Monarch," Mikala said, her voice barely above a whisper. "That's the name I'll use for the organization, and our logo will be a butterfly. What do you think?" She tilted her head.

"Monarch." Jake nodded. "I like it."

"Actually, the name is perfect." She pulled away

and spun, looking at the beauty surrounding them. Her hair floated around her, and the butterflies took flight and danced among her auburn curls. When she focused on Jake, her eyes shone. "A few days ago, I opened Molly's baby trunk to put away her baby book. I found a small book on butterflies you gave her. I flipped through it and read some people see a butterfly as a symbol of endurance, change, hope, and life. Other people see the butterfly as a symbol of transformation. Don't you see, Jake? Something good, really good, will come from the horror we survived."

Jake swallowed passed the lump in his throat. He nodded. Jesus, this woman brought him to his knees. She thought she'd survived because of him. But the truth was, she'd saved him, changed and transformed him.

Grabbing his hand, she squeezed it. "Think about how a butterfly develops, Jake. It starts as an egg, grows into a larva, and then a caterpillar. In a span of a month, a tiny egg becomes a glorious butterfly. The transition is massive. The butterfly looks nothing like the egg it started as. It changed, grew, and survived. Then the butterfly unfurls into something spectacular."

Jake brought her hand to his lips. "Just like you, baby," he said in a husky voice. "You're spectacular. You survived, changed, and grew. You brought me along with you. You're a monarch, my love. God, how I love you. I'm humbled by your resilience, strength, and beauty."

Mikala slid her hands up Jake's chest and wound them around his neck as his arms wrapped around her. "Can this beautiful life be real? Is this really *my* life, now?" Her eyes were wide. "I never thought I could be this happy and this hopeful ever again. People said time heals, but I thought they were crazy. I didn't think I would ever find peace and true joy again."

"Look around, Micky." Jake scanned the vicinity. "This is as real and as miraculous as life gets. Every day we wake up is a gift. How we choose to handle the minutes, hours, days, months, and years we are given is up to us. Every day I'm grateful I have you in my life. I love you, sweetheart."

"Every second counts, Jake. Let's never forget that. Every second, every heartbeat, and with every breath, I will love you my Super-man."

A word about the author...

Mona Sedrak lives a double life. By day, she is a suit-wearing, prim and proper, professor, administrator, researcher, and lecturer. By night, she is a PJ wearing dreamer and writer of books that make people sigh, smile, cry, laugh, and fall in love. She lives in Ohio with her husband of thirty-two years, a cranky, geriatric maltipoo, and an obnoxious Amazon parrot who runs the house and terrifies its inhabitants.

Mona discovered the joy and escapism that comes from reading at the age of twelve and swears books saved her life and her sanity. Through reading, she has travelled the globe and learned all kinds of equally useful and useless skills such as: crocheting, the proper way to eat a pomegranate, carve a watermelon, or bathe an elephant. These skills she has passed down to her two daughters who are incredibly supportive, but often wish she had a wider scope of hobbies.

Mona has a long publishing history in academia, but she started writing fiction recently.
http://www.monasedrak.com
Facebook:
https://www.facebook.com/MonaSedrakAuthor/
Twitter: @AuthorMSedrak
Instagram: authormonasedrak